Craft Fair
December 3rd
1-2pm
raise money for
trip. Be there or
be square

Jonathan's Summer

by

Randa Wise

authorHOUSE

www.authorhouse.com

This book is a work of fiction. Places, events, and situations in this story are purely fictional and any resemblance to actual persons, living or dead, is coincidental.

© 2004 Randa Wise.
All Rights Reserved.

No part of this book may be reproduced, stored in a retrieval system, or transmitted by any means without the written permission of the author.

First published by AuthorHouse 05/31/04

ISBN: 1-4184-1103-5 (sc)

Printed in the United States of America
Bloomington, Indiana

This book is printed on acid-free paper.

ACKNOWLEDGEMENTS:

Well I must admit I enjoyed writing this novel. In my endeavors to get myself published, I have received so much support from friends and family, encouraging me to "get my novel out there" and quit hiding this dramatic tale from everyone. Those people I will never forget, as I continue writing and even if I decide to quit. Hey! I'm no quitter! Writing is my joy and I am blessed to have those around me who have been my strong support system. You know who you are but I will still acknowledge you in this piece I created:

Daddy, you are the most wonderful father and man in the world!

Jeff Wise, my dear brother and wacky writer like myself. You know how dedicated you have to be to sit down and devise a tale that didn't even happen in real life. Like they say, both of us have always been dramatic story tellers.

Sharon Wise, my dear sister-in-law and mother of four of my wonderful nieces and nephews.

Mary Walker, my best friend since I was eleven. You've been there for me during tough times and when I was talking your ear off about what I've recently written. Your patience is something to be reckoned with. Love ya, girl!

Florene M. Thompson, my former next door neighbor from back in the days in Springfield, VA. Thanks for the editing advice. Thanks for all the advice you've given me, including your encouragement.

Last but not least, Khadijah Karim, who has been so patient with Mommy during some of those times when I was trying to complete that dramatic chapter. If it were not for you, I don't even think I would have gotten the impulse to write a novel.

Thanks to the models who posed for the front cover of this book. And many thanks to my publisher for seeing my dream come true.

Peace!

PROLOGUE:

Jonathan stared across the table at her. They dined in an elegant restaurant in Potomac, Maryland. Society folks frequented that establishment, for there was nothing on the menu under one-hundred dollars. All summer, Jonathan had seen to it that Jackie was treated to the best. Even under the candlelight, he could tell how beautiful she was – cinnamon complexion, dark eyes, full lips and her breasts drove him insane, especially this night. She donned a low-cut number that showed the right amount of cleavage that made him hungry.

She smiled back, letting him know that after dinner, she had a little something in store for him. Where they sat overlooked parts of Montgomery County. They could see tall office buildings and the streets below the sixteenth floor restaurant were busy as others enjoyed the nightlife beneath the star-studded sky.

Jackie gave him her all, for three months. But she had not gotten all she wanted from him. She had waited long enough for him to voice his commitment to her. What was he waiting for? She had finally landed a good man. He was not only handsome, but powerful and wealthy. There was no way in the hell she would pass up this opportunity.

"Jonny?" she spoke, giving him that wanton look she usually did when she wanted to wheedle something out of him. This time, she would not ask him to pay her mortgage or two months of her car note. This was that question that made most brothers squirm in their seats.

"Are you ever going to propose marriage to me?"

She was right as she noticed him squirm in his seat. He glanced out into the night. Irritation showed in those piercing eyes. She had him now!

Marriage was something he would consider but not now. Not with her. It was not only too early, there were some things in their relationship that still needed straightening out. She needed to understand that they should give this more time.

"Jackie, I feel we should give it some time."

"Give it some time?" she snapped, her voice rising. Others in the restaurant looked their way and embarrassment overwhelmed him.

"Honey, keep your voice down." he leaned over and told her. He could see that you can take a 'hood rat out of the ghetto but you couldn't take the ghetto out of the 'hood rat. "Let's talk about this when we get back to my place." He thought that would appease her. It didn't.

"Why can't we talk about it now? By the time we get to your place, there will be no time for talking." she said, giving him a knowing stare-down.

"We will talk when we return to my place." he said with the finality that did not go over well with her. She was not accustomed to not getting her way with him. She looked at his answer as a way to sidestep her question.

"I thought you'd have more class than some of the guys I've been with but I can see I was wrong."

"What you thought is that I would give in to your every demand." Jonathan was never one to back down, especially when it came to dealing with gold diggers. He knew what her aim was – had heard her telephone conversation with her girlfriend, Lisa the night before. He decided not to bring that up. But he was fully aware of what she was trying to do. He loved her but that didn't mean he would punk out every time she snapped her fingers.

"All you wanted was some ass, didn't you?" she said, leaning back in her chair, disdainfully looking at him.

"Pardon me?"

He was shocked by her statement.

"Yeah, pardon you, all right." She tossed down the linen napkin. "You're just a playa. Others warned me about you. Yeah, all you wanted was some ass while you were up here taking care of your father's business. Once you got back to Greenville, you won't even remember I exist."

"We can discuss all this at home!" he said, noticing others around them had begun staring again.

"Just answer yes or no! Are we getting married or not?"

"We'll talk about this later. If you can't wait until then, I'm sorry."

"Fuck you, Jonathan!" she shouted.

He could hear gasps from those who were within earshot.

She stormed out of the restaurant, leaving him there alone to deal with the curious eyes around him. The Maitre d' came out, asked him if there was a problem. He told the man that the problem had just left.

He paid the bill with his platinum credit card and left the restaurant. On the drive home, he thought about stopping by her place but decided he would allow her to cool off. He headed to his parents' guesthouse, where he'd been staying for over three months. Once he stepped out of the shower, he called her. She did not pick up the phone.

By the time he was headed back to South Carolina, four days later, he realized that it was over. During his last days in Maryland, he was unsuccessful in reaching her. She refused to pick up her phone and when he went by her place, her car was not parked in front of her condo. He didn't like how this ended. However, marrying someone in haste would not resolve it either.

CHAPTER ONE:

Jonathan Wesley hurried from his Jaguar once he parked in front of his parents' mansion. He had arrived in Rockville, MD in just enough time to get his parents to the airport. His father, Maurice was ordering one of his domestic employees to place their luggage into the van. Jonathan mused that no matter where they were, bossing others around came naturally to his father. He joined his mother in the sitting room since his father's concentration was trained on the young man carrying the luggage.

"Hi, Mom," He encompassed Donya's petit frame in his strong arms. "Are you guys set to go?"

"As ready as we'll be." she said with a dimpled smile.

"Hey, son." Maurice joined his son and wife in the sitting room. "It's so nice of you to hold down the fort while we're in the Caribbean." he said, sauntering in Jonathan's direction and hugging him.

Jonathan gave his father a warm smile, for he was honored that his father entrusted him to the business while he vacationed. "Every year you tell me that, Dad and you know I will hold down the fort."

"Well, you know how your brother is." His father furrowed his brows for emphasis. "I cannot rely on Jerome to do anything except for what pleases his soul."

Jonathan smiled as his eyes traveled quickly from his father to his mother. He understood what his father was saying, how unreliable Jerome was when it concerned handling matters of the family business. Jerome loved to vacation, spend money on himself and treat women to lavish gifts.

"Jerome is the economics major in the family." Jonathan felt compelled to come to his brother's defense. "Maybe he's better off on Wall Street."

Maurice Wesley is CEO of the parent company, *Ethnic Information Corporation.* When he launched the publishing company, one publication was in circulation, called *West Africans in America,* a publication that prints monthly issues and discusses the history of blacks from West Africa before slavery, during slavery and segregation until modern day. The publication features black celebrities and black entrepreneurs. Since that time, twenty five years ago, the company has grown and four subsequent publications to *West Africans in America* have been conceived. The company brings in tens of billions in revenue each year.

"Are you all settled in the guest house?" his mother asked.

"I've taken my things there but I haven't had time to unpack. I'll do it after getting you and Dad to the airport."

Donya patted her eldest son's cheek affectionately and gave him a kiss on the cheek and said, "Don't wait too long, son. You wouldn't want the young lady to be upset because you're late for that hot date with her tonight."

She knew that her son must have made plans to go out with some nice young woman that night. It was expected because she had the most handsome and eligible son in the world.

Contrary to what his she may think, Jonathan hadn't had much luck with relationships in the past couple of years. Although handsome, he was one very lonely brother.

"Mom," he playfully said, "I'm not seeing anyone."

He and his mother followed Maurice to the van and Jonathan got behind the wheel, heading for BWI Airport. Maurice could have had one of his drivers take them to the airport but he elected to have his own son drive them. Not only did he have company matters to discuss with him, he wanted to see him before they left.

"Jonathan, when you get to the office Monday, call a meeting with all managers, editors and department heads." Maurice ordered.

"Is the concerning plans for the new publication you briefed me about over the phone the other day?" he asked, glancing at him through the rear view mirror.

"You bet!" Maurice boasted. "This will be number six! You know the sky is my limit when it comes to publishing. But the love of my life is that pretty gal sitting to your right."

Jonathan glanced at his father again. He grabbed his mother's left hand, bringing it to his lips, giving her a light kiss on the back of her palm. "You're the lady I've been admiring for thirty-eight years."

She smiled, looking at him. "Jonathan Michael Wesley, you're the only playboy that can get away with saying something like that without getting knocked over the head with a purse."

Jonathan chuckled at his mother's wit as the van reached the airport. He removed the luggage from the van, packed the cart and wheeled it towards the airport. The day was sunny, the temperature hitting the seventy mark. He loved this time of year, late spring. The nice weather always brought with it the best time to start a new relationship. Spring always renewed his spirits. During the winter, it was rare to catch the sight of an attractive woman strolling down the street in a pair of shorts or a skirt that displayed the beauty of her legs.

He hugged his parents. "Have a safe trip, you two. And no hanky panky while your children are up here in the states, suffering from not having the company of a significant other." he said, speaking more of himself. Both his sisters were married and his brother never had any problems attracting women. He didn't know what was wrong. He either attracted the wrong type or it seemed no one looked his way – at least not the ones he wanted attention from.

Donya quickly retorted, "If we didn't do the 'hanky panky', we would not have four of you brats to begin with."

Jonathan was her eldest and he knew she meant he was the number one brat.

He embraced them again after seeing them to the gate. He headed back to Rockville, MD, where his family's multi million-dollar home was located, surrounded by twenty-nine acres of land. Once he parked the van in the east garage, he walked about a block to the guesthouse, where he would be living for the next three months. His main career is journalism – interviewing celebrities for *West Africans in America* and *Nubian Entertainment*, both published by his father's company. Life is extremely busy but he would not balk at the idea of buying out time for a date although nothing ever turns out to be anything worthwhile. Each summer, he is acting CEO while his father vacations one of the exotic islands. During the winter, other than journalism, he coaches high school basketball.

Once inside the guesthouse, he winced at the seven suitcases and garment bags laid casually around the parlor. The loathsome part about traveling to Rockville from Greenville, SC every summer is packing and unpacking. He cursed, as if he thought the expletive was enough to give him energy to begin unpacking.

Summer knew she'd catch her father doing something forbidden once she returned from the grocery store. He was outside painting the porch steps. She wondered if he thought that her short trip to the store would give him enough time to finish so that she would not catch him. Although painting the steps was not strenuous work, she considered it to be. Forgetting about the groceries in the trunk for now, she pranced towards him with her hands placed on her hips. She stood behind him a good two minutes before he was aware of her presence.

"Daddy!"

"Hummn?" he said, lightly touching up a spot he'd formerly missed.

"What do you think you're doing? You're supposed to be taking it easy. Doctor's orders. Besides, we made a deal."

He'd recently recovered from a heart attack and Summer had been worrying for him ever since. Each time she left the house, he would perform some chore he was forbidden to do. And each time, she caught him in the act before he could complete it.

"And you're supposed to be out on a date somewhere. It's Saturday evening." he retorted with an impish grin as he stood up, admiring his work.

"Very funny, Dad. Now put down that brush and I'll finish the job as soon as I put dinner on." She pranced back to the car and removed the groceries from the trunk.

After getting the bags from the car, Summer took the rear entrance so that she would not ruin the fresh paint on the porch steps. She had to admit, he did a good job. While she removed the items from the bags, her father snuck into the kitchen and snatched off her burgundy and gold Washington Redskins baseball cap.

"Hey!" she shouted, as if he'd exposed her to a group of people. She placed her hand over her head in order to conceal her beautiful crown of long flowing curls. "I need that." She reached for the cap but he kept it out of her reach. After a few attempts, she quit trying to reclaim it.

He tossed the cap onto the kitchen table. "Why do you need it, Summer?" he asked. "To hide that beautiful face and those pretty eyes. Sometimes I think you behave as if you're ashamed of your own beauty."

Summer laughed with her father. But her mirror contradicted his opinion. She never saw the "beautiful princess" he'd been insisting she was since birth. Summer loved her loose-fitting jeans, sneakers and baseballs caps. "Dad, you told me that as long as my clothes are clean and pressed I'm fine."

"And you still look like a runaway teenager! For God's sake, I would love to walk to you down the aisle of matrimony. Maybe I can get a coupla grandkids outta the deal. But you refuse to allow a young man to see how pretty you are."

"I'm only twenty-five. I have a few years to consider all that."

"You won't be twenty-five forever. In just nine short months, you'll be twenty-six. Then thirty in a few years, and they will creep up on you before you know it. And the way this old body of mine seems to be betraying me, I'm not sure I'll be around to see my only child raise her own children."

"You just turned fifty-nine, darling. That bout you had back in March was probably an isolated occurrence."

"Princess, that was a bout with your old dad's mortality." he cautioned.

"Well, if you'd quit painting steps around here and mowing lawns while I'm at work, you'll add more years to your life."

Laughing, Allen tugged on her long ponytail and said, "You're just like your stubborn mother was."

Summer didn't retort his last comment. She hated being compared to Cynthia Douglas, who had abandoned her own child and husband when she was fourteen. Her father still loved her although she blamed her for her father's failing health since she took flight on the family in order to pursue her own dreams as an actress. Cynthia never really made it, other than a couple of commercials. After that last laundry detergent commercial four years ago, she never appeared on television again. Adolescence was a tough experience for Summer, the time when she needed her mother most and so did her father because he had not a clue how to deal with her during that time.

Allen was even more broken-hearted when Cynthia left. Summer missed how he would call her mother whenever he wanted something, how his voice echoed throughout the house, "Cin-day!" he would call so affectionately, his tone always emanating love.

"I'll make the salad while you prepare the chicken." he told her as they started their regular evening ritual of cooking together – a ritual that had been going on for over ten years.

When Summer looked into her father's eyes, she saw her own: light brown, large and questioning. He'd blessed her with not only an attractive face but a splendid personality. She'd inherited her generosity and self-sacrificing ways from him, not her selfish mother.

After dinner, Summer phoned her best friend and co-worker, Nadia Cruz. She slipped into the recliner near her bed while listening to the phone ring three times before Nadia picked up.

"Hey, you!" Nadia returned in her dramatic Puerto Rican accent. "What's new now?"

"I overheard Mr. Wesley talking to one of the editors yesterday about plans for a new publication. Can you imagine how exciting it's gonna be for some of us who'll get a chance to show our talent?" She was speaking of herself, who wanted out of the position she was in at *EIC* and this was her big chance to show her true talent.

"And?" Nadia prompted.

"Well, I have a good idea for a new publication."

"Summer!" Nadia interrupted before her friend could go any further. "You know you shouldn't eavesdrop on the big boss's meetings with those higher ups. He will personally give you the axe if he ever found out."

Summer sighed, becoming upset that of all people, Nadia just didn't understand or seem as though she would be at least be supportive about it, even if she didn't get anywhere with it.

"I know, Nadia but I couldn't help listening when I passed his office." She went into her spiel with her friend anyway, as if she was talking directly to the boss himself. "But a good publication would be something that we could market to black senior citizens. You know, health and all that positive stuff."

"I understand you have a personal interest in marketing a publication for seniors because of your interest in your dad and the fact that he suffered a heart attack. But you don't hold a position where Maurice Wesley would even want to hear what you have to say."

"I won't be a deposit clerk for the rest of my life, Nadia. That's a straight up dead end position. I took journalism classes. I feel that when I started working for this company and took that position it was to get me in the door in the first place. I *will* get what I really want one day."

Nadia could hear the determination in her voice but she still said, trying to be realistic, "If an idea like the one you just pitched to me came from higher up, Mr. Wesley would certainly consider it."

"What is that supposed to mean?" Summer cut in.

"You know what I mean."

"No, I really don't." Nadia could tell that her friend had her heart set on this idea. "I'm not worthy or intelligent enough to add something to that company. I have an idea that I want proposed and if it gets far enough, marketed to the public."

"I'm not saying you're not intelligent and that you can't add anything." she defended. "I'm just telling you what you may not know. Mr. Wesley doesn't pay too much attention to lower-level employees like us. It wouldn't be taken seriously it if came from me either. I'm *only* a customer service rep for *Latino Outlook*."

"That isn't my point, Nadia. I still want my idea promoted. I could even share it with my department managers." Summer's tone was so relentless, Nadia knew she wasn't giving up and this fight she would not win.

"Summer, you're brand new and there are some things you need to understand. Abu Sosseh and Jacqueline Shannon will laugh in your face. Besides, you'll have to wait three months, sista-girl because Mr. Wesley is on vacation for the summer."

"Really?" Now this was news to Summer.

"Yes, he goes every summer. This time, he'll be touring the Caribbean."

Summer rolled her eyes heavenward. She didn't want to wait that long. Maybe she could find out where he was and have the proposal shipped to him.

"So who'll be taking over while he's gone? Don't tell me that wicked witch Jackie Shannon will." she said, speaking of her department manager.

Laughing, Nadia said, "No, that will never happen. Besides, his son, Jonathan is CEO every summer. Now that I think about it, he might be the only person who'll turn an attentive ear to your idea." she suggested. "Think about it. Jonathan is nice."

Summer's call waiting beeped. When she returned to Nadia, she told her that her father had a long distance call from Annapolis.

She pondered long after hanging up with Nadia. She knew she could never convince a stranger to accept her idea. This Jonathan Wesley was probably pompous and had an ego larger than the state of Maryland. While his father had worked hard to build *Ethnic Information Corporation*, Jonathan probably had an easy ride his entire life, benefiting from his father's hard work.

CHAPTER TWO:

After unpacking, Jonathan turned on the television in the extra bedroom and sat down at the oak desk. "Let's get started," he hissed to himself, gathering the huge stack of notes his father left him. He grabbed himself a bottle of Champaign from the small cooler behind the oval-shaped bar and returned to the room.

After two hours of poring through his father's orders, he took off his shoes and shirt and decided he would relax for the remainder of the evening. It was Saturday and he thought that maybe he would catch up with a few friends since his time would be limited once he walked into that huge, seven floor office building that his father owned. He knew there would be endless meetings and long days at the office, not to mention the list of celebrity interviews he would be conducting during his stay in Maryland.

He decided he would call his old flame, Jacqueline Shannon. Her answering machine picked up. He hung up without leaving a message. *What am I doing calling her?* he thought, slipping into reverie, remembering how she behaved last year which propelled him to break it off with her in the first place. When he met her, he thought she was the one but she turned out to be a beautifully wrapped package covering an empty box.

When Jacqueline Shannon reached home, she opened cat food and fed her three cats. She'd had a long day shopping with her mother, something that was always a trial some experience for her. All her mother did was nag the whole shopping trip. Her mother even went so far as to say that Jacqueline had caused that "good man Jonathan" to walk out because her daughter was so evil. She couldn't stand the old woman. If she was so evil, she must have inherited it from her, which stood the reason her father had walked out on her mother too. Nothing she did with her mother proved to be a pleasant experience. So, when her mother called her that afternoon because she wanted Jackie to take her to Potomac Mills, she thought she would pass out. The drive from Maryland to Potomac Mills was roughly forty-five minutes and all she heard during the trip, at the mall and the trip home was her mother's severe criticism of how she could not hold on to a man.

She kicked off her shoes and grabbed a glass of orange juice from the refrigerator. Holding the glass, she padded across the carpet of her three bedroom condo and headed to the phone, checking the caller ID. When she spied the Wesley's phone number on her ID, her heart launched to her throat, excitement and a feeling of warmth overwhelming her.

Memories of her and Jonathan spending time together the previous summer raced through her mind. She knew she'd made wreck of their relationship but was determined to make up for it. Maybe he was calling because he wanted to give her that second chance. She looked at the ID display again, making sure she made no mistake about where that call came from. It was the number to the guesthouse. He was back in town. She was ecstatic.

She called the guesthouse but there was no answer. Maybe he went next door, she thought, dialing the number of the mansion. Nelda, the housekeeping supervisor picked up on the third ring.

"Hi, Nelda. This is Jackie."

"Oh, hello, Jackie. How are you?" rang the voice of the fifty-seven year old.

"I'm doing pretty good. Would Jonathan happen to be there?"

"He took my daughter, Candi home. He should be back here in about a half hour. Want me to tell him you called?"

Jackie bit her bottom lip. How could he? she thought. Jackie hated Candi because every chance the nineteen year old got, she flirted with Jonathan. She had accused him one time of sleeping with her although her accusations were unfounded and based on her own insecurity. She should have known that he was not the type of man who would betray her. After the incident when she almost physically attacked Candi, she realized what a fool she'd made of herself. Jonathan gave her a piece of his mind because of the ghetto behavior she'd displayed in front of his family at the Wesley mansion during dinner that evening.

"Are you there?" Nelda repeated.

Jackie hadn't even realized that she zoned out. Her jealousy had gotten the better of her then and it hadn't completely died now when she thought about Jonathan taking Candi home. She imagined Candi sitting in the front seat, openly flirting with him now. What was there to stop her from even touching him this time?

"Yes, I'm here. Sorry, Nelda. Yes, of course. Tell him I called. Thanks."

She could not contain herself. Jonathan called and that meant he wanted to talk to her. That also meant that he wanted her back. She picked up the phone again, dialing her best friend Lisa's house.

"What's current?" Lisa asked, knowing something was brewing anytime Jackie called her.

"Jonathan's back in town!" she blurted out. "I thought he would be back next weekend but maybe he's decided to come in early. Now that I recall, someone told me yesterday that Maurice would be taking a flight out this morning."

"Jonathan?" Lisa said, as if she was trying to remember who her friend was speaking of. "Oh, the one you had an affair with?" to her, Jackie only had affairs, not real relationships. Like the others, he took flight too once he realized what a first class bitch she was.

"Lisa, in my book, only married people have affairs. We are both single and unattached."

"How do you know he's still single? I mean the guy hasn't called you since last September. And here we are in May."

"Someone would have told me by now. Besides, his father would have proudly announced it to the entire company, being the type of man Maurice is."

"Well, you're right about that." Lisa agreed. "So what are you going to do?"

"You know what I'm gonna do, girl. I'm gonna reclaim my man!" she boasted. "One look at those dimples and he makes me wanna melt." she added, putting a hand gently over her chest.

Lisa giggled carelessly. "Yeah, he always did have that affect on you."

"Lisa, you know how handsome Jonathan is. And let us not forget about the money. When he walked into that company last year, every hussy in there wanted a piece of him, even some of the older ones like Nettie Fraser."

"You never did tell me why y'all stopped seeing each other." Lisa said, curious about what had taken place. She always knew Jackie was holding something back because she had always been so vague about it.

"Because he returned to Greenville and I wasn't tryna go there with him." she said, which was only a half truth. If he had invited her to return to Greenville with him, she would have had her bags packed and ready. "Neither of us ever said we were quitting."

"I guess you guys need to pick up where you left off then right?"

"And you know I know how to work my shit."

"I hear ya!"

Jackie knew there were problems in their relationship before he returned to Greenville. By August of last year, Jackie was demanding a commitment and he kept on suggesting that they give it a little more time. Angry, she cursed him and stormed out of the restaurant, leaving an embarrassed Jonathan standing there while customers stared curiously at him.

Because she was so upset, she would not answer his calls and when he left for South Carolina, the sun had set with them both in a provoked state. She wondered if he had any flings between that time and now. If he had anyone in his life even now, it was over because she would make sure it was. No woman would replace her. There was no doubt he would drop whoever she was and resume a relationship with her, otherwise, he wouldn't be calling her or the woman in his life would have come to Maryland with him – that is, if she had any sense.

She knew he would never forget her knockout figure and beautiful face. She knew he would never forget the delicious home-cooked meals and incredible sex. Sometimes, after a date, they would head to his place, both ripping at each other's clothes, neither being able to ignore or control the heightened sexual desires that had built up from a few hours of being together in public. She was ready and she knew he was too.

* * *

Monday morning, Jonathan's thoughts were loaded down with the meeting he would hold on Tuesday with all department heads, editors and marketing staff. They had been briefed through memos by his father about creating a new publication but would certainly need reminders.

He donned a dark blue Armani suit, white Armani shirt and matching silk tie. He slipped on his Rolex and Italian loafers. After grabbing his briefcase, he left the guesthouse, heading for his late model black Jaguar. He turned on the radio and sat in beltway traffic from Rockville to Landover, where his father's corporation was located.

Jackie didn't miss a beat when she dressed that morning. She'd looked through her closet Sunday night and grabbed the most daring outfit she could find that she could also get away with wearing at the office. She stood in front of her full-length mirror in a red low-cut silk dress. She put on the right tone of makeup to enhance her features. She knew once Jonathan saw her, he would forget all about the episode in the restaurant the last night he laid eyes on her. As she drove to work, he dominated her thoughts. She mentally devised the wonderful summer that lied ahead. This time, he would propose to her as they walked through the park. This time, he would tell her he loved her when they made passionate love.

Summer galloped downstairs in her usual attire, jeans and a cotton blouse with Nike's on her feet. Her father could hear her, she sounded like a fourteen year old running down the stairs. He shook his head. Once he took note of her appearance, he mused to himself, *how could this young woman expect to ever be taken seriously by anyone?* Sometimes, she headed out of the house looking more like a runaway teen than a woman going into a professional environment.

She gave her father a quick kiss on the cheek before sitting down to eat breakfast. "Hi, Daddy. How'd you sleep?"

"Fine, princess. Up quite early, aren't you?"

"This is the time I'm supposed to be getting ready to leave. I want my supervisors to start believing that I care about my job from now on." She poured a bowl of cereal and noticed his quizzical expression.

"So what brought about the sudden interest in your job? I thought you hated the place. And let us not even go into the dislike you have for that woman you say is your supervisor."

Summer tried ignoring that comment because she didn't want to discuss Jackie this early in the morning. By the time she arrived at work, she would be mentally drained. "I want to present that proposal one day." she said, hoping that maybe Jonathan was as affable and easy-going as Nadia claimed he was. "The one I told you about Saturday. Maybe if I start being on time it'll help."

No matter how far up the ladder she wanted to go, nothing could ever replace her father. He was priority. Now that his health had improved, she saw no reason to be late again. She could now start concentrating more on her career.

"OK." he said. "And call me around lunch time."

"Sure." She gave him another kiss before bouncing out of the back door and to her car.

When Jonathan arrived, Jackie and Abu were already in the break room getting coffee. He passed the break room. Neither of them noticed him when he passed as he sauntered casually to his father's office. His father's assistant, Kim Justen had already arrived and was awaiting his arrival.

"Hi, Mr. Wesley." she greeted.

"How many years are we gonna go through this, Kim." he said as he strode pass her workstation and into his father's private office. "You may call me Jonathan if it's not too difficult."

She got up and followed him into his office. She stared blankly at him. He thumbed through several messages that sat on his father's desk. He looked up and gave her a quick wink with a smile. She smiled back. He had always found Asian women attractive and wondered sometimes why Kim hadn't gotten married after all of these years.

"I see Betty Newman will be here around one o'clock. When she arrives, lead her to the conference room and call Chris Moyer down."

"OK." she said, jotting it down on a pad.

"Send out a memo to everyone's email about the meeting tomorrow as a reminder." he concluded, finally sitting down behind the desk.

Kim pushed up her wire-framed eyeglasses, giving him a quizzical stare. "Meeting? Tomorrow?" she asked.

"Yes, Kim. Tomorrow."

"Are you sure anyone would have any proposals this early for the new publication? Mr. Maurice Wesley just put this out on Friday."

"This is in case anyone has come up with any proposals over the weekend. You know these people around here never quit working. It's also to get our marketing staff ready. I want to put this out as priority before some of them decide they want to take vacations. Even if they leave town, we can always send them updates on what's going on here."

"That too. OK." She added that to her notes.

"Thanks, Kim."

Before reaching the door, she spun around and shot him another perplexed look. "I'm sorry, Jonathan. Did you say something?"

He smiled and repeated, "Thank you, Kim."

She smiled. "Oh, you're welcome."

She had been with the company five years and never received the type of graciousness from Maurice that she had from Jonathan. Working with Jonathan was always much different. He emanated such kindness that she could not describe.

Jackie read the memo in her email that came from Kim only minutes ago. Jonathan was having a meeting Tuesday morning. That meant he was in the building. Just as she was about to leave her desk, Gwen Franks, one of *West Africans in America's* customer service reps and her main lookout entered the office.

"You busy?" Gwen asked.

"No, actually, I'm not. What's up?"

Gwen took note of Jackie's outfit and cracked, "I see somebody knows that Mr. Jonathan is here."

Jackie smiled. "Is he here?"

"Yes he is. I saw him getting on the elevator this morning."

This confirmed what Jackie believed once she read Kim's memo. She smiled "What time was that?"

"I would say about thirty minutes ago."

"He must have gotten here right after I did then." Jackie said, elated and excited.

She rushed to the bathroom. She had to check herself before Jonathan saw her. She checked her chin-length bobbed hairdo making sure that no hairs were out of place. She refreshed her lipstick and took a deep breath before leaving the bathroom and heading to the other side of the fourth floor, taking the long, winding corridor. At least she did not have to leave her floor, for Mr. Wesley's office was also on that floor.

Before she got within twenty feet of Maurice Wesley's suite, a thought occurred. *Let him come to you, girlfriend! Don't you know better than to chase down some brotha even if he is wealthy and the catch of the century?* With that in mind, she made an about-face and headed back for her department. Before she passed the computer room, a man who stood six-two emerged from the room, nearly stepping right into her path. He talked over his shoulder to one of the programmers as he stepped out. Jackie stopped cold. He was not wearing his suit jacket and the muscles that bulged out of his shirt nearly caused an explosion to go off inside of her. Seems he had grown even more handsome within a year. Life must have been treating him well!

She could not stop the insecurity that bubbled within her when she thought that he looked so good because maybe some southern diva down in Greenville had been responsible for it. Most men looked better when they had a woman in

12

their life. He wore a fresh fade haircut and his mustache was freshly trimmed, enhancing his chocolate complexion. She noticed that he did not wear a ring on his third left finger but that did not mean he was not engaged or involved. *What the hell*, she thought. If some country-ass woman was in his life, she'd better step aside because Jackie was determined to get her man back.

She tried to turn around and get out of dodge before he saw her but it was too late. "Jackie Shannon?" She spun around slowly after hearing that sexy, melodic voice. She always loved the way he spoke her name, as if it was something sweet on his tongue. He said it with ease and with so much rhythm behind it. She stared at the man the voice belonged to. He was igniting her fire. She couldn't stop the warm rush.

"Oh, Jonathan." She extended her hand nervously. Her sister had always told her that you could always tell when you loved a man because no matter how many times you saw him, he would make you nervous. "Been a long time." she spoke around a lump in her throat.

He smiled, shaking her hand, his manly grip sending more fire through her and she prayed he would snatch her into his arms and her head would come to rest in his broad chest. But he didn't.

They slowly released each other's hand and she said, "Nice to have you back."

"I'm delighted to be back." As if he suddenly remembered what had transpired last year and never resolved, his expression suddenly grew serious. She noticed his eyes bore right through her.

He hasn't forgotten! she thought with much alarm.

She tried ignoring the change in his countenance and attempted to steer his thoughts elsewhere as she began babbling about all the things that had gone down in the office while he was away. She told him that Dee got married; William quit working there to launch his own business and that Stacy had a baby. He knew all of this, for there were others who kept in touch with him during the months he was in Greenville.

She stared at his dark honey skin, voluptuous lips and probing eyes as she talked, prolonging being in his presence. What else was she supposed to talk about? Was she supposed to say something like: *Oh, Jonathan, I know I acted like a complete ass the last night we were together, but I'm here trying to make it up to you?*

When Summer reached the building, as a custom, she went to the third floor to say few words to Nadia before heading to the fourth floor to her department.

"Have you met our temporary boss yet?" Nadia asked.

"No." Summer said with aloofness in her tone. "Where is he?"

"He's on your floor so get up there. You'd make a good first impression on him if you're on time. And on top of that, Jackie won't have nothing to say to you." Nadia admonished.

Summer twisted her mouth and asked, "Is he gonna fire me or something?"

"Sista, take yourself seriously. Remember what we discussed Saturday and what you plan on doing. I hope you're not going to chicken out on this one. Because when I think about it, I think it's a good idea."

Renee suddenly emerged from the elevator after the chime sounded. She cut into their conversation rudely. Renee worked in Nadia's department as a customer service representative for *Latino Outlook*.

"I'm so sick of that car," Renee whined to Nadia. "I wish I had money to buy a new one."

Just like the selfish heifer she was, she didn't even acknowledge them with a good morning before she wanted everyone to hear her problems, Nadia thought.

"You could buy a new car if you didn't have such an expensive wardrobe." Nadia replied sarcastically.

Renee twisted the two-carat diamond ring on her third right finger and said, "Nothing wrong with a woman liking the finer things in life."

"Nothing at all," Summer interjected. "especially if you can afford them." She noticed the fresh hairdo, the Donna Karan skirt suit and shoes, three hundred dollar Coach bag and thought about how Renee's boyfriend must be stacking some paper in order to support her high-maintenance lifestyle.

"Anyway," Nadia said, glancing at her watch. "my department is about to turn on the phones, so I'm bouncin'." Renee followed Nadia down the hall while Summer took the elevator to her floor.

Once she reached the department, she cautiously passed Jackie's small office. When she realized the witch wasn't there, she looked heavenward, thanking God for looking out for her that morning. She knew Jackie's warning about tardiness would be enforced even if it meant being five minutes late. She hadn't realized how much time she'd spent talking to Nadia.

Summer headed down the hall to the computer room to grab the transaction reports from Friday's work. "Jason?" she called. "Do you know where the reports are for the *West Africans in America* publication?"

"Mr. Wesley's assistant came and picked them up this morning." he answered. "I think he wanted to get an idea of how much revenue was taken in from subscribers on Friday."

"That's great." she hissed, rolling her eyes, wondering how she was going to retrieve those reports without disturbing some important meeting he could be having. If Mr. Wesley's son was handling Mr. Wesley's job, she knew he would be busy. She reminded herself that this might end up being the person she would have to pitch her idea to. She couldn't wait three months until Maurice Wesley returned from his cruise.

When she reached the suite, Kim was sitting behind her PC, typing more memos. Summer rapped on the door twice before she passed the half-opened door. "Excuse me. I need the transaction report for the *West Africans in America*." She told Kim.

Kim swirled around in her chair without saying a word as she got right up. She headed into Maurice's private office and Summer's eyes followed her. A gentleman who looked to be in his mid-thirties stood up when Kim entered the office. She could tell they were talking but the words were muffled and she could hear the deepness in his voice. Nadia told her a long time ago that when a man had a deep voice that meant virility and he had a high level of testosterone. She didn't know if that was true or not, for Nadia said a whole lot of things. Like a true Scorpio, the girl talked a lot of garbage.

His height literally took her breath away once he stood. He was well over six feet, his profile well structured with a strong jaw line and nice nose. His attire demanded respect and his stance told anyone that he was proud, dignified and would protect if he had to. Although in a suit and tie, he looked like a fighter. Maybe Nadia was right. Many times, Summer had to admit, she was right about men. He was quite handsome, although much older.

So long for dumb little fantasies! she thought as Kim returned with the report and ended her crazy imagination of being in bed with Jonathan.

Summer returned to her small window-less office and closed the door. She could see Jackie staring at her from her peripheral vision but paid no attention. She knew that all Jackie wanted was to catch her making a wrong move and that would be the end of her employment at *EIC*. Once, Jackie even accused her of being responsible for missing petty cash in the accounting department. Though Summer was never given access to the safe, Jackie's suspicions were founded on the fact that Summer was good friends with Veronica, one of the accountants in that department. It turned out that Veronica was the one responsible.

Summer balanced the marketing report with her transaction report. After finishing the recap sheet, she made copies.

Summer was quite shy. She didn't socialize with most of the employees either at work or outside of work. Her best friend, Nadia was the only person who saw through her shell and understood her. Most of the *EIC* employees looked at her as if she was strange. Most men thought she was strange. Even when Nadia took her out to a nightclub, she could not muster up the nerve to talk to any of the men at the club. They ogled over her no doubt because she was a "redbone" with long hair and an enticing derriere. She knew all they probably wanted was sex and there was no right man out there. After that time she'd gone to the club two years ago,

Randa Wise

she never went into another one again. How did Nadia expect her to find a decent man at a club?

CHAPTER THREE:

"Who was the young woman that came in here this morning looking for that report?" Jonathan asked Kim. He had been itching to ask Kim that for over an hour and could not contain his curiosity any longer.

"Her name is Summer Douglas, I think. She's been with the company about three or four months now. She handles the deposit for the *West Africans in America*."

Jonathan gave her a curt nod and returned to his office, thinking that she looked a little young for that type of position. Since when did his father hire teens to work there during the winter? This was only May and if she'd been there three or four months, that meant she worked there during school months.

At lunchtime, Summer met Nadia in the cafeteria. They headed outside to enjoy the spring weather while having their meal.

"So, have you met Jonathan yet?" Nadia asked with an impish smirk. Summer knew something was behind Nadia's eyes, they were full of mischief. She had been trying for years to get her hooked up with some eligible brother.

"I got a glimpse of him." Summer answered. "He seems okay."

"I know how you feel about Jackie —"

"Nadia, please." she interrupted. "If I wasn't eating lunch, maybe we could talk about her."

"Just listen." Nadia insisted. "I know Jonathan. He's a very good listener. I'm telling you that if you don't think that idea for a publication for black seniors can be be presented by you with the backing of Jackie, go straight to Jonathan."

"Abu Sosseh listens to me." she retorted.

Nadia erupted with laughter. "Summer, Abu does what Jackie tells him to do. He's one of those African guys who'll chase down an American sister thinking he'll get a green card out of the deal if he goes along with her demands."

"What are you saying?"

"If Jackie tells that guy to toss your idea out the window and that the bosses wouldn't want to hear it, he'll do just that. Everyone in this company has an agenda. Her agenda is making sure you don't move up that ladder. I've been telling you that for four months now."

"Really?"

Nadia leaned over the table and whispered to Summer, "And he's in love with that witch. But all she likes about him is being able to order him around like some child."

"That's wrong."

"You tell me. It's also selfish. She knows she can wrap men around her dainty little finger and she uses it for her own selfishness."

To solve his curiosity, Jonathan called the Human Resources department and requested Summer Douglas's file. Many people lied about their ages in order to obtain employment. This Summer looked like a seventeen year old. He looked through the file until he located a photocopy of her Maryland driver's license. So it was legit, she was not some kid working there. Once he added up the year she was born to the date, he saw that she had turned twenty-five February ninth. He heard three short raps at the door. "Come in." he called out.

The door swung open and in pranced Jackie, walking seductively in his direction. He had to shake off the sexual response that he got from looking at her in that fitting dress.

"You wanted to see me?" she asked.

He had forgotten that he'd called her extension an hour ago. His thoughts were so monopolized with Summer that he hadn't had time to remember calling Jackie.

He closed Summer's file and said, "Yes. Have a seat."

She closed the door, sitting in one of the green leather chairs facing his mahogany desk. Jonathan glared into her partially deep-set piercing eyes before speaking. His eyes then traveled to her stubborn lips, though straight, full and seductive. She's pretty, he thought, *but what a nasty little attitude!* In his experience, some of the most attractive women were always the most difficult or they thought that a man would never leave because they were gorgeous. How wrong some of them were! It took more to being a fox than beauty. To him, a true fox knew how to respect a man. He wondered about Summer. Was she a true fox or an empty box?

He cleared his throat, dropping his pencil on the desk. He said, "So what happened, Jackie?"

Smiling, she answered, "What exactly are you talking about, Jonny?"

She leaned over, displaying the fullness of her voluptuous breasts, peering at him from above the V-neck dress. She knew one of his many weaknesses for her was her breasts. His large hands fit perfectly whenever he encompassed them in passionate strokes. He hated being called "Jonny". That was the name one of his ex-girlfriends gave him when he was twenty. He'd allowed Jackie to get by with things his mother wouldn't have even thought about doing. It was time to put an end to it, especially if he thought this relationship was worth resuming. He was exhausted with landing into these dead-end relationships. He didn't want to bed-hop or have one night stands. He at least had been in a relationship with Jackie. Maybe she'd changed once they split. Maybe she had time to ponder over her mistakes because he'd had time to ponder over his. The last few months should have given them both enough time to regroup. He missed her.

"Why did you behave like such a mad woman on our last date?" He wanted her to get off her chest whatever was bothering her so that they could put it all behind them and renew their friendship.

For moments, she dropped her head and stared at the fancy design on her air-brushed nails. "I asked you a simple question and you evaded It." she finally answered.

"I didn't think, 'let's give it some time' was evasive, Jackie."

She stared into his large, penetrating eyes. All she could remember was being in his strong embrace, kissing him and her heart accelerating during passionate lovemaking and sometimes pure, raw sex.

"I love you, Jonathan. You know that. I know I was being unreasonable. But I thought after all the time we'd been spending together, you wanted what I wanted."

Was that an apology? he thought before saying, "I never said I didn't want to get married. However, I had only known you three months. You're talking lifetime commitment here."

Though marriage was something he wanted most in his life, he wouldn't take a hasty trip down matrimony lane just to stand before a minister with a strange woman to his left. It wasn't worth it. He wanted to make sure that the woman he took vows with was the right woman for him.

"Listen, if you'd like, we can start again." she said with the arrogance he did not miss. Did she actually think she was doing him a favor if they resumed a relationship?

Her words then trailed off, her body language now had his full attention, the way she raised her head proudly, as if he was begging her. His eyes jumped to her cleavage quickly and back to her face. Now, before him, he saw a woman sporting a long black dress, pointed hat, and a broom stick in tow.

"Name one woman who can give you what I have?" she said with too much confidence for him to stand.

Ironically, his thoughts shifted to Summer. He didn't know where that came from, but now that his thoughts had gone to Summer, he wondered about her. Could she offer him more than Jackie? He didn't know the woman but that could change. He did not always exercise his ability to get what he wanted but he was entertaining thoughts of doing so as he further thought about Summer.

"At this point, I don't know, Jackie." he said as if he'd heard everything she had said. He hadn't. He'd zoned out on her and didn't care. "I'm your friend, always will be. But I was deeply hurt and embarrassed by your behavior. And not answering my calls was the topping on the dessert."

Humph! she thought. She was hardly settling for a mere friendship, especially after what he'd given her last year. She would make it up to him. Nothing would stand in her way!

He couldn't get pass the fact that she was selfish. He should have heeded the negative signs back then – the way she would cling to him whenever another woman was present. He thought about Candi, Nelda's daughter. How could she believe that he would sleep with a nineteen-year-old child, someone half his age? Her possessiveness and self-centered displays were all red lights that Jackie was about herself and no one else's feelings mattered, including his. He remembered how hurt Nelda was when Jackie tried to jump on Candi. Nelda wanted to strangle Jackie and even threatened to quit and his mother, Donya had to beg Nelda not to quit. She had been working for his parents since Jonathan was in elementary school. If it had not been for Donya holding Nelda away, she would have attacked Jackie for trying to attack her daughter. Finally, they were able to calm down the drama that went down in their dining room. Maurice was infuriated by the entire episode and voiced that they'd never had this type of ghettoism go down in his house. Ever!

Above all, Jackie was one of the worst types of gold diggers. She had much to gain if she married into the Wesley family with their history of "old money". Jonathan's grandfather was also a wealthy man. As far back as he could date, the family always had money. So why did he still care for her? Maybe his desires were defeating sound reasoning, he thought. He hadn't had sex since his last episode with her back in late August. Then again, maybe he was watching the clock. In two years, he would be looking at the big 4-0. Like women, men had biological clocks, as his father warned him. He had wealth, prosperity, education, property – he had it all and no heirs to benefit from it. Once a man found himself, he usually wanted someone to share all his success with. Jonathan was enduring the "Adam before Eve syndrome", having all that he needed to sustain life around him, but no woman to comfort him and be his support system. No children to revere him.

"Are you attending the company picnic next Monday?" he asked. He had to steer this conversation elsewhere. This meeting with her exhausted him.

"Yes, are you?"

Sweet memories of last year's Memorial Day picnic crept into her mind. She remembered how she was sitting alone on the bench in a pensive mood when Jonathan had approached her and introduced himself. Noticing her sadness, he asked her to take a walk with him, leaving other employees at a far distance as they talked and she poured out her heart to him. She told him about a man whom she thought used her for sex. He had asked her how long she'd been with the company since he had not seen her the previous year. She told him she started right before Christmas. When she glanced at his left hand and noticed no wedding ring present, she began methodically devising a plan to sink her claws into him. And quick!

Jonathan's Summer

"Anyway," he stood up, turning her thoughts back to present day, "I'll be bringing a dish this year."

"What could you possibly cook?" she asked, laughing. *She had him now!*

"My parents' chef will make something. But I have a purpose for being here and that's CEO until my father returns. So let me get back to work."

Jackie stood up to leave and he called her again. She turned around, facing him. "Don't sweat the small stuff. Let's take this one day at a time. Okay?"

Smiling, she responded, "Okay."

Once she was in the corridor, she fanned herself with her hand. Being in the presence of him made her literally hot. The temperature below was rising.

When Summer returned from lunch, she had the refund report to handle. Some subscribers weren't satisfied with the publication and that meant the company had to refund the unused portion of their subscriptions. The volume of cancellations did not cause the company to rock or suffer, however. They kept over ninety percent of their subscriber base and the incoming orders far out-weighed cancellations for all publications.

After finishing the refund request report, she went to the accounting department to drop off their copy. Afterwards, she headed back down the hall to the bathroom and from there, back to her office, taking a left, heading back down the long, winding corridor. She began humming the first verse of her favorite song to an old cut by Stevie Wonder called *Lately*.

Jonathan had just emerged from the senior vice president's office of *West Africans in America* when he heard the lovely hum of a song he recognized. He looked to his right and noticed a young woman walking down the hall. Immediately, he recognized her. Summer! His member hardened, demanded by the woman although she did not know it. He could not prevent the signals his eyes transmitted his manhood. Her hips swayed seductively beneath the black denim jeans that fitted her perfectly and her lengthy dark brown ponytail kept rhythm with her curvy bottom. Her nuance intrigued him. She was like that forbidden fruit – knowing he could not have her but that was the reason he wanted her. He watched, mesmerized until she disappeared around the bend. Fortunately for him, she never turned around to witness him staring. He would not have known how to explain why he was if she had. But someone else witnessed it. He'd been so entranced that he hadn't noticed he was being watched.

"Why don't you just go for it and get it over with?" cracked Ricky Channing, the senior vice president of *West Africans in America*. He had exited his office and saw that Jonathan was still standing there. He wondered why he was still there until he spotted Summer walking down the hall.

"Oh, Rick. Man, I didn't even see you standing there." Jonathan said, trying his best to play off what he was doing. It didn't work.

"If she wasn't so damned young, I'd go for it myself."

Jonathan chuckled, still trying to minimize the affect she had on him.

"I mean that shit." Ricky added, not caring who heard him. He was in the position he held because of his education, experience and skills and he'd grown up with Maurice.

Ricky placed his arm around Jonathan gently as they headed in the opposite direction Summer took. "You know, man, when I first saw that chick, I thought to myself, 'I'd like to bang her for days'."

"Rick, you're a married man with grandkids. You ought to be ashamed of yourself."

"Hey, I'm a man, not dead. But you're not listening to me. You've got your head so far up Jackie Shannon's ass that you can't even think straight."

Words of wisdom from an older man himself! Jonathan thought, slightly amused.

"I don't know why you even think that, Rick. That ain't fair."

"I've known you since you were born, Jonathan. Don't be such a wimp. Hey, you want that chick, go get her. You only live once, boy. If I thought like you, I would never have gotten Alicia. She's a fox, I must admit. Even in her late fifties, the girl is baaad!"

Jonathan thought there was some truth to what the old guy was telling him. But what if Summer didn't reciprocate?

"If you talk to Maurice anytime tonight, let him know that he needs to call me." Ricky said. "I'll put him on conference with Greg Wilks so we can get this shit rolling. But for now, I'm outta here. Gotta take the lady to dinner tonight or my ass will end up in the dog house." He threw on his suit jacket and added, "For life."

Jonathan laughed. "I will, Rick. Have a good time at dinner tonight."

"I'll try." Ricky said unenthused as he sauntered off in his expensive suit, holding an equally expensive leather briefcase.

CHAPTER FOUR:

Jonathan reached his office and shut the door. He opened her personnel file, trying to make out the face on the photocopy of her driver's license. The picture didn't do much justice in telling how beautiful she was. But judging by what he saw that morning, she surpassed beauty. His hands caressed the outline of the photo copy. Summer! How appropriate the name for that face. His favorite season of the year. That season usually brought along solace in his life. He wondered if the woman named after his favorite season would bring him the joy and happiness the season usually did. There was only one way to answer that question.

When quitting time arrived, Summer quickly grabbed her belongings and hurried from the department to the third floor to get Nadia.

"You would have thought somebody rung a bell for recess or something." commented Gwen, one of the representatives. Summer had shot by her and out of the department, nearly running into her.

"That girl is strange anyway!" Jackie said to no one in particular, also watching Summer shoot like lightening from the department. It was obvious to all sixteen employees of that department that Summer was not happy there.

Abu's eyes roved Jackie's sexy figure as he said, "Yeah, I agree." he laughed. "very strange."

"Who's strange?"

Both Jackie and Abu turned to the voice at the opposite entrance of the department. By then, everyone had left except the two of them. Her eyes landed right in the middle of a broad chest. He wasn't wearing his suit jacket and his muscles outlined his white dress shirt. Jonathan leaned a shoulder against the wall, his hands in his pockets, looking as if he'd stepped fresh out of a GQ magazine. She stood in a trance.

"One of the employees." she answered smoothly.

Abu returned to his desk, logging off his computer, pretending to be fishing around his desk while he overheard them talk. How he wished Jonathan Wesley would leave and never show his face there again. But he knew that would never happen. Even if he never worked there again, he'd be up for company parties and visits. As long as Jackie was there, so would Jonathan be, Abu thought. Jonathan reminded him of a panther and she was his prey. As the time neared for Jonathan to return, Abu's anger grew with each passing day. He always hated this time of year because it meant he would have to compete with this playa named Jonathan.

"Which employee?" Jonathan wanted to know, giving his ex-girlfriend a quizzical stare that demanded a direct answer.

"Some kid who just started working here in January." she said, waving a dismissing hand.

He wasn't satisfied. "Who might that be?" he insisted.

"Summer Douglas!" spoke Abu's voice from across the department. By this time, he had moved to the copy machine, still pretending to work.

"Oh," Jonathan said, cocking an eyebrow while thinking of how gossip had no place in the company, especially by those who were supposed to present exemplary behavior for those they supervise. "Anyway, I came here because I wanted to know if you had anything planned for this evening, Jackie."

Abu's ears perked up at Jonathan's request and he silently prayed that Jackie would turn down the invitation. One thing he admitted and that was this other man proved to be more than formidable competition for him.

"No, I don't have any plans." she said while Abu bit his bottom lip. "Why?"

"Because I'd like to escort you to a jazz club in Takoma Park."

Jackie's face broke into a big grin, displaying perfectly set teeth. "Thanks, I'd love to go."

"Does seven agree with you?"

"Seven's perfect."

What a player! Abu thought. He wanted to call Jonathan every single curse word in the book. He thought that if he was as tall, handsome and rich as his enemy, he could be of some competition. To him, Jackie went after what was tangible, the good looks, height, a fat bank account and a flawless body – everything Jonathan represented and everything he did not. Abu however thought that he could offer her something this other man could not – love, a subject lover boy himself needed to take a real life course in.

After Jonathan left the office, he headed to his Jag, tossing his suit jacket on the back seat. He slammed the door, wanting to punish himself for that move he'd just made. He would have preferred asking Summer instead of Jackie. But what the hell was he supposed to do? Sit around the house all evening? He sat in the car for a few minutes, rationalizing. *A person had to work with the cards they're dealt with,* he thought. Maybe this was it, the hand he was dealt. He could have asked Summer out and she turned him down. Besides, he did not know Summer, she could have been married or already involved with another man for all he knew. He started the ignition and popped in a CD, resigning himself to the possibility that she was involved. How could a woman like her not have a man?

After dropping Nadia off at home, Summer headed home. She met her father in the kitchen cooking. "Hi, my king!" she playfully greeted with a kiss on his cheek. "How was work today, princess?" he asked, removing the baked potatoes from the oven.

"Okay. Any calls for me?" she sorted through her mail while awaiting his answer.

He put the potholder back in place and answered, "Tina called. She wants to know if you'd be available to watch the kids on Saturday."

"Anything for Tina. Besides, I love her kids." She headed to the phone in the living room.

Her father turned around and shouted behind her. "If you love her kids so much, maybe you ought to have some of your own."

She tossed back, "Marriage first, Daddy."

"Then get married!" he shot back.

Summer waved his last comment away and picked up the telephone. She told her cousin that she would baby sit the children while she and her husband went to Hartford.

After dinner, Summer went upstairs and began working on her proposal for the boss. She turned on her computer and put on her wire-framed specs. Later, she called Nadia to update her on the information she'd found on the internet about good eating and healthy living.

"I've told you endless times that Jackie isn't going to listen, Summer." Nadia insisted.

"I've even found ideal vacation spots for black seniors." Summer said, openly ignoring Nadia's warning. "The ones with the means can make a trip to the mother-land. Do you realize how beautiful the Ivory Coast is? And what's unbelievable is the different healthy foods seniors can consume that are also good on the taste buds. We have to consider that an overwhelmingly number of black folks suffer from diabetes and high blood pressure." Summer was so excited that she didn't hear Nadia say something in between. "I've looked at different hair styles our older sistahs can wear that are sporty, yet conservative. And here's the good part: sexy black seniors and good exercise. Who would not be interested in a publication like this? Even if you subscribed to it for your parents."

"Tell all that stuff to your father." Nadia was finally able to get a word in. Summer noticed the sarcasm loaded in her tone.

"Nadia, why do you have to go there?"

"Because you won't go to Jonathan!" she tossed back. "You know Jackie is not going to back you up and turn a deaf ear. She doesn't want to see you make progress on that job. She'll probably even tell you that they're not looking for that type of material. She'll tell you anything just to make you feel like shit and kill your enthusiasm."

"I cannot go directly to Jonathan or even Maurice without first proposing my idea to my department manger. It's not that simple and you know it."

"You can do it during non-working hours, that way no one will see you having a meeting with him. You can behave like someone on the outside who doesn't work for the company. No one can tell you who to talk to after work."

"But this is about work! Anyway, Jonathan isn't going to listen to me if I don't go to Jackie first. He'll probably ask me if I've run it by my managers first."

"I'll say this and then I'm going to bed. You wear me out sometimes, Summer." Nadia said with a yawn. "Jonathan won't give a damn if you went over Jackie's head and went directly to him. He is not the snob his daddy is. That chain of command bull is his father's rule. Jonathan allows more liberty than that."

"I'll think about it then."

"You promise?"

"Yes, I promise. Will I have to pick you up tomorrow morning or is Jose bringing you to work?"

"Jose will take me. Goodnight, sistah."

Summer lied in bed hours later, thinking about her idea. She was confused. She didn't know how Jonathan would respond to the idea though Nadia kept insisting that he would be receptive. Nadia had never lied to her of course but anyone could be wrong – and she could be wrong about Jonathan. Summer felt so intimidated by him. Maybe it was because he was so handsome and emanated an air of pride. Men like that made her run in the other direction. What the hell was she thinking? *All* men made her run in the other direction. Could this man's appearance bring along the cocky attitude and overgrown ego? She drifted into slumber in the grips of pondering.

* * *

After leaving the jazz club, Jonathan took Jackie back to her condo in Hyattsville, MD. He stopped the engine, hopped out of his Jag and opened the door for her.

"Thanks, Jonathan. I had a wonderful time." she said, peering into his regal face.

He glared back and his lips began searching hers. He jerked away when he recalled a telephone conversation he happened to overhear one afternoon. Jackie had never known he heard it. She was telling her main sidekick, Lisa that if she got pregnant by him, that would expedite a marriage proposal for sure. That conversation occurred the day before she stormed out of the restaurant, after he'd told her that he needed time to consider marriage. He wanted children – Jackie was aware of this. But he would have preferred input as to when to become a father, not forced into it. Deceptiveness was always something he detested. Until that very moment, he had dismissed what he overheard. Suddenly, it came flooding back. He didn't like ending a relationship simply because the woman had flaws. However,

Jonathan's Summer

his mother always told him that there were three things in a relationship a person should never violate: love, trust and respect. Love was something he took rather seriously and respect and trust he took equally seriously. He had to resolve one fact now: Jackie was a stealthy woman.

"What's wrong?" she asked, rattling his thoughts.

"Nothing." he said, looking away.

"Then kiss me, you handsome boy." She jerked at his necktie and forced his head down. He gave her a kiss, closing his eyes. He then took a deep breath and said, "Jacqueline, it's late. I'll see you tomorrow."

She knew that when he called her "Jacqueline" something was wrong. She hastily tried to do something to change his mind. "Why don't you come in for a little while. I got a little something for you."

"It's late, Jacqueline. We'll talk tomorrow."

He saw her to the front door before walking back to his car. As he drove, thoughts of Summer began assaulting him again. Jackie and Abu claimed she was strange but he could not agree. On the contrary, she ignited desires in him that had lain so dormant for so long, he didn't know it was possible to feel that way about a woman again. The feelings he had for Jackie when he'd first met her didn't compare to the ones he had for Summer so he knew this would not be a temporary admiration. There was something awfully unique about her. She seemed so fresh, so innocent and so "foxy" as his father and his father's best friend Ricky would say. She was high caliber, nothing like the dime-a-dozen chicks he'd run into while spending time in the DC area, that would only be after trying to figure out what the total digits were in his bank account.

Tuesday morning, Summer woke up refreshed. A little sleep did wonders for her, refreshing her sense of reason. Nadia was right. She felt even better about her idea. She went downstairs, greeted her father and ate breakfast.

"I have to go, Daddy." she announced, rising from the table.

"OK. Call me later."

She hopped into her father's van and sped off to work. When she arrived, she stopped on the third floor, said a few words to Nadia and rode the elevator to the fourth. When she entered the department, she noticed Jackie and Abu near his desk, engaged in a private conversation. The department was open-space and didn't afford most of the employees privacy. The only private areas of the department were Jackie's office and hers. She thought about pitching her idea to them but thought maybe now was not the time. After tossing her back pack onto the extra chair in her office, she went to the computer room to collect her daily reports.

Both Jackie and Abu took notice of her Washington Wizards baseball cap, blue jeans and red cotton pullover. She could feel their eyes pinned to her back but maintained her cool air. She continued on her path to the computer room and a repeat of the day before presented itself. The report for her department's publication was missing.

"Jason!" she called out.

Her lack of consideration that he could be busy annoyed him. The day before, she had disturbed him from handling something urgent. "They're in the big boss's office again, Summer!" he called from one of the terminals he sat behind. He'd be damned if he would get up and face her. His countenance showed the anger he was feeling. That woman had some real issues, he mused silently, wondering why the airhead didn't think of the possibility that Jonathan could have her reports again.

She wondered why the big boss kept taking the reports. She stormed down the corridor. This only slowed down her being able to get her work done early so that she could bullshit in her small private office the rest of the day and talk to her friend, Nadia over the phone. Her job did not always require a full eight hours. She made sure it stayed that way. Sometimes things were hectic and she didn't finish all of her work in one day. But most times, she was finished by two or three. Now, this idiot was making it harder for her to get her day started and complete.

When she opened the suite's door, Kim was not there. She decided to do a quick scan around the office, hoping she'd spot the reports lying around somewhere. She could grab them and get out of dodge before anyone saw her.

"Looking for something?" asked a voice entering the suite.

Summer jolted at the melodious voice of the man standing behind her. "I-I, I was looking for my reports." she stammered, turning around and her eyes locked into the chest of a man dressed in an expensive dark gray suit, white shirt, and a tie that complemented the suit.

She tilted her head back and caught a full view of the boss's son. *What a heavenly sight!* she thought as her mouth hung open. *Talk about a smooth but masculine complexion.* She took in his unusual hue, sort of like a dark honey. He had probing eyes, as if there was a constant question in them. She could feel her nerves jump, her stomach tightening up in little tiny knots. She never imagined she would be this close to him. She could feel his heat, his gaze causing her to feel as if she was under some type of microscopic scrutiny. Her heart drummed violently in her chest and she could feel it all the way in her feet.

Jonathan stood there, gazing into her golden-brown complexion. She had those young, innocent eyes – bedroom eyes. *Beautiful!* he thought. *Splendid! Not a flaw on that face to be seen. But that baseball cap has got to go!*

He swallowed a laugh before he spoke up. He knew she was nervous and it amused him because she had nothing to be nervous about. He should be the one shaking in the presence of this masterpiece God created. "They're in my office." He walked toward the office.

Jonathan's Summer

She stood, her feet were so rooted into the forest green carpet that she could not move. She decided she would wait in Kim's station for him to return the reports. He turned around, rewarding her with a warm smile. "I don't bite. You may come back and get them." he spoke, as she noticed him giving her an admiring once-over. Summer reluctantly walked into his office. This was the first time she ever walked through the door of Maurice's airy office.

She noticed a compact refrigerator in the corner that was exactly the color of the forest green carpet. Next to it was a bar. In the other extreme corner was a round mahogany conference table that perfectly matched the desk with three high-backed green leather cushioned chairs seated around it. The person responsible for doing the color schemes of the masculine-looking office did a marvelous job, she had to admit. It reflected the personality of the occupant of the place, which spoke power, wealth. Summer glanced through the balcony, which overlooked the executives' parking lot, spying the freshly cut shrubbery lining the side street. The certificates and plaques lining the walls then captured her attention. The only object in the room her eyes could not seem to meet was the tallest figure in the room, the man who stood before her. His presence made her tremble.

"Each day, I tell Kim to collect these from the computer room. I'm trying to get a heads-up on how much revenue is brought in by subscriber new orders and renewals. But don't fret, after this week, you'll be able to get your reports without my interference." he spoke softly, although the bass in his voice was still not hidden.

Her hand trembled as she reached for the report. "Thanks." she said around a dry throat.

"By the way," he said before she could make a hasty departure. No! He was not allowing her to take flight before he had a conversation with her, although since she'd come in, he felt as if he was speaking to himself. "I don't think we've met. I'm Jonathan Wesley, taking over for Maurice until he returns." He extended a hand and she reached out and shook it, a little embarrassed by her sweaty palms.

He chuckled, trying to loosen the tension in the room. "Would you happen to have a name?" he asked, knowing what it was but wanting her to tell him. Wanting to hear her speak to him, although his question would only get him a two-word response, her first and last name.

"Summer Douglas. Nice meeting you, sir." she said.

"Jonathan would be more acceptable than sir, Summer."

When she finally looked at him, he was smiling, showing perfect white teeth. Summer cleared her throat. She decided at that impromptu moment she would tell him, tossing the idea of going through Jackie and Abu. She never got the chance. Four people abruptly entered Kim's workstation. She heard them talking and laughing loudly.

"I gotta go!" she said, dashing out of the office, colliding right into one of the editors of *Ethiopian Journal*. She dropped her report. "Oh, I'm so sorry, sir. I hope I didn't hurt you." she spoke humbly.

"You didn't, young lady." said the kind East African older man. "Just don't hurt yourself." He picked up her report, handed it to her and smiled.

She smiled back after thanking him.

Jonathan looked on as she clumsily made her way out of the suite. He hadn't meant to make her nervous.

The editor gave Jonathan a toothy grin and said, "Such a nice kid. But I don't know why she's so quiet all the time."

"This is the first time I ever even heard her talk." the managing editor of the *Journal* said, laughing as she spoke.

So she was a quiet one, Jonathan mused to himself. Did that mean he could have a clandestine relationship with her? Unlike Jackie, who broadcasted to the entire company that he was seeing her, Summer could prove to be different. He pushed all of those thoughts from his mind as he and the other four sat down to have their short meeting.

"Where's Ricky?" he asked the managing editor.

"He's on his way down." she said. "He and Chris Moyer had something to iron out."

CHAPTER FIVE:

Summer's heart was still racing when she reached her department. She quickly realized that Jonathan Wesley could strike nerves no other man had ever been able to. Those young thugs in her neighborhood couldn't compare to him – he was a real man. She hoped she didn't have to work closely with him. Her thoughts were so occupied with Jonathan, she never realized Jackie and Abu's absence until they returned. As long as Jackie had a complaint, she knew she would never get a promotion unless she transferred to another department.

* * *

Jonathan met with most of the writers, editors, marketing staff and department managers in the third floor conference room for a meeting. The meeting lasted for nearly two hours. Most of the writers were the ones who had questions, which prolonged what otherwise would have been a one hour meeting. The writers showed more interest in establishing a new publication because it gave them something new and exciting to work on. And Jonathan could tell that all twenty-nine writers in that meeting were bidding to get a spot or column in this new publication, each secretly trying to out-bid the other. This new publication could mean many things for the writers, such as being promoted to actually running the publication itself. However, no one had ideas yet. Just before the meeting adjourned, Kim Justen reminded them of the upcoming company picnic and told everyone to email her what type of dish they would be bringing to the gathering. Everyone then headed back to their departments.

The two hours Jackie was in the meeting were the best hours of Summer's whole week. Maybe they should have meetings every day, she thought with amusement.

"Summer, I need to speak with you a moment." She looked up and Jackie had entered the deposit room, closing the door behind her.

What did I do this time? she wondered, staring blankly at Jackie. "How can I help you, Jacqueline?" she asked.

"I know you're not a manager or team leader of any sort."

Oh, no kidding?

"But your manner of attire will have to change." Jackie said, glancing at her baseball cap.

"Perhaps I should dress like you?" Summer raised a brow and glanced at the low-cut neckline of Jackie's navy, hooker-style wrap-around dress that was five inches above the knees when she sat down.

Bitch, you could never be me! Jackie thought but said, "No, but you'll have to quit wearing those silly baseball caps. This is a professional environment and we have many visitors coming here from outside companies. You need to dress more presentable for this company. It represents Maurice Wesley."

"He's never said anything to me about my attire." Summer shot back.

"That's because he leaves it up to us department managers to straighten out matters such as this. The jeans are fine from time to time but don't come to work as if you're headed to a ball game or something."

Summer knew this was just another avenue Jackie used to pick on her. It had to be something at least once a week. She gave Jackie a curt nod of acknowledgement before she was left alone.

She was furious by the time the witch left. She would leave the baseball caps at home. However, she wasn't trying to look like some of them hoochies that came to work all G'd up and wearing those tracks in their hair just to impress their male co-workers. She didn't need hair extensions – she was blessed with an enviable length of hair that Jackie and all the rest of the them hoes wished they had. She knew they were hating on her big time. She hadn't done anything to any of them and wondered why they always found a reason to laugh at her and try and make her feel stupid whenever she asked a question. She'd overheard the whispers, the so-called inconspicuous conversations that took place in the bathroom. What Nadia said was true: "They hate you because you don't share all your personal business with them."

At lunchtime, Summer gave her father a call before getting something to eat. Afterwards, she met Nadia in the cafeteria and they joined a few others who decided to enjoy the late spring weather outside while feasting. She told Nadia about her meeting with Jonathan and then Jackie.

"Why didn't you say something to him about the idea?" Nadia quizzed.

"Because…Oh, I don't know. Like I said, I have to go through the chain of command first. That means going through Jackie."

Nadia waved a dismissing hand and picked up a French fry smothered in ketchup from Summer's plate. "Forget about Jackie, will you. Nothing you do is going to please her. You may get rid of the baseball caps, lose the jeans and pullovers and dress like Hillary Clinton, and that whore will still find something to pick on you about."

"What I need…"

"You need to go directly to the top dog before Maurice returns. You don't got much time, girl." Nadia interrupted.

"Well, I don't know."

"Have you suddenly lost your nerve? I guess nothing I've been telling you for the past few days has reached that brain of yours yet, Summer. What? Do you feel stuff rattling around when you shake your head?"

"That's not fair, Na-Na." Summer said with a laugh.

When Nadia looked up and across the parking lot, she spotted Jackie and Jonathan getting out of his Jaguar and heading in their direction.

"Maybe I was wrong about what I said about going to Jonathan." Nadia said.

"Why?"

"Look," she said, inclining her head in the couple's direction.

Summer's eyes followed Nadia's. All she could see was a couple that looked as if they enjoyed each other's company. They walked closely as Jackie must have been laughing at some corny joke he told. Women were so phony! Summer thought. She felt suddenly betrayed. She had begun trusting what Nadia said. As it appeared, he betrayed the trust of both of them. She realized now that anything she told him would go straight to Jackie. There goes the idea right out the window, she thought. If Abu would not listen to her idea, how in the world would Jonathan? To Summer, Jackie was just a pretty woman who had mastered the art of luring men and altering their thinking – even when it concerned purposeful matters. How could a woman like her build up a man like him? She would bet that if Maurice ever retired and Jonathan took over the company, the place would be in trouble because the new CEO would have a dangerous woman by his side.

Nadia openly rolled her eyes at them. Jonathan disappointed her by getting back with that tramp. He had told her some of what happened regarding his break-up with Jackie. He'd called her all the way from Greenville and asked how she was doing. When she asked about his relationship with Jackie, he told her it was over. She heard the sadness and depression in his voice, for he was deeply hurt. Now Nadia thought that he was back to using his balls while his brain took recess.

The couple walked towards Summer and Nadia but when they were within a few feet, Jonathan slowed down. Waiting for him, Jackie stopped and stood next to him, her stance and body language openly expressing her possession of him.

"Summer?" Jonathan said.

Summer brought her head up slowly and met his dangerous gaze. "Yes, sir?"

He laughed lightly. "I thought we went over this just this morning? Call me Jonathan. How are you, by the way?"

"Fine." she spoke softly. The tone of her voice was as meek as a lamb.

"That's good. And how are you, Mrs. Nadia Cruz?"

Nadia looked up, giving him an openly flirtatious grin. "Fine, Mr. Jonathan Wesley. Practicing your Espanol lately?"

"I'm a little rusty now." He smiled back.

"I'll be happy to oil you down and give you a refresher." Nadia said, noticing Jackie's jealous expression and openly ignoring it. She knew it was pissing her off and kept going at it.

Jackie glanced the other way and both women could see her jaws tightening.

"That's a thought." he said with a laugh, knowing Nadia was always quick when it came to taunting Jackie. But what could he do? Nadia was his friend. "You ladies have a nice afternoon."

"Yeah, you do the same, Jonathan and give some serious thought to my offer." Nadia called behind them as they headed off.

Nadia was laughing so hard when they left, her side ached.

"Girl, what were you doing?" Summer asked. "That was the big boss."

"Like I don't already know that! But did you see the look on that bitch's face? She knows she don't have him nailed down. She never will."

Jackie's jaws were so tight by the time they reached the elevator, her temples were aching. Seems he basked in all the attention he got from other women and rubbed her nose in it.

"If you saw Summer just this morning, why are you speaking to her again?" she asked suspiciously, wondering what they talked about earlier.

Jonathan glanced down at the five-six woman, his eyes went towards the ceiling, heaved a sigh. "I don't know some of the new employees here. I want them to feel comfortable working here. After all, they'll have to work for me the next three months. Or did you forget that my main reason for being back in Maryland in the first place was to run the company?"

"Those young girls have crushes on you. And you're just standing there enjoying every sick moment of it." she shot back curtly.

"Jackie, why are you reading so much into this? And from what I gathered, they're not young girls, they look more like young women."

She would be damned if she would let him slip through her fingers at this point. She was going on thirty-four, ready to get married and have a couple of babies.

He could clearly see that she had not changed an ounce. He'd been there before, now recognizing the signs. This time, it was not new to him but rather familiar. He couldn't go back to her, only to end up miserable in a relationship simply because they were already on familiar ground with each other. So many stayed in relationships because they felt it was safe. Not him – he would cut his losses and be done.

She pressed the elevator button and turned her back to him.

"Are you giving me attitude again?" he asked.

"No. Forget it. I guess I behaved a little impulsively."

Repulsively was a more appropriate word to describe her behavior, he thought. And he would not forget this time, as he'd done a year ago. Her attitude will continue slapping him in the face, reminding him that she was a selfish woman. Why would he even expect her to change? Maybe she would be ideal for some other man but not him. They headed their separate ways once reaching the fourth floor. Jackie was still fuming by the time she reached her office. She slammed her purse on the desk and slumped into her chair.

"Is everything okay?" Abu asked, always at her beck and call. He entered her office and shut the door.

She stared at him several moments before saying, "I'm okay. Can you get me a copy of June's issue of *Nubian Entertainment*?"

She wanted the issue because she wanted to get new ideas for hairstyles. Now that Jonathan was back in town, it was time for a new do. But she couldn't help the alarm that went off within her, the sound of her own words echoing, asking her how long would she be able to hold on to him.

"I'll be right back." Abu left the office to fulfill her request.

She stared from the window, watching vehicles enter and leave the main parking lot, thinking of Jonathan. It was no doubt that he found Summer attractive but what irritated her was that he seemed so open with it. And what *had* they discussed this morning? Why would he find that broke-down chick so appealing? She was fashion-challenged, having no idea what style was. Hell, she didn't even walk like a lady. How could she fit into the Wesley family if Jonathan wanted her as his wife? She didn't believe him when he said he was simply trying to get acquainted with some of the new employees. To hell with that! She saw the excitement in his eyes when he spotted Summer and Nadia sitting on the bench. The only way to get Summer out of the way would be to fire her. She had to concoct something, start a paper trail, come up with a valid reason before Jonathan became too "acquainted" with her.

When Summer returned to work, she noticed Jackie's door was open as she passed. She would not let Jackie know that she intimidated her – that would be like giving her the stick to whip her with. She didn't care if Jonathan seemed to have been flirting with her or Nadia. If so, Jackie deserved every second of it.

After finishing the reports, Summer made copies of the work sheet and started her rounds to the marketing and accounting departments. On her way back, she met Jonathan heading down the corridor in her direction. Her first instinct was to turn and run the other way but she didn't. She walked toward him in an attempt to pass but he apparently wanted to stop and talk to her.

"Summer?"

"Yes, Jonathan?"

"Is everything okay? I mean, with your job?" He asked, glaring down at her with a look of concern in his handsome features.

"Fine." she shrugged.

"I was briefed about what you do. But if you ever have any concerns, feel free to talk to me about them. I'm not untouchable."

He felt compelled to say that, knowing how Jackie was. Since the incident during lunchtime, he didn't know what type of trick she might pull from under her sleeve. Jackie was only concerned about one thing – that was holding on to him and she would be ready to resort to any measure to remove any woman who stepped into her path.

Summer smiled, showing her teeth. Just as quickly as she smiled, she closed her mouth. Not only did she show her teeth, she showed her wire orthodontic retainer she had worn since having her braces removed two years ago. It didn't surprise him though. He smiled back and patted her shoulder lightly, causing a brush fire to rush through her body.

At four, Summer was feeling quite elated. Her feelings were due to the fact that there might be some hope she could talk to Jonathan regarding her idea for a new publication. Nonetheless, part of her had to admit that when he smiled he aroused that virgin body of hers.

"So, are you going to do it?" Nadia asked, sitting next to Summer in the caravan.

"I will but not for a couple of days. Friday seems like the perfect time because if Jackie finds out, her entire weekend will be ruined, thinking about how smart I really am."

"You little devil!"

"I learned from the best, Nadia."

Nadia opened the door and hopped out, telling her friend goodbye. Before Summer pulled off, she noticed Renee Lyles's car sitting in front of Nadia's house. She wondered what Renee was doing there. Summer didn't approve of Nadia hanging out with Renee because the woman was trouble. But good old loyal Nadia Cruz thought she could save the world and turn a misfit like Renee into a child of God. If Renee didn't want to help herself, there wouldn't be anything Nadia could do to help her either.

CHAPTER SIX:

It was close to seven when Jonathan arrived home. He kicked off his shoes, poured himself a glass of orange juice, intending to relax the remainder of the evening. He perused some of the ideas that had been proposed to him that afternoon. None seemed that original except a proposal for a periodical for Asian-Americans Kim Justen had given him that day. He decided he would fax it to his father's stateroom.

He went over the ideas three of the writers had given him and made a mental note to stay open for ideas. The game had just begun.

He stood up, thinking of nothing in particular as his eyes roved the many African carvings lining the walls in the parlor of the guesthouse. His thoughts were interrupted when he heard at knock at the door. He uttered an expletive as he headed for the door. His brain had been disturbed from the short break it took. Since returning to the office, his mind had been taking on so many different matters – work, dealing with Jackie and Summer often sailing through his mind.

"Mr. Wesley," said Will, the chef, "I thought you could use some dinner so I brought you some."

Will came in, ceremoniously placing the tin-covered containers on the small kitchen table. He began removing the covers but Jonathan stopped him.

"I'll handle it from here, Will. Thanks."

"Certainly, Mr. Wesley." he said with a smile.

Jonathan didn't like being served. He'd been away from it for so long, he was used to being a bachelor without people serving him.

Once Will was gone, Jonathan removed the covers and the smell of baked fish, Au Graten potatoes, and biscuits assaulted his nostrils. Will also left a huge slice of German chocolate cake for dessert. His hunger pains were becoming violent now. He hadn't had lunch and didn't realize he was hungry until the chef delivered dinner.

He thought of Summer and how he would like to share this delicious meal with her. Loneliness sometimes consumed him and whenever he thought of her, the feelings of loneliness were even stronger, especially at quiet moments such as this one.

She seemed so shy, but there was more to her than what most people saw. Jonathan saw it. He saw innocence, class and the right ingredient of sexiness to drive him insane. He thought about the incident in the corridor, when she smiled but obviously embarrassed she mistakenly showed her wire retainer, quickly closed her mouth. He was much older than she, for women in his own age group usually attracted him. This was the first time he had been so attracted to someone more than six years younger, and she was twelve years younger. He wondered if she would date an older man. He wanted to marry and have children – she was young enough to still have them. He wanted a family more than life itself.

The doorbell chimed again. Jonathan put down his fork and headed to the door, hoping that Jackie didn't happen to appear out of the blue. That woman would do something conniving like that, announce her presence without calling first.

He darted towards the door. His brother and youngest sibling, Jerome stood there, a garment bag tossed over one of his broad shoulders, another suitcase on the doorstep. Jerome was younger by four years. There was only about a year between each sibling.

Looking pass Jerome, Jonathan noticed his brother had carelessly parked his brand new BMW off to the side of the house, on the lawn.

"Mom's gonna kill you if she finds out you parked your car there." he told him. "You know how much she loves her lawn."

Jerome shrugged and smiled, his sunglasses tilted, touching his nose. He hugged Jonathan. "'Sup, bruh-man!"

"I saw your Jag parked in the west garage so I knew you were here. Although I thought you would be out with Jackie. How are things with that situation?" Jerome queried. "Has she rekindled that male drive in you?"

Jonathan wanted to tell him that someone else had caught his attention. He decided not to – was not sure where Summer's head was.

"No, man. I can't really say we're going out like that anymore."

Jerome poured a glass of wine. "Well, I didn't come all the way from New York to get into your personal life. Of course, this is my monthly home-coming and I need to get started working. Got a meeting with Chris Moyer in the morning." he said, speaking of one of *Centric's* editors. "I have most of the chart completed for the month of July." He paused, taking a sip from his glass. "I know how my subscribers rely on the investing tips I put out each month."

"Gotta keep making that money." Jonathan added.

"You know some of them call me all the way up on Wall Street for specific advice. Being a stock broker is hard work, man."

"Money and women have always been your favorites. I figured you rather loved the life. Would you like some dinner? There's plenty here."

"Sure. Speaking of women, once I finish up here, I have to be going. I promised Amanda a trip to Maine before the weather starts getting cold. You know summer ends up there around August."

Jonathan shook his head. He loved women and was considered virile by many. But Jerome played the field!

Jerome sat at the table with his dinner on one side of him and the laptop on the other, concentrating more on what was on the monitor than the plate. Jonathan began loading the dishwasher. Thinking of Summer was causing him to swell.

Because he knew it was impossible to have her body next to his, he worked off his stress in the weight room and put an end to his wanton desires with a cold shower afterwards.

* * *

Two days had gone by since Jonathan spoke to Summer. He wondered if she was avoiding him. An alarming thought that Jackie may have fired her struck him hard in the chest. He called Summer's extension and when she answered the phone, relief swept through him.

"Hello, Summer."

Her right hand fingers paused on the adding machine. That voice! She wondered why he was doing this to her. She couldn't be his type – he seemed to go after the fly women, the ones who wore the trendy clothes and all the banging hairstyles. She was too plain for his style – he was a man who sported Faragamo, Versace, Vitton and Armani. Not only that, didn't he consider her a little too young?

"Jonathan?"

"Yes. I just called to say hello. Haven't talked to you in a couple of days. How's life treating you?"

Her lips trembled at his question. She was still too nervous to mention the proposal. Though she had already taken Nadia's advice to pitch the idea to him, she still chose a cowardly method of doing so. "Everything is fine."

"Good. Good," he said hesitantly and she could tell he felt equally awkward. "I just wanted to say hello. And hopefully we'll talk later."

As soon as he hung up, Kim entered his office. "Finally, you're off the phone." she said, dropping a large brown envelope on the desk in front of him.

There were times when he got the impression that Kim had a crush on him. He wondered if she overheard his conversation with Summer. When Kim entered his office, her face displayed a look of envy and confusion.

She turned around and left the office without a word, although he thanked her. When he opened the envelope, he pulled off a yellow sticky note attached to the contents that stated:

If you want ideas, call 301-555-4330.
Elaine,

Jonathan stuck the phone number into his suit jacket. He then looked through the contents of the envelope and there were photo copies from publications about vacationing, exercise and food. He slid the contents back into the envelope and tossed it onto the round table adjacent his desk. Who was Elaine? The name didn't sound familiar and he had never met anyone in the company by that name.

At five, he left the office. He could feel himself burning out already. There had been endless meetings, constant phone conversations and long days and he hadn't been there a whole week yet. Once he reached home, he called Elaine.

An older man with a jovial southern accent answered the phone.

"May I speak with Elaine, please?"

The man on the other end burst into laughter and Jonathan wanted to ask the old guy to share whatever joke had gotten him so tickled.

After laughing, the man regained his composure. "I'll get Elaine for you, sir. Hold on."

Moments later, a young unfamiliar woman's voice spoke into the phone. "Hello?"

"Is this Elaine?" he asked impatiently.

"Yes. You are?"

"Elaine, this is Jonathan Wesley with *Ethnic Information Corporation*. You left a message with my assistant for me to contact you."

"Yes, I certainly did, Mr. Wesley." she said, continuing to disguise her voice.

"I'm listening, Elaine. In fact, I don't have much time here."

"I would rather meet you in person to discuss this."

"Is this a joke?"

"No, it isn't, Mr. Wesley. I really have an idea that could skyrocket the profits of *EIC* and broaden its subscriber base."

He stopped cold. This was someone who worked for the company, otherwise why would she refer to the company's abbreviated name. He hoped Jackie was not behind this, using this as an avenue to meet him somewhere. If she was, she could forget it.

"Where would you like to meet?" he asked, knowing that he had to take this meeting.

"I'll let you choose the place."

"How about Aretha's Rib Joint?" he suggested.

"What time?"

"In an hour. Will you recognize me when you see me?"

"I will, Mr. Wesley."

"Now how will I know who you are?"

"You'll recognize me also."

After hanging up, Jonathan thought about calling her and canceling that meeting. But what if this person was all about business? He would soon find out.

After hanging up, Summer gave Nadia a smile. "Did he agree to meet you?"

"Yes."

Jonathan's Summer

"I know you're going. Now that's the kind of voice you need to use when you speak to him in person – that sexy voice."

"Yes, I'm going."

"Good. This could mean a promotion for you, girl."

Changing the subject, Summer asked, "By the way, how's Renee?"

"Okay, I guess." Nadia said, turning her back while answering.

"You guess?"

"Summer, you're going to be late for your appointment with the boss."

Summer dropped the subject for now, but still wondering what Nadia was thinking.

Nadia was hoping Renee wasn't serious about carrying out what she told her she was planning to do. Her plan was a stupid move and suicide would be even worse. There had to be a way to pay off those loan sharks without resorting to extreme measures. Renee had told her that they would kill her if she didn't pay up by the end of May and they were rapidly approaching that time.

Summer took Nadia home before heading to the restaurant. When she arrived, she parked in the only spot left, next to a black Jaguar with shiny silver rims.

"Nice car," she said to herself, putting the strap of her backpack on her shoulder and entering the restaurant.

She could hear smooth R&B as she entered the "joint". Most of the tables were taken, couples sitting, enjoying soul food and the company of each other. *Now this is what I'm talking about*, she thought, taking in the environment. Just then, another thought occurred. She wondered if Jonathan would have brought Jackie with him. Since this was more like an intimate place for couples, it would make sense for him to have the meeting and his date, killing time in the process. Why else would he choose this place to have a business meeting?

She finally spotted him sitting alone at a table for two, nursing on a glass of wine. She was glad he was alone. She took a deep breath and headed in his direction. When he looked up and noticed her coming, he almost choked on his drink. He wondered what she was doing there, although seeing her was a pleasant surprise.

She noticed the look on his face, realizing that he still had not figured out whom he spoke to over the phone.

"May I join you?" she asked.

"Of course." he said. "But I am expecting someone shortly."

Summer stifled a grin and took the chair across from him. A waiter came over to take orders before they started their conversation.

"Can you give me a little time before I order?" he asked the waiter.

"Sure." the young man said as he left the table.

Jonathan glanced at his watch and back at Summer. He was thinking that Elaine should have arrived by now.

"So, how are you?" he asked, breaking the thick ice. "Haven't seen you in a couple of days."

"Fine. Yourself?"

He looked into her eyes but her eyes would not meet his. The way she avoided eye contact annoyed him. He couldn't determine if she acted this way because she was shy or because she disliked him.

"Summer?" he said, the bass in his voice cutting through the music.

Her head shot up and her eyes danced around him. "Yes?"

"I'm going to be heading the company for the next three months. I would appreciate eye contact when I'm speaking to you. I'm not going to bite you."

"Sorry, Jonathan."

He just didn't understand. She had suddenly lost her nerve. He was not aware of how dangerous he appeared to her. If it was a crime to be as handsome as he was, this man would be brought up on felony charges.

He tried another approach, "Do you ever have plans of moving up in this company?" he asked. "You know, most of the employees see many opportunities to get promoted. The company is growing constantly."

"Sure, one day."

"Then if you cannot handle me, you certainly won't be able to handle Maurice Wesley." he said in a joking manner. "I'm only warning you now."

Not only that, whatever company she works for, she would have to lose that shell if she wants to move up. He wondered for a fleeting moment if she had ever been abused by a man. Women who were timid were sometimes that way because they either endured the violent hands of a man or her esteem was shot down by nasty words spoken from the tongue of a man. Psychological damage could last for years.

"What steps would I need to take in order to move up?" she asked.

"What do you feel you could do to be an asset to the company?" he shot back. It now was obvious to him that she had been pondering a promotion. He noticed her eyes light up when she voiced her question.

Without speaking, she reached into her backpack, noticing that he was checking his watch again. She pulled out the proposal she arranged, handing them over to him. He removed the documents from the brown envelope that was the same type as the one Elaine left with Kim.

She watched as both his eyebrows shot up with interest. She smiled to herself. She knew he liked those ideas.

Jonathan had a personal interest in promoting this type of information. Both his parents were in their sixties and it wasn't just the profits that a publication of this nature could bring that interested him.

Finally, he looked up at her and said, "You came up with this alone? Did anyone assist with this?"

"They're all mine."

"Have you told anyone else in the company?"

"Just Nadia Cruz." she admitted, wondering why he was asking her these questions.

"I would suggest that you not tell anyone else," he said, flipping through the pages of her proposal again. "and make sure you impart that to your friend."

"Why would this be such a big secret? I thought I had to relate my idea to my immediate supervisor. That's how it's always been. Mr. Wesley has always done things that way."

"I'm not Maurice, I'm Jonathan. I want the person who creates an idea to get full credit. That requirement about going through your immediate supervisor isn't agreeable with me."

Nadia was right after all. Summer should have listened to her long ago. By now, she would have had it over and done with and not have to sit here before this man who made her thoughts run wild and her body go haywire.

"I'll get full credit for this?" she asked.

He smiled warmly. "They're all yours! And if it's accepted, you'll get a promotion. But why aren't you doing something in marketing and editorial? I noticed how excellent your writing skills are. So much precision – how you get your point across without me having to re-read what you've written."

"Because balancing the deposit was the only position open at the time."

He reached over, gently placing his large hand on hers, causing that brush fire she'd been feeling to intensify. "You're intelligent, Summer. I have no doubt about that. I'll definitely promote this idea to Maurice and the senior vice president. I believe a publication such as this could be profitable." he said, touching the documents on the table.

She eased her hand from under his and stood slowly. Her mission was accomplished and it was time for her to "bounce" as Nadia would say.

"Thanks for your time."

Confusion immediately set in, he was now wondering if she was "Elaine." And since they were in this nice, homelike restaurant, what a perfect setting to have a date, although impromptu.

"Wait a second!" He stood up, grabbed her wrist. "Were you the person that left the number with my assistant?"

"Yes."

"Why did you give me a fake name?"

"I didn't give you a fake name. My middle name is Elaine. And if I told you who I really was, you probably would have laughed at me."

This now confirmed what Jonathan believed regarding the possibility of a man abusing her.

CHAPTER SEVEN:

"Summer, can you sit back down again?"

She eased back into the chair while he still held on to her wrist. "I don't laugh at anyone. You probably consider yourself a nobody. But young people like you have much to offer society and their whole futures ahead of them.

"Not only that we all have potential. Your idea could prove to be something productive for the company and the more I think about it, the more I become a little annoyed with you."

"Why is that?"

"Because you were sitting on this idea, that's why." he said jokingly and she had to laugh.

Now that's what I'm talking about! he thought. *Does she look even prettier when she smiles or what!*

"Now I hope this isn't just a one-time thing you plan to do here and stop. I want your ideas from now on. Your idea could prove productive for the company and I admonish you to continue."

"How can this prove productive for the company?" She folded her arms across her bosom and he didn't miss the gesture. His attention was held for a moment before he spoke.

Once his eyes traveled back to her face, he said, "We could end up with tens of thousands of subscribers who would find a periodical of this nature informative."

A slow, determined smile crept across her golden face and he could see the wheels turning in her head. Right then, he *knew* that all the comments he heard about her were not true. This woman was no airhead.

"Do I have your permission to pass this idea to my father?"

"Sure."

He waved to the waiter, saying, "Now let's eat."

Jonathan ordered the house ribs and Summer wanted barbecue chicken. He felt himself growing aroused, watching her devour the meal. Those huge, bright eyes entranced him. He forced himself to maintain control as he felt himself swelling. He began speaking again, in order to stop this torture.

"What made you come up with such an idea?" he asked.

"My father had a heart attack in March. That's when I became conscientiously aware of the needs and health of people over fifty-five. I have to look out for my dad. He's all I have now."

"Is your mother deceased?"

"I don't really know at this point." Not that she cared either. After what her mother had done, she didn't care if she ever talked to her again.

Jonathan's eyes grew perplexed. "You don't know?"

"I haven't seen her since I was fourteen. She walked out on us. That's been about eleven years now. And my father hasn't been right since. Stressing, worrying all the time, forced him into early retirement." Jonathan nodded, acknowledging that he understood. "What about you? Your parents are still together, right?"

"Coming up on forty-one years." he boasted.

Summer laughed again. She was beginning to feel more at ease with him.

Hearing her laugh was like smooth jazz to his ears. Her chuckle was sexy, yet innocent. That interested him – she was sexy and innocent. He could not explain that radiance emanating from her and he'd never met a woman like her before. She seemed so pure.

"Would you like something to drink other than coke?" he asked.

"No, I'm driving."

"Do you drink any alcoholic beverages?"

"No."

That was all right with him. Didn't have to worry about her losing her senses due to drunkenness – something Jackie and previous girlfriends seemed to have problems with.

After finishing dinner, they stood. Jonathan tossed down a tip on the table.

"Will you be okay getting home? You know it's after nine."

"I'll be fine. Thanks. And thanks for dinner, it was delicious."

"Maybe I should follow you to make sure you're safe." he suggested.

"I'll be fine, Jonathan." she insisted. "I'm a grown woman."

Now she had him wondering if she was going home to a man. Why would she refuse his offer to make sure she arrived home safely? He thought to ask if she had a man but it was too early for that now. He would have the opportunity one day to inquire about that. Jealousy set in when he thought about it.

"I agree that you're an adult, over the age of eighteen and all that wonderful stuff but that doesn't erase the fact that there are some idiots out here."

Was there a possessive tone in his comment? she couldn't help wondering, almost laughing out loud.

She headed to the door and she was so quick that he had to take long strides in order to catch up with her. He stopped at the register to pay the bill and they headed outside. He walked her to the caravan. The night was around sixty degrees, clear skies, stars peering down at them. This would be a nice night for him to drive her down to Virginia Beach and walk along the boardwalk or stroll Atlantic Avenue. A perfect night for perfect romance.

When she hopped in the van, he shut the door for her. She slid down the window to tell him goodnight and thank him again. He said goodnight, burning to taste her voluptuous lips. He settled for the handshake she offered and headed to his car, feeling his manly desires overwhelming him.

He thought of her his entire trip home. Though they discussed business most of the evening, being in her presence alone instead of that busy corporation was gratifying and he felt they'd made a step forward. He had learned a lot about her.

"Where were you?" Jerome attacked once Jonathan stepped inside the guesthouse. "Jackie called here about twenty times and I started to unplug the phone. That ho better be glad I was expecting a call or I would have."

"Out with Summer."

"Who in the hell is Summer?" Jerome asked, an impish grin creeping across his face.

"Now you better not mention this, but she's a young woman that works for *EIC*. I like her. I really hate to date someone on the job but this is one I simply cannot help being interested in."

"I knew something was up with you. The reason you just basically dumped Jackie. When you said you two weren't going out anymore, I knew something was going on. You can't fool me."

Laughing, Jonathan said, "What makes you say that?"

"'Cause I know you, Mike." he answered, referring to him by his middle name. When Jerome was a small child, he could not pronounce his big brother's name so his parents had taught him his middle name because it was easier. Ever since, Jerome never broke the habit.

"I just have so much going on at the company. But this girl is so different, she acts differently...I can't tell you, Jerome."

"And her name is Summer? What does she look like? How old is she? Give me some details and don't leave nothing out!"

Jonathan looked at him suspiciously. He hoped Jerome wasn't planning on making a move, as he'd been known for doing in the past. His brother's reasoning was that all was fair, as long as a woman was not married. If her man could not hold on to her, then that was his problem if it was that easy to take her away.

Jonathan described Summer in vivid detail after threatening to break his neck if he ever tried to push up on her. Jerome listened, occasionally nodding.

"That's all good, but I've never known you to be smitten with someone that much younger than you. Even when you were twenty-five, you always preferred them older. Aren't you going on thirty-nine in November, pretty close to forty now." he taunted.

"So what?"

"Sure this isn't some silent way of stroking your own ego – making sure you still got what it takes? Some mid-life crisis a shade under forty."

"Someone like Summer can't simply stroke my ego. I see something in her that has fully captured my attention. That much I know."

"But some of your description of her left an impression in my mind that she's a tomboy. Now I could be wrong but what's up with a woman that doesn't wear dresses and skirts and sports jeans and sneakers all the time wearing goddam baseball caps."

"That's why I don't like telling you shit, Rome. I said I've always seen her in jeans." *Jeans that enhanced her curves at that!* "You don't listen to nothing! I haven't been there a week yet. Who knows what next week might bring?"

"Still the same as saying she doesn't wear feminine gear." he said with a wave of his hand. "But I recall you dating them sexy, sophisticated type."

"Well, Summer is all of the above in a natural kind of way. She's not superficial, high maintenance."

Laughing, Jerome retorted, "That's if you plan on settling down do you get with her kind. You know Mommy ain't letting you come home with a fast bitch without giving you a piece of her mind." With his eyebrow lifted, he added, "Are you planning on getting engaged again?" Jerome knew he taunted Jonathan when he made comments like this. He knew his brother didn't want to be reminded of Andrea Rose.

"Andrea was the personification of high-maintenance." He didn't want to think of her right now. He wanted to knock him out for even bringing that up.

"If she taught you the lesson you claim she has, why would you even think about going out with Jackie, that modern day Jezebel?"

"I didn't know how Jackie was until I dated her. What a waste of three months."

"You'll be all right. Just make sure you're not going to the other extreme." Jerome patted him on the back. "For your sake, I hope this Summer chick isn't a butch-made woman – you know, more man than yourself."

Jonathan stood there, feeling worse for talking to his brother than he'd felt before he confided in him.

"But I need to finish up. I want to get this info to editorial and be out of here by the middle of next week." He left Jonathan in the parlor and headed for the study.

* * *

Nadia took her husband's car and met Renee in Adams Morgan, an uptown district of Washington, DC. "Here's the money," she told Renee, handing her what she had withdrawn from her personal savings.

She'd been saving for years because she and Jose planned to start having children when they both turned twenty-eight. As it stood, Nadia only had two and a half years to go before that happened. She could accumulate the money again by that time. Right now, Renee's safety meant more to her than what she saved the money for.

Renee counted the money, looked at Nadia and said, "It's two thousand short."

"But at least they'll know you're trying."

Renee conceded and Nadia headed back to her car and drove down Columbia Road, thinking of a way to help her friend get out of the mess she'd finagled herself into.

When Summer reached home, she met her father sleeping. The central air-conditioning was quite cool so she pulled the comforter to his chin and kissed him.

"I love you, Daddy."

He smiled at the familiar voice and resumed sleeping.

She adjusted the temperature on the thermostat and headed to her private bathroom. She took a long hot bath and turned into bed. Jonathan dominated her thoughts as she lied on her back, staring into the darkness of her room. An alarming thought rattled her musing. What about Jackie? It was obvious to Summer that Jackie either liked him or they were dating. What if Jonathan liked her instead of Jackie? If he did, what if Jackie found out and found a reason to fire her?

Summer thought it was time to transfer from that department before it was too late. She needed her job since her father was on a fixed income now. Now that there was a promising future ahead, she cared more about her job.

* * *

The next morning, Jonathan ran to his ringing phone. When he heard his father's voice, he knew he had to wake up. He knew how annoyed his father would become if he still sounded like he was sleeping. He'd been tossing and turning the whole night thinking of Summer and hadn't gotten much sleep.

"Oh, good morning, Dad," he tried sounding awake.

"Has Jerome arrived yet?" Maurice asked. Jonathan could hear noise in the background – water splashing and voices of some of the vacationers on the beach.

"Yes, he's in town but he's already at the office. You know how swift he is. He breezes in, takes care of business and off to New York again or some woman's bedroom."

Maurice laughed before asking. "I suppose you're getting ready to head in?"

"As we speak. I have plenty to do today since Monday's a holiday."

"Anything new?"

"I thought you'd never get around to asking." he said with a laugh. "In fact, one of your humble employees tossed me one of her ideas." He reached for the envelope Summer had given him. "I'll fax it to you once I arrive at the office. The one at the mansion's acting up again."

"OK. Get Lance to come out and look at the fax machine. Otherwise, go buy a new one. I was having problems with it when I was home. And who is this humble employee?" Maurice was curious to know.

"Summer Douglas."

"You can't be serious!" his father resounded. "You mean that quiet little girl that works for *WAIA* department?" He had trouble with this one and he would definitely have to question his son about this. How had she ended up knowing about plans for a new publication?

"Well, Summer is incredibly bright and intelligent. She has great potential though some may not see it until they talk to her."

He could sing her praises all he wanted, Maurice thought. He had some questions he wanted resolved.

"I'm not doubting your word, son." Maurice said, the question still nagging him but now was not the time to inquire. "Anyway, I have to be going. Your mother wants to go swimming today."

"Have you spoken with Debra and Theresa?" he asked.

"Your sisters have called each day since we left. They refuse to let us forget that we're not home. But I gotta go. Talk to you later."

Once Summer arrived at work, she was so elated, she couldn't conceal the smile she wore on her face each time thoughts of her and Jonathan having dinner the night before crept into her mind. Some of the employees in the department even noticed how she seemed carefree and more at ease.

Gwen, Jackie's main girl in the department noticed it and it reminded her to inform her boss of something she had witnessed the evening before.

"What's up?" Gwen said as she stepped into Jackie's office.

Of all the representatives, Gwen was the only one allowed off the phones when she was not officially on break or lunch. She had it like that. No one else, including Abu were given the liberties Gwen was given and he was her assistant department head.

"Nothing, just finishing up this marketing report for Ricky Channing." Jackie said as she swirled around in her chair and faced Gwen.

Gwen took the seat facing Jackie's desk. Wait until girlfriend hears this shit! she thought before she began spilling it.

"Girl, I went to Aretha's Rib Joint last night." Gwen said. "Me and Ayden decided we would go out finally."

"Oh, really? Did y'all have a good time?" Jackie said with less interest than she should have had. Since she and Jonathan hadn't been doing anything exciting, she could care less what Gwen and her man did. In fact, she would rather not hear about their night out.

"Well, that's not the good part!" Gwen said, her mouth watering to tell her girl what was up. "We had to park across the street because there was no other place to park in Aretha's parking lot. So as we're getting out of the car, you won't guess who we saw coming out of the joint."

"Who?"

"Ready for this, Jackie, because I don't think you are?"

"Just tell me who!" Jackie said, now anticipating whom Gwen was talking about.

"Jonathan and…"

"Jonathan?"

"Yeah, just let me finish. Dayum, Jackie, you never let people talk. Yes, Jonathan and Summer. They were laughing and shit and check this: she wasn't acting all quiet and anti like she be doing at the office. She was all up in his face, like they were going out like that."

A burst of anger exploded inside of Jackie. Her body quaked as the anger caused a violent thump of her heart and her stomach cut somersaults. Her teeth clamped together and right at that moment, she felt like getting up and going inside that little office in the rear of the department and choking the hell out of Summer. She knew the bitch was sneaky, she just hadn't anticipated how sneaky. She would pay for this!

"You're lying?" Jackie said, maintaining her composure outwardly. But inside, she was fuming. "I don't believe you."

"Well, my eyes were not deceiving me and neither were Ayden's. He even said something."

"Like what?"

"That Jonathan was a player. I had to punch his ass for making that comment because he was saying it as though he was praising your boy."

"Did they ever see you and Ayden?"

"No. In fact, we practically walked right pass them. I didn't want them to see us. Not that he would have anyhow, 'cause he was busy all up in her face when she got in her car."

"Maybe they didn't go there together. Maybe they just happened to run into each other once they got there." she said hopefully.

"You know Aretha's ain't no place to go by yourself, that mostly couples go to that place. And if they did happen to run into each other, where was both of their dates?"

That was true and Jackie wanted to question him as to why he'd gone there in the first place. She had known him to order take-out from there but not go there alone. That had been a place he'd taken her to on one of their first dates.

"So what you gonna do?" Gwen asked, a slight tone of instigation in her question.

"I'll find out what was up." Jackie tried to act like it was no big deal but this information was assaulting her heart. Of all the chicks in the office, he would decide to hang out with the one she hated most. And he knew she despised Summer.

"Yeah, you find out. And make sure your boy stays away from her. Now she walking around here like she just won the Maryland lottery or something."

Jackie had noticed Summer's attitude that day. Even when someone cracked a joke and Summer happened to be passing through the department, she laughed. It was rare that she'd seen that hussy laugh. Jackie would straighten him out and straighten out Summer. Now she knew why he was not home when she called last night. Not that Jerome would share anything with her, but she wanted badly to ask him where his brother was.

Summer headed from the accounting office and on her way, she spotted Jonathan heading in her direction. He was donning a pair of jeans and Nikes and a dark blue Polo shirt. He looked handsome even when he dressed casually. Excitement set in as she headed towards him. Seeing him made her heart beat so fast, she thought it would jump out of her chest. He smiled as he neared her. She smiled back.

"Hey, darling." he said softly.

She didn't miss the term of endearment. Was she his darling now? She sure hoped she was.

She rewarded him with a dimpled smile and his was equally dimpled.

"Hi, Jonathan. Are you working hard?" She was clueless what to ask him and knew her question probably sounded a little silly.

"Harder than I've worked my whole life." he joked, peering down at her affectionately. He liked what he saw. She donned a pair of jeans that fitted her more than the others she'd worn before. He could see the contours of her breasts through the cotton blouse she wore. The baseball cap had disappeared days ago. Her beautiful crown was pulled into a ponytail that hung down the side of her face, pass her ear and mid-way down her arm. He loved her hair and was tempted to run his fingers through it.

"Oh, Jonathan, you're so funny." She laughed.

"I'm serious." He smiled and added, "When you get into a higher position, you'll see what I mean."

That sounded promising but she would not get her hopes up too high at this point. Anything could happen, such as someone else coming up with a much better proposal. It was way early in the game, in fact, it had just begun.

"I'm looking forward to it." she said.

"Well, let me get back to the grinder. Sometimes this place feels like a concentration camp."

Summer laughed really hard this time. He had that awkward sense of humor she didn't find in most black men.

"Okay."

Before they walked on, he asked, "You're not having any problems with Jackie, are you?"

It seemed that question either came out of the blue or he'd been pondering it for some time. The question seemed well thought out. Why was he asking her that?

"How come you're asking me that?"

"I'm perceptive." he shot back, looking serious now, his eyes looking straight into hers. She averted her eyes. "I sensed some things the day I met you and Nadia outside eating lunch."

He also knew something Summer may not have – her inability to get along with those she supervised. Last year, she'd had a problem with another young woman who handled Summer's position. Nadia had told him when he returned to Greenville that the woman quit because of the way Jackie talked to her.

Summer's eyes finally traveled back to him. She didn't want to answer that question directly, did not want to cause any problems for anyone. She said, "I don't bother her and she doesn't really bother me."

That still did not answer his question but he let it go. He had to accept it. No use probing if there was no real problem.

"Okay, darling. I'll speak with you later." he said.

Now she was sure she didn't make any mistake about that term of endearment.

"All right. See you, Jonathan." she said in a childlike voice that melted him.

CHAPTER EIGHT:

Saturday and Sunday shot pass so quickly, Summer was thankful Monday was a holiday, otherwise her weekend would have been over too soon for her to stand. She had been babysitting her cousins while their parents traveled to Hartford, CT for the weekend.

Before she realized it, Monday had arrived and it was time for the picnic. She and her father dressed alike, wearing jeans shorts and white tee shirts with New York City logos scrawled across them. They packed the potato salad and steamed crabs in the caravan and made their way to Rock Creek Park.

"Don't indulge in fattening foods, Dad." she said, getting behind the wheel.

"Girl, you sometimes make me think my mother is still alive."

"I'm just reminding you of what the doctor ordered."

"Aye, Captain Summer!" he said with a playful salute.

Once they arrived, at least two hundred employees and family members were already there. Some were sitting at benches eating, some playing cards, a volleyball game was in full progress and there were some who were simply socializing.

"Are we late?" Allen Douglas asked his daughter.

"No, Daddy. These co-workers of mine just like to eat. Stands the reason they would be on time for a picnic. Besides, it's an all day picnic. I heard Maurice always reserves this place on Memorial Day."

"He has clout like that hunh?" Allen said with a grunt.

The crabs were on the table less than a minute when people started grabbing from the basket.

From some distance, Jackie noticed Summer holding her father's hand. She introduced him to several people before she led him to one of the wooden picnic tables.

"Hey, Gwen, look at the scank now." Jackie said, tapping her girl on the shoulder.

"Did you ever speak to him about that shit the other night?" Gwen asked.

"Haven't gotten a chance to. The bastard won't answer the phone when I call. I should just go over there and surprise him."

"Don't do that. You might find something you don't wanna see."

"Like what?"

"Him in bed with Summer." Gwen joked but Jackie took that comment to heart.

"He ain't interested in that little slut."

"Sure about that?" Gwen said, her face suddenly breaking into a frown as she looked pass Jackie. What she saw, her friend hadn't seen yet.

"Of course, I'm sure. I'm not even gonna get myself all worked up. Besides, she ain't his type."

"I wouldn't count on that, Jackie. Look." she said, gesturing at Jonathan making is way to Summer.

Jonathan donned Khaki shorts, black FuBu shirt and a pair of Air Force Ones. Most of the women present couldn't take their eyes off his muscular, hairy legs. Jonathan knew he had spectators but never showed semblance of knowing he was being observed and admired. His attention was on Summer. He wanted her to admire him.

Jackie sat her soda can on a nearby table and began making her way through the mass of employees, heading towards him.

"How are you today?" Jonathan asked Summer, his eyes hooded, sliding up and down her figure approvingly.

"I'm okay. Are you having a good time?"

"I'm fine. See you brought crabs. Who cooked them?"

"Me and Daddy did."

Allen joined them, obviously wanting to know who this man was that was up in his daughter's grill. Not that it bothered him but Allen was old school. Whenever the time came that his daughter *finally* met a guy, he wanted to know all about him. Allen tugged on her ponytail playfully.

"Oh, Daddy, this is Jonathan Wesley, the one I proposed that idea to the other night. And this is my father, Allen Douglas."

"You're the one that called the house looking for Elaine!" Allen said, tilting his head back, laughing loudly.

Jonathan laughed with him and extended a hand to the older man. "It's my pleasure meeting you, Mr. Douglas."

Allen returned the same treatment to Jonathan as he had Summer at the office last week. "Oh, call me Allen! Mr. Douglas sounds so impersonal."

"Hopefully, I'll see you enough to grant that request, Allen. Your daughter has gained much favor with the company and we're hoping to…"

"There you are." Jackie said, crashing the conversation. She put an arm around his waist. "How are you, Summer?"

Her tone was so transparent, it made Summer want to spit in her face and it didn't take her father but a second to realize who this woman was – the one his daughter despised so much. She was putting on such a show for the two men, she should get a Grammy.

"I'm fine." Summer said with the aloofness none of them missed.

"This must be your father." She extended a hand to him and introduced herself. Allen returned an introduction, shaking her hand.

Jonathan stood silent during the interaction. His jaw ached because his teeth were locked so tight. He realized this woman was treacherous and would go to great lengths to get what she was after. Why was she suddenly interested in Summer and her family? It was bullshit to him.

He decided to be civil and not curse her out right there in front of everyone. He eased out of Jackie's embrace, noticing the stress in Summer's face. Her eyes never lied, she was hurt – he hated seeing the pain in those large eyes. He wanted to reach for her. He took a deep breath and looked away, no longer listening to Jackie making conversation with Allen and Summer. He began counting the number of people in the park wearing white tee shirts, trying to swallow the anger he felt.

Some of the employees brought their parents and they had four card tables set up. Allen noticed the games and wanted to claim a seat, maybe he could win a little money.

"Princess, I'm going to play some cards with some of the old-timers." He kissed his daughter and made his way.

Summer stared behind her father as he headed towards the table Nadia's mother and two others were setting up.

"Princess," Jackie echoed Allen's term of endearment. "I think that's rather cute, don't you, Jonny." she said, giving him a sexy look.

He refused to look at her as he nodded, still watching others in the park.

When Summer realized what a fool she looked like standing in front of the couple, she politely excused herself. During Jackie's performance, she didn't know what to say or how to handle the situation. Maybe if she threw herself at him like Jackie did, he might find her interesting. She found Nadia but her best friend and husband Jose were about to leave the park. With her father off playing cards with newly-found friends, Summer ended up alone.

She went to the van and opened the sliding door. She felt sad. She felt hurt. Most of all, she felt like a fool! Had she forgotten that just six days ago she saw them returning to the office from a lunch date? How could she have believed a handsome, wealthy black man like him would replace sexy Jacqueline Shannon with an insignificant sistah like her? She couldn't be compared to that other woman and this caused relentless insecurity.

Summer leaned back, reclining in the seat. She closed her eyes. When she opened them, she realized she had been sleeping. She looked out the window of the van, noticing that some of the employees who were present before she drifted off had left. Some she hadn't seen earlier were now present. An hour had passed since she'd gotten in the van.

She sat up straight, rubbing her eyes. She observed everyone. Five minutes after waking up, she spotted Jonathan and Jackie getting in a dark blue Mercedes, some distance from where she parked her father's van. He opened the door for her, went around to the driver's side. He cranked the engine and drove off with the witch. Maybe she forgot her broomstick! Maybe they came to the park together. Why else would they leave together?

"I thought I'd find you in here." spoke the voice from outside.

Summer jerked around and there stood her father. He was smiling, holding out his hand. She gripped his hand as he helped her from the vehicle.

"Sorry, Princess," he said. "I was so busy playing Spades, I almost forgot to look for you."

"That's okay, Daddy. I was just a little exhausted. Didn't realize how Tina's kids had worn me out over the weekend."

"Let me know when you're ready to leave. We don't have to hang around long."

"I'll be ready when you are. Besides, I want you to enjoy yourself. You don't get out that much." She affectionately patted his arm.

And he was having a lot of fun. If she only knew why he was having so much fun, she would probably discipline him like a child.

They held hands while pacing around the park, dodging a volleyball while heading toward the farther end of the park, leaving others at a distance.

"Tell me what's on your mind, Summer." he spoke softly.

"Nothing, Dad."

Her answer was not convincing enough so he said, "I'll tell you what I think is going on. That young man, Jonathan has a thing for my daughter."

Summer smiled, looking up at her father. At five-three, she was seven inches shorter than he. Though over fifty, he was still the most handsome man she had ever seen. That was, until Jonathan Wesley came into the picture and turned her world sideways, causing her quiet little world to rock, erupting her volcano.

"I think he has a thing for Miss Thang herself." Summer said with sarcasm.

"And I think that thought frightens my daughter away from Mr. Wesley."

"You really don't believe they're in love? Geez!" Summer asked, stopping in the grass. Seems her father could see it if no one else could.

"I'm an old man, Princess." he looked into her eyes and continued, "I've been in love before and I can tell when a man really loves or adores a woman. And I've seen women fight other women over a man."

He was speaking about personal experience. When he'd met Summer's mother, Cynthia's neighbor pulled all types of tricks to get him away from her. But Allen knew whom he wanted and he got her.

"I won't fight her over him."

He smiled and pinched her cheek. "I don't think you would, baby girl. However, I believe it's the other way around."

"You think she's fighting me for him?" She shook her head.

"A little advice from the old man?" he offered.

"You will even if I didn't want it."

"Take care of yourself as I've always taught you to do. Don't get caught up in a love triangle and watch your back."

Summer nodded. She was blessed to have a father like him. Before long, he was making his way to another card game, itching to gamble some more. He knew his daughter felt better now. She tried mingling with some of the other employees but it seemed no one really wanted to converse with her. Things hadn't changed at all, though they weren't at the office. Some of these people hated her. The only ones she could relate to and seemed to have any interest in her were the high-ups and most of them weren't there.

With night falling, everyone started packing and leaving. Before stepping into the van, Summer noticed Renee from a distance talking with a young man she had never seen before. Judging by their body language, this didn't seem like a friendly conversation. Summer sat there, hesitating to turn over the engine as she watched Renee and the young man argue. She didn't have to hear the words exchanged between them to figure that out.

"That's none of our business." Allen warned, referring to Renee and the man.

She turned over the engine and they headed home, still curious about what was going down in the park with her co-worker and that thug-looking nigga she saw.

* * *

When Jonathan arrived home, his blood was coursing through his veins so vigorously, he felt he would explode. Anytime he had an encounter with Jackie, he was always left so exhausted. That witch had the nerve to question him about his evening at the restaurant with Summer. He asked her if she'd followed him but she refused to tell him how she knew about it. He told her that what he did was his business and she had no right to question him. Jackie then cried, knowing that it would weaken him. He had to do something to keep from seeing her cry so he pressed the accelerator harder, speeding down the beltway, getting her home as quickly as possible. He didn't want to see the tears, hated to see a woman cry, especially if he was the cause.

He cursed Summer for leaving him standing there with that she-devil. If Summer stood her ground, Jackie would not have found it so easy to claim him and monopolize his attention. He cursed himself for not going after Summer when she left. But if anyone should have excused herself, it should have been Jackie. She had told him that she came to the park with Gwen and was left there without a ride because Gwen's husband called her cell phone stating an emergency. Jonathan knew it was staged. Jackie probably told Gwen to go on without her once the other woman was ready to leave.

She allowed Jackie to chase her away – Jackie used power and intimidation to do so. He would soon fix this! When he stared at his reflection in the mirror, he hated what stared back: a coward. Why hadn't he stood his ground? Because he had not expected Jackie's award-winning performance, had not expected her to be so bold. But he learned a little about her each time he was around her.

He ached for Summer, she turned his world into a volcano. That little switch she had when she walked made him want to ravish her and feed his sexual hunger. He'd gone long enough, held out for the right woman and had found her now. His interest in Summer was not solely based on sex. Although making love to her would not do him an injustice, his interest was still genuine. Her intelligence, warmth, beauty, unselfish spirit and unbridled sexuality turned him on.

He darted into the bathroom, turned on the cold water and stepped in, allowing the cool spray to work its wonders. Those cold showers were not fun. They were harsh and merciless – unlike what he was sure Summer's body and soul represented. He had to convince her how much he was falling in love with her.

When he stepped from the shower, Jerome had made his way in. "How was the picnic?" he asked.

"You should have gone. Then you would have met Summer." Jonathan answered curtly. He wasn't man enough to keep her from slipping through his fingers, maybe Jerome was, he thought with much frustration.

"Naah!" Jerome teased. "I'm not one for crowds. Sounds weird coming from a guy who's been setting up residence in New York the past seven years. But maybe that's the reason. And I'll probably get to see Summer tomorrow. I have a meeting with Chris Moyer, my editor."

After their brief conversation, the brothers went into their rooms and retired to bed. Minutes later, Jerome was snoring – unlike Jonathan. Knowing the younger brother, he'd probably gotten himself a piece while he was out, wherever the hell he was, a hotel, motel, the chick's house or maybe even the back seat of his BMW. Nonetheless, Jonathan knew he'd had his evening meal.

* * *

Tuesday morning, Summer slammed the alarm clock, silencing it before easing out of bed. She wanted to break that alarm clock for announcing to her that Tuesday arrived and she had to go in and face Jonathan and Jackie. The bit of hope she'd had that he liked her was short-lived. Now she felt like a fool and was embarrassed to see him. She thought about spending the day with her father and calling in sick but he had already promised some friend he claimed he met at the picnic a day fishing. After eating breakfast alone that morning since he'd already left at six in the morning, she hopped into her Chevy Cavalier and cruised to work. She entertained the thought of turning around and heading back home.

Abu entered Jackie's office and shut the door behind him. "I found these in Summer's desk drawer," he announced, handing her two personal checks subscribers had sent. "I don't know how long they've been there but they're dated back two weeks."

Jackie examined the checks, noting that they were not signed. "Why didn't she send these back to the subscribers? They're not signed." she told Abu.

After looking over the checks, she promptly went into the deposit room, thinking that maybe she could find other things to incriminate Summer with. She entered the room, glanced at the clock, noted that she had at least thirty minutes to search the room before the other woman arrived.

What she found in the top drawer of her desk was even more interesting than the measly unsigned checks. It was a large brown envelope. She opened it, wondering what it was. She read it, realizing that it was a proposal to the boss. A slow grin spread across her face.

"A magazine for black American seniors huh, Miss Douglas?" Jackie spoke to herself, already mentally devising a plan to screw her over. Since Summer thought she could play this game, Jackie thought she'd teach her what the game really entailed. Before this was all over, Summer would know not to ever fuck with her again. After she was done schooling her, she would terminate her.

"Write up a reprimand!" Jackie ordered Abu. "It's high time we start a paper trail on her."

"That's a little extreme, Jackie." Abu said, not particularly wanting Summer out of the way.

"We got a case. But she's clever. She knows her probation is over. I should have taken action all those times she'd been late for work." Had she known Jonathan would take a liking to her, she would have. Summer would not even be there and Jonathan would not have met her.

She headed back to her office and sat down behind the desk. Abu followed.

"But, Jackie," he said in a voice that sounded pleading. "her father had been ill. What if she has to care for him again?"

"That's her problem!" she snapped. "This check incident is her last damned warning. I don't even think your idea about giving her a mere warning about the checks is suitable. We have grounds for termination right in our power."

CHAPTER NINE:

Abu gave Jackie a sidelong look. He knew it was more to it than Jackie simply doing her job. This woman had another agenda. He didn't agree that being late because of family emergencies and a person's parents being ill warranted being fired. Being from Africa, he had been taught the importance of caring for ailing and aging parents.

Above all, he didn't want Summer out of the way so Jackie could have full access to Jonathan. He was beginning to believe that Jonathan and Summer were interested in each other because he had seen them conversing in the hallway Friday afternoon. Jonathan stood there with his hands in his pockets, leaning against the wall, obviously comfortable with holding a conversation with Summer. Once he learned Jackie's angle, he realized that Summer was formidable competition for the woman he pursued. He liked Summer giving Jackie that competition.

"Whatever you say, Jackie." he said with a frustrated huff.

Abu decided he would give Summer a verbal warning and not a written one.

"But I had all intentions of sending them back, I swear, Abu." Summer said, sitting at her desk while he stood in front of her.

"Just be careful, Summer. Be careful. I was told to write you up, but I'm not going to do that. I don't want this stuff going into your file. Okay?"

"Okay, and thanks a lot for looking out."

"You're welcome. Anytime."

Summer managed to successfully avoid Jonathan for two days straight. On the third day, she was not as successful. When she completed the deposit, she took a different route back to her department, the route that she had been taking for the last two days. She glanced at her watch, making a mental note that it was almost three-thirty and she'd gotten through the day so far without running into him.

She returned to the department, grabbed the mail to be metered and took the shortest possible route to the mailroom. She didn't feel safe until she was inside the private room with the door shut. Too bad she couldn't lock it because others often came in to use one of the three metering machines.

"Hello."

Summer turned toward the voice and smiled at Deana, one of the few employees in the whole company that treated her like a human being instead of like a plague.

"Hey, Deana. How's it going?"

"Fine." Deana took a seat in front of the computer terminal.

The women talked while working, mostly talking about the weather and what plans they had for the summer. Her mind was temporarily taken from Jonathan. Deana picked up the mail from the post office each morning and was constantly roaming the halls, distributing mail.

Summer heard the door open as someone abruptly entered the room. Her worst fears were confirmed when she looked up and saw Jonathan. "Deana," he spoke, glancing in Summer's direction. "I need you to Fed-ex this package to my father in Tobago for me." He handed the woman a large brown package.

"Sure, JW. No prob."

Summer heard the order but kept working, as if she didn't know him. She continued metering the mail. The sound of the door closing behind him relieved her. She hoped he wouldn't still be in the vicinity of the mailroom once she was done.

"He's so cute!" Deana couldn't help declaring. "Makes me wish I didn't have a boyfriend. But that wouldn't make a difference because I'm sure he got somebody."

Summer listened to Deana, thinking that he did have someone, the wicked witch herself, Jackie!

Once Deana left, Summer sighed and wiped the line of perspiration from her forehead. He was still striking those nerves, lighting her furnace. She removed the gold scrunchy that held her ponytail in place. She brushed her massive curls with her hands. Instead of putting the scrunchy back on, she put it on her wrist like a bracelet. She stacked the trays onto the cart in preparation of taking them downstairs to be picked up by the post office.

Before she could make a clear escape from the room, Jonathan burst in again, startling her.

"Did I scare you?" he asked, noticing her hair had been let free. He saw Deana leave the room and knew Summer was alone now. Did she think he'd just saunter off without hanging around until she was alone? No, he wasn't going out like a chump this time. Not only that, did she think that he hadn't noticed her ducking him since Tuesday? He knew that building, all the short cuts and different routes.

"No, you didn't scare me." she said, placing a bundle of mail into one of the trays.

"Summer, will you please look at me." he gently ordered but that bass was still in his voice. He could try to talk softly all he wanted, he still sounded like a tuba.

She slowly brought her eyes up to meet his. When she looked at him, she clearly saw the annoyance in his features. He tried to hide it but couldn't.

"Yes?" she answered.

"Is there a problem?"

She wanted to say, *Yes! I saw you getting in the car with Jackie only three days ago and drive from the park. You've got the nerve to be questioning me about a problem!* Instead, she voiced, "No." She was never bold enough to give others a piece of her mind, especially him.

Jonathan released a long-awaited sigh and tossed his eyes upward. What would it take to convince this woman that he was interested? He glared into her face. The hair crowning her face put a different spin on her whole appearance. It complemented her long eyelashes and bedroom eyes. Those lips were enough to send his imagination over a cliff. He mused how sweet her lips were to taste. She toyed with the scrunchy on her wrist nervously.

"Sorry."

"For what?" he asked, his stern gaze slowly turning soft. "You haven't done anything that you should be sorry for." He added to himself, *I'm the one who's sorry for letting you get away from me at the picnic.*

Summer blinked at him. He was approaching an erection at full speed and he had to do something to bring this to a screeching halt. She was the demanding force, causing his manhood to respond in ways he couldn't stop.

"Summer, I faxed those ideas to my father. He liked them. I would have told you earlier but you were working full time avoiding me."

"I wasn't avoiding you, sir." she said, clearing her throat.

"Jonathan!" he insisted. "My name is Jonathan."

"Sorry." She hung her head, staring at her LA Gears, still toying with the band on her wrist.

"I told you the first day we met, I don't bite. Why are you behaving as if you're a rabbit trying to escape the predator of a tiger?"

"I'm not behaving like that." she protested.

Jonathan had to smile in order to loosen the tension. He changed the subject. "I hope you enjoyed the picnic?"

She smiled back. "Yes. Did you?"

"I forgot the package you gave me, Jonathan." Deana said, entering the room, interrupting their conversation. While she eased pass Jonathan, Summer used that opportunity to leave, telling him that she would talk to him later.

Jonathan didn't move as he watched her exit the room with her cart in tow. He shook his head, making his way to his office after she disappeared down the corridor.

That evening, Jonathan arrived home, parked his father's Mercedes in the east garage and joined his brother, who had already made it home.

"Jackie called," Jerome said when he met Jonathan at the bar, pouring a glass of wine.

"What else is new?" Jonathan hissed while loosening his silk tie. He made himself comfortable and took a sip from his glass.

"I saw Summer today." Jerome blurted out as if he was waiting for the right moment to reveal it.

This snatched Jonathan out of his sunken mood and his brother's words were like a glass of ice water being tossed in his face. Just the mention of her name made him hard.

Laughing, Jerome continued, "She must have thought I was you. She saw me and damn near took off running. That's when I realized who she must have been. Why is she so shy?"

"How do you know she's shy?" Jonathan asked suspiciously.

"I know women. She's very shy. Wonder if she's ever had a man fuck her real good?"

"Nasty Negro."

It was easy to mistake the brothers. They sported the same low cut hair, had the same dark honey brown hue, and full lips. Jonathan was only an inch taller than Jerome. Their broad shoulders and slim waistlines told the story of the Wesley man for sure. Though Maurice was sixty-five, he had maintained his waist, only accumulating an inch and a half over the years.

"Anyway," Jerome added as if he intended to tap dance on his brother's nerves. "I say go for it, man. The dress code can always change. But that girl got an ass on her that could send a man's imagination into overdrive."

"I am not surprised in your behavior or your words, Rome. You will never rid the Doberman Pincher in you. Will always be a dog."

"Can't help being a dog. You only live once. But check this, I'm leaving tomorrow morning. I say we should go out and have some fun. Maybe we can hunt down a coupla fine sistahs on our mission."

Jonathan didn't feel like going with Jerome but he had to do something to get out of that house. So he accompanied him. Once he arrived in the club, he talked to a few women but didn't give out his number, didn't accept any. He had a couple of drinks before the brothers returned home.

Jerome on the other hand had a list of phone numbers he'd collected. Jonathan questioned him about how he could remember some of those women he met and he showed him a databank with names, numbers and descriptions of the women so that whenever they called, he could always say something like: "I like that teal dress you had on the other night when I met you."

* * *

A week later, Jonathan finally got the chance to relax. He had been interviewing celebrities for the *Nubian Entertainment* publication and hadn't had the chance to call Summer. When he woke up that morning, his mind was occupied with the meeting he was supposed to have with Jackie and Abu. Jackie called him two days ago and informed him that she wanted to propose this "fabulous" idea to him. Jonathan could not refuse the meeting, though he figured this was another avenue she used to finagle herself into his presence. He wondered what she could possibly create as an idea.

He was already waiting in the conference room when Abu and Jackie joined him at nine that morning. They sat on each side of him. He noticed the daring tight dark green dress she wore, another one of her schemes to capture his attention. It wasn't working. Maybe some other man would find her irresistible, but that other man would soon find out she was nothing but a nasty, conniving person.

"Okay, let me hear it," he said, not trying to hide his aloofness. He folded his large hands, rested them on the conference table.

Jackie looked at his hands. She could not help remembering those same hands caressing her body during wild sex and passionate lovemaking. She missed him!

Jackie removed several documents from her briefcase before speaking.

"How does a publication for African American senior citizens sound?" she asked.

Jonathan felt his temper rise that very moment. He furrowed his brows until he wore a complete frown. *How dare her!* came the thundering thought. How in the world had she and Summer come up with the exact same idea?

"It sounds great." He cleared his throat. "But is this original?"

She released a careless laugh. "Of course, it is. Abu and I constructed this one the other day together."

"Really?" he asked with disdain. "How long have the two of you been working on this?"

He wanted a specific time. Her "other day" answer was too evasive. Summer already appealed to him over two weeks ago with that idea. Now here she and Abu come with the same idea? He smelled a rat.

Ignoring his last question, she said, "Now the cost would probably be cheaper for subscriptions since many of the prospective subscribers for this type of publication would likely be on fixed incomes." She added, "But think of how many mailing lists you could buy and sell because of it."

He admitted that she had a knack for marketing. She also had the natural-born ability for stabbing others in the back.

"I'll give it some consideration and inform Maurice, Jackie." He then nodded at Abu. The other man hadn't said anything during the entire meeting and Jonathan wondered why.

She stood up right after the men. "So, what do *you* think? I want your personal opinion, not Maurice's."

"I think the person who drafted this idea is a genius." His answer meant Summer and Jackie hadn't even picked up on his inference. This told him that she thought he was a damned fool.

By the time he reached his office, his blood had come to a vigorous boil and he could feel a headache attacking his temples. He figured Summer had ignored his advice and gone through Jackie anyway. His father should have never established that chain of command rule. That way, others wouldn't find it so easy to steal the ideas of the originator. Four years ago, that had happened. One of the writers came up with an idea and here comes another writer with the same one. He had tried getting to the bottom of it, both writers claiming that it was their idea. He couldn't determine who was telling the truth. This time, he would handle it differently. He had more authority in the company now than he did then. If it took maneuvering his way around Maurice to get to the bottom of it, he will.

Summer was trusting, not realizing that Jackie would stab her in the back. He would have to remind Summer again not to be so trusting!

He called Kim Justen and told her to have Summer come to his office. When she came in ten minutes later, his temper had lowered but his heartbeat accelerated.

"Did you want to see me?"

"Yes, I wanted to let you know that I thought your idea was great and so did the old man." He didn't know where to begin this conversation. Didn't want her to think he didn't believe in her.

She giggled and looked at him quizzically. "You told me that already."

"But now I want you to tell me something. Where did you get that idea? Was it really yours?" She nodded affirmatively and her expression grew more perplexed. "You didn't happen to overhear that somewhere?" he asked and she nodded again. "No one told you about it?"

"Jonathan!"

"Summer, I have to be certain."

"Certain of what?"

"Company policy. Whenever a person drafts an idea, we have to make sure it isn't stolen. That way the originator is protected."

Summer stood up, her hands placed on her hips and he wished she hadn't. Those fitting jeans revealed her curves and the cropped top revealed her slim waistline and a hint of golden flesh on her belly. Her youthful radiance was causing his manhood to pulsate now. At that moment, he felt like tossing her on the desk and making love to her.

"Jonathan, if it wasn't my idea, I wouldn't have told you about it. Not only that, I have more ideas for simple articles. I don't have to copy other people's stuff. And I haven't told anyone except Nadia."

He began growing harder. He couldn't have her – she had made that clear because she hadn't said so – so why in the hell was she torturing him this way? Why couldn't she sit down and give an explanation instead of standing there, displaying her figure.

"I'm only checking, Summer." he said sternly.

"I understand now. I just hoped you didn't think I was not smart enough to construct an idea."

"Not smart enough?" He laughed. "Your IQ is probably somewhere right around one-sixty."

"OK. I see."

"Listen," He stood. "thanks for coming in. You may return to your department. We'll talk later. I think we're done here."

"Your father rejected it, didn't he?" she asked solemnly. She knew it was too good to be true. Maurice didn't like her. She knew he didn't. Each time he saw her in the hallway and she spoke, he would give her a curt nod of acknowledgement without speaking. This would be something great if it came from another source but since it came from her, Maurice would reject it.

CHAPTER TEN:

He sighed, glancing away from that beautiful being. Why couldn't she leave? He had another issue to resolve, forcing himself down. He couldn't do that if she kept standing there before him.

"Summer, my father liked that idea and I will get back to you."

She finally yielded, turned to leave. Relief swept through him. It took every bit of control he had to resist the urge to stare at her curvy derriere when she exited the office. Too bad his father's office didn't have a private shower room.

He pondered a while after Summer left. If she didn't tell Jackie and Abu about her idea, how did they come to find out about it? He covered another ground and called Nadia's personal extension.

"Hey, Jonathan. What's up? Are you firing me or something?" Nadia joked.

"No. But you are aware of the idea Summer proposed to me, am I right?"

"Yes. Why?"

"Have you mentioned it to anyone?"

"Hell no. Jonathan, you of all people know that I know better than that."

"All right. I was just checking."

After hanging up, he grew more furious. If Summer or Nadia hadn't told anyone, there was only one conclusion he could arrive at – Jackie may have been snooping around in Summer's office while she was making her rounds to different departments after she completed the deposit. He found it quite difficult to believe that Summer would snoop through Jackie's office.

When Jackie realized Summer returned, she stormed into the deposit room and slammed the door behind her. The sound startled Summer. She looked up and witnessed the disquieted countenance of her immediate supervisor. She wondered why this woman came storming into her office that way. She could see the smoke billowing from her face.

Jackie approached her desk and spoke, shaking her finger at her as if she was talking to a four year old. "Whenever you leave the department, you have to let your supervisor know you're gone!" she spat. "I looked for you and no one could tell me where the hell you'd gone."

Summer wondered why this was all of a sudden a department rule.

She stood up, facing Jackie. "Don't curse at me. And if you want to know where I was, I had to go and see…"

"I don't care!" Jackie interrupted rudely. "I don't care if you had to pay the

Pope a visit. You have to let us know. You're already in hot water. Don't let me have to take measures to reprimand you."

It was time Jackie turned up the heat. She had to find a way to get Summer out of there. Now that she had the idea, she would get the promotion and by the time Maurice returned to get things rolling, Summer would be gone. What's more, she would have Jonathan back.

Summer wanted to slap Jackie. She had no business pointing that finger at her and if this transpired outside the office, she knew she would probably jump on Jackie and whip her ass.

"Is that understood, Summer Douglas?"

Summer narrowed her eyes at her and said, "Yes." She choked back tears.

When Jackie left, she slammed the door so hard, the customer service agents, website manager for their publication and Abu all looked up in silence, wondering what was going on. She then realized that she had lost her cool and caused a scene. If it had not been for Summer, none of them would have witnessed her behaving unprofessionally. She pranced to her private office as if she didn't notice them all looking at her and closed the door.

Summer gave in to tears once Jackie left. She didn't want to lose her job now that things were beginning to appear to take a turn for the positive. Two months ago, she would not have cared. She did now.

During lunch, Summer sat alone on one of the outside benches. This was the day she needed Nadia, who had left for a doctor's appointment. Each time she thought of how Jackie treated her, she cried. She allowed her lunch to grow cold. She didn't feel like putting anything on her stomach. She wiped her eyes with a paper napkin. The people getting in and leaving their parked vehicles all looked blurred, her tears were blinding her.

"Eating alone today?" said a deep masculine voice.

Summer didn't see the face of the person before she noticed the size twelve expensive Louis Faragamo shoe propped onto the spot on the bench next to her. Her eyes traveled to his neatly pressed dark slacks, matching leather belt around the tight waistline, white shirt, finally landing on the face that made it all correct. The eyes of the face stared intently at her. A smile played at his lips but slowly vanished when he noticed she had been crying.

"Hi." she spoke just above a whisper.

He placed his tray on the table and sat next to her.

"I know I wasn't invited, but since I do own half of this property you're sitting on, I think I'll just sit right here and make myself at home." He wiped a tear away with his thumb. "What's the matter?"

She sighed and said, "Nothing, really."

"Summer, you can talk to me about anything. I promise not to bite if you tell me." He raised an eyebrow, a smile playing at his lips.

Summer giggled at his joke. He always had a way to cheer her up when she was feeling depressed.

"That's a little better than that pout you gave me a moment ago." He smiled. "Where's Nadia?"

"She had a doctor's appointment."

"I'm so happy to hear that!" he declared.

"Why?"

"Because I wouldn't have this special privilege of eating alone with you if your nosy girlfriend was here. No offense but the worst challenge in the world is trying to get with a woman and her inquisitive girlfriend all up in the mix. I love Nadia like she was my own sister but she's as nosy as a seventy year old widow with a young couple living next door."

Summer's soul bubbled with laughter. She wanted to tell him how Jackie treated her that morning and how she'd been treating her nearly five months. She decided to keep her mouth shut. He told her that she could come to him with any problem but she was still reluctant to tell him what was really going on.

"What do you normally do in your spare time?" he asked.

"Take care of Daddy." Her tone reminded him of a nine year old when she referred to the most important man in her life.

"You and your father are close, aren't you?"

"How can you tell?"

"The day you were at the restaurant, he was all you could talk about. And I noticed how tight you seemed when I watched you at the picnic."

She didn't know he'd been watching her like that.

"He's my life, Jonathan."

He brought his index finger under her chin, guiding her face to him. Her eyes lowered and he gently pushed her chin upward. She looked at him and he said,

"Summer, may I ask you a personal question?"

"Sure."

"Other than Allen, is there a special man in your life?"

"Like who?"

He laughed. She was not going to make this easy for him. "Like a husband or boyfriend?"

"No. How about you? Do you have a wife or girlfriend?"

"No." He paused momentarily, looking into her face. "You're beautiful."

Bashfully, she lowered her eyes again. "Only my father tells me that."

"At least he isn't a liar."

She grinned, at a loss for words. His forthrightness was embarrassing her.

"There's no lady in my life." he felt the need to repeat. "Hopefully, I'll run into her before I return to Greenville." He looked at her and added, "Maybe I've met her already."

"I would have thought you were married or had a girlfriend. You're so handsome."

"Only my mother tells me that." he shot back and they both laughed. "But you know what?"

"What?"

"Relationships extend beyond looks." He had learned that dealing with Jackie. "Have you recently dated?"

Summer raised her eyes skyward. Why was he asking her embarrassing questions.

"I know it sounds a little retarded, but no. I have never dated anyone at all."

He would have thought that she would have dated at least once in her life.

"How come?" He hoped she wasn't a lesbian as Jerome had pegged her. "You don't have to answer if you don't want."

"I don't know. I'm just busy making sure my father is okay. I love my dad."

Didn't he know she loved her father! But didn't she have a life of her own too? He lightly touched her hand, sending her twenty-five year old virgin body through a heat wave.

"I'll be very honest with you. I'm interested in knowing more about you other than another employee in my father's corporation. And I hope my interest doesn't go unrequited."

Summer saw no reason why they shouldn't get to know one another. In fact, she wanted him more than he thought she did. Then she thought of the witch who ran her department.

"I thought you and Jackie Shannon…"

He placed his finger over her lips before she could finish. "Shhh. Me and you, Summer. This has nothing to do with Jackie. She is not my wife. We no longer have a relationship. I dated her last year but she and I have nothing between us anymore and I will keep it that way forever."

"I saw you and her leaving the picnic together. I thought you came together and maybe you were seeing each other."

"I took her home because Gwen had left. She came with Gwen and needed a ride home."

He didn't think it was appropriate to tell her that he and Jackie also had a heated argument because of how she showed her behind at the picnic. No use bringing any burdensome issues into this friendship.

"Now, would you feel comfortable enough to take a trip with me two Saturdays from now?" he asked.

"Where will we go?"

"I have to go and check on my parents' farm house up in Frederick. I would like you to ride up with me. I'm going up a week and a half from today. There's no livestock but my mother still grows a huge garden up there."

"I'll have to make sure my father is okay first."

Jonathan's features showed concern. "Is he okay?"

"Yes, but I'll have to make sure he's well enough for me to leave him and won't need me for anything."

"Okay. I can understand that. In the meantime, think about it. And please think about what I said about us."

They got up and he grabbed the trays, emptying them in the garbage receptacle. Summer was able to eat a little since he helped relieve her depression.

He escorted her to the building, opened the door for her. "May I call you tonight?" he asked.

Summer peered into his face, giving him a warm smile. "Of course, you can."

Once the elevator arrived at the fourth floor, they stepped off. So this is what heaven felt like, she said to herself. Even when she passed Jackie in the department and the woman rolled her eyes at her, she didn't care. Couldn't find a way to care. Her focus was on the proposal and the man she was falling in love with.

CHAPTER ELEVEN:

"You and Jonathan ate lunch together?" Nadia's voice resounded through the phone.

Summer fell into a reclining position on her bed, mentally reliving the time she spent with Jonathan. "Yes, and he asked if he could call me tonight. And he wants me to go with him up to Frederick to check on his father's house."

"I should have doctor's appointments more often." Nadia said. "Because I know he said something about being glad I wasn't there so he could have you all to himself."

"Why are men that way? You know, selfish?" Summer wanted to know. Jonathan was the closest she had ever come to falling in love.

"Because they're like little boys." Nadia added as an afterthought, "Matter fact, they are little boys."

Both fell into giggling convulsions.

"All jokes aside, watch your back for real now. Jackie is the devil's daughter and if she ever catch the vapors that you're seeing her ex-boyfriend, she will come after you with the hatchet for sure."

"I don't think she'll catch the vapors. Jonathan said that he and Jackie have nothing anymore."

Nadia rolled her eyes as if Summer was standing right before her. "Girl, that's not the point. Jackie knows you're a threat. You might think this is a clandestine thing between you and Jonathan but people in that company have a way of finding out things and that hussy has eyes and ears all over the place, starting with that damned Gwen that works right in your department."

"Since you put it that way, let me make tracks out of that department. I'll start checking around to see where I can work until this deal goes through."

Abu pulled his Honda in front of Jackie's condo. He got out and headed up to her front door, rung the bell. She opened the door and said, "This is strictly concerning business."

She wanted to make it clear to him that she had not invited him over for a social visit. He may as well get that out of his head. Once she was done using him, she would make sure he was out of *Ethnic Information Corporation* too.

"Then why couldn't we discuss this at work?" he asked, disappointment showing in his face. However, he had to admit that being invited to her home seemed promising. He noticed the dress she wore – a red short satin number with thin shoulder straps. She looked stunning!

"Because you never know who's listening." she said, walking toward the bar. "I just want to make sure we have our shit straight."

Abu patted her soft cinnamon brown cheek, smiling admiringly at her. "We've got that covered, cutie. Jonathan won't believe an imbecile like Summer before he believes us."

She turned slightly away from him, a worried look washing over her face.

"I wouldn't count on it. Jonathan seems to be enthralled with Summer and that little innocent act she portrays. Do you know I found out where she was when we were looking for her high-yellow ass this morning."

"What does that have to do with the proposal, Jackie?"

"She was in his office, Abu!"

"Maybe that had nothing to do with the idea. You're growing paranoid. Just get that through your head. He doesn't give that girl too much credit for having any intelligence."

Abu knew what Jackie's angle was. He had caught on weeks ago. Yes, he wanted that promotion as much as she and was willing to muscle it from Summer but he didn't want Summer fired.

"Just make sure you do what I told you!" she snapped. He could tell she had grown not only desperate but also irrational. "This idea being mine means a lot to me. We have to make sure we are on the same train in case Summer musters up the nerve to tell Jonathan about it. Now I found the proposal in her drawer so that could mean he hasn't gotten it yet."

"Good. Now you're thinking more positive."

"The way things look, she just might become comfortable enough. Jonathan may even remain with the company. If he does, there go all of Maurice's policies right to hell."

Jonathan and his new-fangled bullshit! Abu thought. Knowing the son of the CEO, he would change things so much that many would end up being out of that company. Some of those comfortable in their positions would not take the change lightly but what could they do?

"What are you saying?" Now her statement alarmed him.

"The so-called rumor about Maurice retiring in October turns out to be not such a rumor. Maurice has been planning this for years now. Why do you think his bitch-ass son runs the company every summer? Summers are practice sessions for Jonathan. He'll be running the company when Maurice quits."

"What makes you so sure?"

"Maurice told me, Abu. Whatever the case, make sure you tell Jonathan what I told you to tell him in case he decides to ask you where it came from. He's savvy, Abu, and keen."

When he failed to respond, she added, "Or your job will be on the line."

He hated her threatening him but he conceded with a slow nod before leaving. What if Jackie and Jonathan resumed a relationship as the result of him remaining in Maryland? Abu could deal with him being all the way down in Greenville, SC. If he told Jonathan or Maurice that Jackie stole Summer's idea, she could be fired. He didn't want to treat the woman he loved that way. Jonathan's permanent return to the company was his greatest fear.

* * *

Renee thought everyone had gone home. She headed back to *Ethnic Information Corporation.* It was time to make her move. She'd been watching their moves for weeks now, knowing who left at what time and knowing which employees tended to stay later than others. Most of the writers and editors usually left later but their offices were on the second floor. Her destination was the seventh floor, where the accounting office of *Centric* was located. She had taken Nadia's entrance card to enter the building. After entering, she inconspicuously took the stairs and moved stealthily down the hall of the seventh floor. She knew there were cameras on the grounds, staircases and halls but didn't care because she wore a disguise. She used an inactive credit card to open the door of the intended suite.

What a disappointment! She realized this was not the office where the petty cash safe was located. She closed the door and began creeping down the hall. When she heard voices behind one of the suites on the right side of the corridor, she darted back toward the office she had just left and shut the door, pinning her ear against the door, checking for sounds. A door of one of the suites opened and the voices grew louder, getting close to the suite she hid.

Oh shit! She knew the voices were headed her way. She looked around quickly for a hiding place. The only place to hide was under the desk. Piles of disorderly paperwork fell from the edge of the desk, landing on the floor next to her. She attempted to pick them up but it was too late to make a sound. She held her breath. The door opened, the light snapped on. The voices were right over top of her. A pair of size eleven Stacy Adams shoes walked right over next to her.

"Jerome doesn't keep the charts in here, Brenda." a male voice said.

"He told me to look in his files, Darryl. I know what I heard him say." a female voice said.

Darryl's voice grew impatient, dealing with the chicken head that had him running all over the place looking for something they could not find. "He means his system files, not his hard files. You could probably access it on one of the computers in *Centric's* common library right down the hall."

"I didn't think of that. You're right, let's go. Even if they were in here, we'd be until next month trying to locate something in this junk yard he calls his office."

The light went off. The door shut. Renee released that breath she'd been holding. She waited until there was complete silence before dashing out of Jerome's office. She went down the hall, entered the accountant's office. What were Brenda and Darryl doing still here? They usually left around six. She could not concern herself with that now – she had a mission to accomplish.

Her nerves didn't calm until she reached the highway, heading to DC. She had encountered another close call after that one with Brenda and Darryl. Once she left the accountant's office, she spotted Chris Moyer headed down the hall in her direction but he was so wrapped up in the documents in his hand, reading them as he walked that he paid no attention to her as she hid behind the encased wall. He walked right pass her, sauntering carelessly until he bent the corner leading to the other side of the seventh floor. Even if he saw her, he would not have recognized her because of the disguise she wore.

When she stopped at a red light on the corner of 14th and Park, NW, she opened her mirror case to check her hair. Immediately, she realized that one of her $700 earrings was missing. Roderick, her boyfriend had brought them from Africa a year ago. She feared that she'd lost it in the building or Jerome's office. If she did, she would be in big trouble because someone would know it belonged to her. Everyone who noticed her wearing those earrings complimented her. She looked around in her car once she parked in front of Stix's house, hoping it fell off there. She didn't find it. She got out, went to Stix's door and knocked.

"This better be in our favor." Stix's boy, Lew said after opening the door.

"I have the money." she hurried to tell him.

Without a word, he ushered her into the two-story town house and down the hall to the smoke-filled dining room, where Stix and three of his partners played cards. Stix glanced up, mashed out his cigarette and got up. Walking toward Renee, he told Lew, "Take my seat."

Afterwards, he escorted Renee to the den, where she handed him an envelope and he counted the money. She waited nervously. He smiled at her curtly and said, "Your debt is clear."

She began heading out but he grabbed her arm tightly. "And if you ever try to screw me over again, I'll kill your ass! I'm not gonna cut you any time just because you're Roderick's girl. Is that understood, bitch!"

"Yes, Stix, it's understood." she spoke humbly.

"Good. Now get the fuck outta here before I have my boys back there run a train on that luscious ass of yours."

She hurried from the house the moment he released her arm. She got to her Toyota, nervously sticking the key in the ignition. Now that Stix was no longer a worry, she had to get Nadia's pass card back to her before she realized it was missing and find that earring.

Jonathan couldn't find it in himself to relax after arriving home that evening. He had been home almost two hours, thinking of Summer. He told her he would call around ten. He glanced at the slow-moving clock in the kitchen.

Never had he dreamed that at almost thirty-nine years old, he would be acting like a high school boy who found his first love. He didn't want to come off like he was desperate either. After pondering a few minutes, he made determined strides to the telephone. *To hell with seeming desperate!* he said to himself, picking up the phone. He wanted her, needed her, loved her. Summer was special.

The telephone rang twice before he heard Summer's greeting. His heart betrayed him with violent thumps, hearing her relaxed, sexy voice.

"Good evening, Summer."

Hearing his voice made her secret place go wild with desire, a warm feeling rushing through her. No man had ever set her body aflame as he had.

"Hi, Jonathan. It's not ten yet."

He could tell she stifled a giggle. He had to save face now. "I got in a little earlier than I anticipated. Have you eaten yet?"

"Dad and I ate about an hour ago."

She wasn't hungry, he thought, that narrowing down his options. He tried to think of a place they could go at this hour that would be to her liking. It was summer and they could even take a walk through the park. "How about I come over, pick you up and we go to a movie?"

"It's sort of late. I don't usually go out after this hour on weeknights."

She set him to thinking on his feet now. "Well, how about I come over and bring you back here?"

"And do what?"

"Watch movies. Maybe I could give you a tour of my parents' mansion."

"Okay." she said.

She always wanted to see where Maurice Wesley lived. She had heard many stories from others how beautiful the home was. But whenever Maurice had those social gatherings at his house, she was always excluded. She was never part of the "in crowd".

"I'll be there in thirty minutes." he said.

She jumped out of bed and got dressed. She decided to wear a pair of white cotton slacks and a black satin short-sleeved blouse. She slipped on a pair of black low heels and stared into the dressing mirror, debating if she should allow her beautiful mane to flow freely or wear that ponytail that Jonathan seemed to forbid. She realized he loved her hair the day he slipped into the mailroom after she'd removed the band that held it in place. Nadia always told her that men didn't verbalize what they felt – just watch their body language and you could tell if you had their approval or not. Well, she knew she had Jonathan's approval because when he saw her hair uninhibited by the barrette, he looked as if he could devour her whole.

She told her father where she would be going before Jonathan arrived.

"Oh, yeah?" he said, sitting up straight. He'd been relaxing on the bed, watching television. "So where are you and Mr. Wesley headed?"

"He wants to show me around his parents' mansion."

Allen smiled. It was about time she stepped out on a date. Not only that, as long as she was occupied, she would not have time to stick her nose in his business. He wanted her to move on with her life.

"Always remember, guard your heart, baby girl."

"I will, Daddy. Besides, we're not going to do anything."

"I know my princess, she always conducts herself as a lady." he said with a smile.

She kissed his curly head. "Let me get the door."

She dashed downstairs to the front door and opened it. Jonathan took notice of her appearance. Her massive curls made her look so natural. She didn't look like the seventeen year old he thought he had seen the first day he laid eyes on her. She still had that youthful appearance but letting her hair free did something to enhance her appearance.

"Won't you step in," Allen offered, standing behind his daughter. Summer hadn't known he crept downstairs behind her.

Jonathan stepped into the living room, his eyes never leaving Summer. He shook hands with Allen and accepted the glass of lemonade Summer offered.

"Would you like to come along, Mr. Douglas?" Jonathan offered, hoping Allen would decline. He wanted Summer to come alone but didn't think it was polite not to invite a girl's father to his family's mansion.

"Allen," the older man corrected, waving a dismissing hand. "Naw, you kids go on. I need my sleep or I'll feel like hell in the morning."

After guzzling down the lemonade, Jonathan took Summer's hand, escorted her to his Jaguar parked in the Douglas driveway. She waved to her father before stepping in. He closed the passenger door for her and went around to the driver's side.

They cruised the beltway in his smooth-riding Jag as they talked.

CHAPTER TWELVE:

Once they reached his parents' home, he parked in the east garage and opened the door for Summer to emerge from the car.

"You know, a girl can get used to this." she said, smiling in his face, turning him on again. She shouldn't play these games with him. Every little so-called innocent thing she pulled only made him want her more.

The motion signals around the house lit up and Summer took a step back, wondering if someone inside the house had turned on the lights. He put his arm around her shoulders reassuringly.

"They're part of the security system. Nothing to worry about. I sometimes don't know why my father had them installed since they live in a gated community."

She stood next to him as he unlocked the door and punched in digits on the security pad. Alone at last! he thought. He began giving her a thorough tour of the house. Summer was amazed by the size of the bedrooms. The smallest bedroom of the nine was still larger than her living room. She was fascinated by the many African carvings from nearly every country in the continent adorning the walls.

What captured her attention most was the large pure gold plaque of Nefertiti's crown on the wall in one of the sitting rooms. The Wesley's had nothing but the real thing – everything was authentic. In Jonathan's childhood bedroom sat a Yoruba drum in the far corner beneath a window.

He gave her the history of some of the items in the house. "That drum was one they used in Nigeria during tribal fests in the fifteen-hundreds, way before slavery." he said.

"How did you get it all the way over here?"

"My father negotiated with a museum owner over there. Money talks."

The house was two-story, with a lower level, what most would just call a basement. The main house contained nine bedrooms, six full baths, a parlor, library, two sitting rooms, a sunroom, major kitchen where the cooks performed their culinary duties and smaller kitchen where Donya sometimes cooked meals for herself and Maurice. The lower level held the domestic employees' quarters, two more bedrooms and two full bathrooms, a huge movie/entertainment room with tens of thousands of dollars worth of Japanese stereo equipment and a 62" screen TV.

Outside was at least thirty more acres of land and the east and west garages, both able to accommodate four SUVs comfortably. When she'd heard from Nadia that the Wesley's lived in a mansion, she knew her friend wasn't exaggerating now. They walked up the wooden slope and entered the house again from the side entrance.

"My father had this slope installed for visitors in wheel chairs." he explained, noticing her curiously eye it.

"That was considerate," she said. "Do you stay here?"

"My mother insisted. But I insisted on staying in the guesthouse. It's more private and I'm not in the way of the crew that works here. I grew up in this house. My brother, two sisters and me. Of course, it wasn't this easy to maintain back then. It stayed a mess all the time when we were kids. I remember Nelda used to paddle our butts all the time."

"Who's Nelda?"

"She's the boss." he said with a laugh. "She whipped our butts more than our parents did."

"Is this you?" she asked, removing a framed picture from a table as they stood in the smaller sitting room. As soon as she spotted it, she knew it had to be him. She walked right over to it.

His face flushed with embarrassment. "I was ten years old then."

"When you were ten," She turned to meet his eyes. "I wasn't even born." She began laughing at her own comment, just realizing how many years he was older than she.

"A pleasant statement, Summer." He shook his head, laughing with her. "But that doesn't matter today, does it?"

She returned the photo to the glass table and folded her arms across her bosom. Jonathan closed the space dividing them, standing behind her, inches away. His warm, sweet breath tantalized her as he lifted her curls and she felt that fire igniting. He brought his arms slowly around her waist, gave her a gentle embrace, tossing more fuel into her fire. Her mind was saying no but her traitorous body was telling her yes.

He brought his hands up again, gently massaging her shoulders. She was so soft to touch, felt like butter in his palms. She basked in the feel of his strong hands, tilting her head back, resting it in his broad chest.

"My feelings are growing very deep for you. Do you realize that?" his soft, baritone voice spoke into her ear.

"Yes. I mean, no. Oh, I don't know."

He laughed, trying to ease her nervousness. When he took her, he wanted her to want to be taken. He didn't want to chase her away so he handled her delicately.

"Having the ability to love is the best gift humans could have." he spoke again before kissing the top of her adorned head of curls.

He turned her around to face him, stared into her eyes. She blinked and glanced around him, avoiding his dark, piercing eyes. He placed his palm under her chin, brought her eyes to meet his. He bent down and pressed his full lips to hers, thrusting his tongue between her lips to meet hers. She followed his lead.

This was the first time she had ever been kissed and it felt strange, yet so right. She could feel herself spiraling out of control, comparing it to a dream she used to have of falling but never hitting anything. His lips were thick, but soft and warm. Summer could not stand it any longer. She threw her arms around his waist and thrust herself forward, closer until she could feel his hardness. *No!* she thought. She was a virgin but she knew when a man was in want, need. She drew back slightly but that didn't do much, his huge shaft still pressed against her. She drew back more until she could no longer feel it.

He pulled her back, caressing her soft bottom with his large hands.

"Jonathan." she whispered.

"Yes, baby?"

"It's almost ten-thirty."

He touched the sides of her face with gentle hands. "I know. You can sleep here if you like. I mean, in the guest house with me."

"It's not proper."

Now where in the hell did that come from? he asked himself. "There are two bedrooms in the guest house."

She wanted to spend the night. She also knew that even if they intended to use separate rooms that night she would end up in his bed, through no forcing or coaxing of his. She wanted Jonathan Wesley to release all of his pent-up pleasure on her. Just then, the phone rang, breaking the silence of the quiet house, startling them.

"Stay right where you are," he said, darting across the room to get the phone.

"Jonathan," spoke Jackie's voice. "I called the guest house but you weren't there. I figured you'd gone next door."

Was she some sort of radar?

"What can I help you with?" he asked abruptly, frustrated that she had thrown a wrench in his groove. If he'd known it was her, he wouldn't have picked up the phone. Something told him to look at the caller ID first but he thought his father may have been trying to reach him so he didn't bother.

"Thanks for the birthday gift."

"You're welcome."

Though he never mentioned the name of the calling party, Summer knew who it was, noticing the impatient way he talked. He seemed so annoyed. She smiled, knowing it was Jackie.

"Listen," he said, as he seemed to cut her off. "I gotta roll. I have company."

After hanging up, he sauntered over to Summer and she teased, "I have to get up early in the morning and so do you."

"Yeah, you're right. I'll take you home, baby."

If only Jackie hadn't interrupted with that meaningless call, Summer would not have had time to debate whether or not to make love to him. Something had him believing that Summer feared Jackie to a certain degree. He wanted her in his bed, dammit! Like an automobile with just enough gasoline to reach its destination, his patience was running on fumes, just barely getting him by each day.

He forced down his raging hormones as they talked during the drive back to her house. He knew the value of taking it slowly and was determined to continue using the head that sat on his shoulders, the one God gave him to think with.

* * *

Friday morning, Jonathan was awakened by the shrill of the telephone. His father was calling. It wasn't six yet and he wondered why his father would be calling so early. He cradled the phone between his chin and shoulder while ironing his Khakis, listening to his father's speech.

"Now I want you to wait until I get back before this situation is handled." his father continued. "Don't do anything without me being present."

"No problem."

"Jonathan, you know these are situations you'll have to anticipate once I retire. That's if you still plan to take over the company."

"I am, Dad…okay…I love you too. Give my love to Mommy."

Once he was done ironing, he stepped into the shower. He pondered the situation concerning Jackie and Summer, knowing it would have to be handled. Why wouldn't Maurice allow him to handle this now – Jackie could do some major damage by the time he returned. Knowing the scorned woman, she was a wreck waiting to happen at this point. It was just a matter of when. She would become relentless in getting him back once she was sure what was going on with him and Summer. Waiting for Maurice was not a good idea for another reason: his new love would endure a lifetime of hell in the process. But if his father insisted on tackling the matter himself, Jonathan would step aside and allow him to. After all, it was *still* his company.

He thought of Summer as he dressed. It had been two days since he'd brought her to the house. During the past forty-eight hours, he hadn't seen much of her because he had been busy interviewing an historian for an upcoming article for *West Africans in America's* publication. He had a few brief conversations with her. But that was not enough.

Fridays he customarily dressed casually. Today, he donned a pair of Khakis and a green Polo shirt.

Once he arrived at the building, he noticed Jackie in the lobby, awaiting an elevator. When she turned around and saw him, her eyes lit up. She was overjoyed to see him, no matter how many times a day she saw him.

"Jonathan, good morning."

He kept whistling as he approached her. "Good morning, Jackie."

"Have you intimated Maurice with the idea Abu and I proposed?"

"Yes."

"Well, what did he say? I'm dying to find out."

I'll just bet you are! he thought and a grin almost came over his face. "He says he'll speak with you once he returns."

The elevator doors opened and Jackie, Jonathan and three others stepped on. The others got off on the second floor. Jonathan and Jackie rode up to the fourth. She was tempted to touch him since they were alone but couldn't figure out where his head had been all these weeks. There had been rumors about seeing him talking to Summer. Someone even told her that they saw the two of them coming in from lunch one afternoon. Jackie hadn't caught them together but the rumors were spreading like wildfire, too much for her to stand. She couldn't help but to believe there was some truth to what others were saying.

"May I see you in my office once you get things settled in your department?" he asked as his question seemed to have come out of the blue.

She glanced around, making sure he was talking to her before she said, "Me?"

Jonathan furrowed his brows in frustration. Now she's going to try and play dumb. "Who else is standing here in the hallway in front of me?" he curtly asked.

"Sure." She swallowed hard. "I'll be there in fifteen minutes."

Anticipation quickly set in. She wondered what he wanted. This was the first time since the first day of his return that he'd asked her to come and see him. Maybe he changed his mind about them. He would give them a second chance. Why wouldn't he, after he'd been dealing with Summer – that is, if he was.

Jonathan strode to his office, whistling the entire time. If Maurice wanted to drag his feet handling Jackie, he would at least toss some questions at her and try to get to the bottom of what's going on. But he knew the woman would go to a great distance to screw another person. And now she was trying to screw Summer. He wasn't having it!

As promised, Jackie made her way to see him in fifteen minutes exactly. Why wasn't he surprised? Kim Justen had called in and said she would be arriving late. When Jackie arrived inside the suite, she didn't see his assistant so she came in, closed Kim's workstation before making her way to Jonathan's private office.

"Jonny," she said, knocking three times on the half-opened door.

He was on the telephone with Summer when she arrived but waved for her to come in and close the door. Jackie strained, trying to hear his side of the conversation. He was talking awfully low and this irritated her. If he wasn't talking to that scank, he was talking to some other tramp. She remembered calling the house two nights ago and him telling her that he had company. However, this was her opportunity to reclaim her man. They hadn't spent any leisure time together other than the night of his first day back with the company but she planned to change that.

When he finished his call, he leaned back in his chair, folding his hands behind his head, showing off his broad chest, muscles outlining the Polo he wore.

"I wanted to apprise you that I faxed that idea to Maurice and he likes it." he told her.

"Oh, that's wonderful!" she cheered.

What a phony chick!

He gave her a quick nod and cocked a brow. "Is it?" he asked. "But he wants to know where you got your idea from?" He was the one who really wanted to know, not Maurice.

"My mother is sixty-six. I thought of it one day when I was out shopping with her."

Jackie was quick but not quick enough. He knew she never got along with her mother, her feelings bordering hatred for the woman who gave birth to her. Her wanting to circulate a publication for the needs of those in her mother's age group just seemed so out of character for her. Maybe he was wrong but it just didn't seem she would want to publish something that would benefit her mother, whom she strongly disliked.

"I have to make sure you didn't overhear that from another employee. You haven't told anyone else besides Abu, have you?" he asked, wondering if she would come clean and tell him the truth.

"Jonny, I know what the deal is with that. I've been with this company long enough to know better. Besides, I don't trust a soul around here."

A person who didn't trust usually was one who could not be trusted.

"I still have to go over this with you, Jackie."

A slow, surreptitious grin appeared on her face. She got up, pranced over to him and eased into his lap before he realized what she was doing. "We haven't been spending any time together, daddy." she whispered.

He placed his hands around her waist, eased her from his lap." That's because I haven't had time to spend on a leisurely basis."

She stood up abruptly, stared angrily at him. "What the hell is that supposed to mean? Does it mean you don't have time to spend with me? Go ahead, tell me what's really going on here!" she snapped and he hoped Kim hadn't made it in yet. Just then, he had a flashback of the day at the restaurant almost a year ago.

"Maybe you've been spending time with that slut who was at your house the other night when I called."

"I am not implying anything." he retorted. "And I never said I didn't have time to spend with you. You read too much into things. That was always a problem with you."

It was on and Jonathan couldn't turn back. "You've accused me of sleeping with so many other women. You've done hurtful things to others and that's the reason I thought it was best not to get involved again. Like I said, we need to go our separate ways."

"I know you've been upset with me since the picnic. But I thought you'd gotten over it." *He always did!* "Especially since you bought me that tennis bracelet for my birthday." her tone was so pleading, he wanted to lurch.

She knew where the gift came from, although the person who sent it didn't leave a name. It was his style to send her something expensive.

"It was simply a birthday present, Jackie. And there you go again, reading more into something than what's intended. I buy birthday presents for friends all the time."

He just didn't have it in his heart not to send her a present – he couldn't be that cold. Now he regretted it. She gave a whole new meaning to the proverbial saying: "Never cast your pearls to swine." Because she didn't appreciate anything, that was not a very wise move for him to send her that present. Instead of her simply appreciating the present and moving on, taking it for what it was, just a present, she took it to mean that he was still in love. He would not do that again because anything he did could be taken as him leading her on.

She heaved a sigh, staring at him. "So, it meant nothing?" she asked.

"Jackie," He rose from the green leather chair. "I don't have time for this. I called this brief meeting to discuss the proposal. I didn't call you in here for an argument."

She brushed her hands down her gray and blue silk pants suit as if she was straightening herself. "Fine, I understand." Without saying goodbye, she pranced out of the office and slammed the door behind her.

She made her way back to her department and went into her office, leaving the door open. When she saw Summer dart pass, she stood up and went to the door, watching her until she disappeared into the deposit room. Summer's new appearance didn't escape her notice – her hair flowed freely down her back, she wore a blue silk mini skirt, showing off legs that even Tina Turner would envy. Why the sudden change after six months?

CHAPTER THIRTEEN:

Jackie's concern was not only about the change in Summer's attire – her disposition towards the job had changed. She seemed to enjoy coming to work now and was even engaging in conversations with others, something Jackie had never seen her do. The only person she ever talked to was that Puerto Rican hoochie who worked for *Latino Outlook* on the third floor. She knew she had to be up to something. "That little bitch!" Jackie bit off before returning to her office.

No one heard her except Gwen, who got up and went into Jackie's office. Gwen was always down for whatever drama was going on and she wanted to know what was up and why her girl seemed so upset.

"What's up, girlie!" Gwen said, coming into the office, taking the empty chair in front of Jackie's desk.

"That hoochie in the deposit room is what's up. I think something's going down with her and Jonathan."

"I been knew that."

"Yeah, but you know how people talk. You can't always believe what they say. Now he's acting all funny and she's acting like her ass just hit the big one."

"So what you gonna do, Jackie? I asked you that before. You can't let her just come between y'all like that."

"What the hell can I do, Gwen?" Now Jackie was snapping at her like she'd done something wrong.

"Hey, I'm not the one trying to get your man. You better channel that shit to the heifer that's after your man."

Jackie didn't know what to do, other than creating a situation that could make Summer's life a living hell. As it stood, she didn't have any grounds yet. Seems that hussy had been watching her back, making sure she didn't screw up. She knew she should not have listened to Abu, who insisted on not firing Summer for the unsigned checks that had been sitting on her desk for weeks and not returning them to the customers.

Jonathan put his hands over his face, resting his elbows on the desk once Jackie was gone. He never intended to hurt her but it was obvious that relationship was not going to work out. What about Summer? He was certain she was gaining as much interest in him as he'd already in her. A short knock interrupted his pondering.

"Come in!" he called.

Kim flung open the door. He'd been so absorbed in his thoughts about Summer, he hadn't realized Kim finally made it to work.

"Mr...Um, Jonathan," She took another moment to catch her breath. "They need you on the seventh floor. There seems to be a major problem."

"What kind of problem?" he asked. He was not completely out of his daydream.

"I think you better go up and see for yourself."

He got up, followed Kim down the hall to the elevator. When they reached the seventh floor, all he could see was confusion at the entrance of the accounting department. People from different departments on that floor were standing around. Jonathan hated being the last to find out something regarding his business.

He hurried down the hall with Kim at his heels. One of the accountants for *Centric* approached him, confusion washing over his face. "I don't know how it happened." Andre said. "No one has keys to this office, let alone know the combination to the safe, except Candice and I."

"How much money is missing from the safe?" Jonathan wanted to know. Andre had better give him a better explanation than the one he just gave.

"There was at least two thousand in petty cash in that particular safe and all of it is gone."

"What do you mean, 'at least two thousand'?" Jonathan snapped at the shorter man, making him take a step backward. "What was the exact total?"

"Tw-two, th-thousand." Andre stammered.

Jonathan's countenance showed the anger he was feeling.

"You'd better find out what happened and how your ass is in hot water." he said before walking off and finding the department's manager. This was the second time money turned up missing from petty cash. What was more mysterious was the fact that nothing appeared broken in to. This was definitely an inside job.

Later that afternoon, Jonathan called an impromptu meeting with building security. He had already questioned everyone in Andre's department, shook them all scared. Now it was time to get on security's case. The entire security team consisted of twenty-four people, divided into three shifts. Until he conducted a thorough investigation, no one would be terminated. Once he found out who was responsible, that person or persons would be let go. It was not fair to fire the entire team for what one person may have been responsible for.

"I have the printout you requested earlier, Mr. Wesley." Carla, one of the team members handed him the printout of all activity entering and leaving the building after seven p.m. over the period of two weeks. Since Andre claimed to have gone home by six-thirty each day, the thief must have struck after that. He looked at the list. Darryl and Brenda's stories checked out. When they were questioned separately, both said they never stayed after seven once finishing the projects assigned to them by Jerome, except for one day earlier that week.

After checking off pass card numbers of persons he'd questioned, he had security check pass cards of employees not assigned to that floor. No one seemed to have entered the building except one person.

"Carla, look up pass card number, 7-6-5-0-1-3," Jonathan ordered.

Carla punched in the numbers and hit enter. "Well?" he prompted impatiently.

"This card is assigned to Nadia Cruz."

Jonathan repeated the number to Carla and she insisted she had the right number once she punched it in again.

"There must be some mistake," he said, not able to imagine Nadia stealing a nickel from anyone.

He peered over Carla's shoulder, peeping Nadia Cruz's name on the monitor. He didn't believe Nadia had used her own pass card, entered the building, ripped them off two thousand dollars, but someone had. Someone who could get close enough to Nadia's card and leave her to take the fall. Someone Nadia would trust.

Jonathan went home and looked over the printout again. He grabbed his cell phone from his briefcase and located Nadia's number in the log. There was no answer at her house. As soon as he hung up, the shrill of the house phone snapped him.

"Hello, Jonny. Carla told me what happened on the seventh floor." Jackie's unwelcome voice attacked his ear. She was really trying to lay it on with the sexy voice but he wasn't biting. "I never would have guessed Nadia would steal from the company. I should have known that tramp wasn't the Miss Goody Goody she pretended to be."

"Jackie," he curtly interrupted. "let's refrain from name-calling and let's get the facts before jumping to conclusions. Nadia may not be responsible for this. Seems since you're in the position of manager, you would know better."

"How could you possibly be that naïve?" she shot back.

He wasn't surprised that she would have heard about it by now. There were some in that company who loved to gossip and as soon as his father retired, he .planned to do some major house cleaning.

"Nadia could have lost her card and someone could have found it and used it." he defended one of his dearest friends.

"Or someone she knows could have taken it and used it." she shot back.

"What does that mean?"

"Nothing." she said, but added casually, "Summer does hang out with Nadia."

"Jackie, the tape I reviewed today didn't show Nadia or Summer on it. In fact, the person was someone nobody recognized."

"People do wear disguises." She would not give up.

Jonathan's Summer

"So it could have been anyone, including you." he sarcastically came back. She would not win this, pin this on Summer or Nadia. She may as well forget it if she thought she could coax him into believing any of them would be that scandalous.

"Don't be silly."

"I've wanted to tell you the same thing since the opening of this meaningless conversation. Anything else you want to say other than something to get another in trouble?"

"Yeah. What are you doing now? Maybe we can hook up and go out to dinner."

"I'm busy. I was before you called and I have to get back to what I'm doing. Jackie, I don't want you to continue getting the wrong impression. I don't know how else to put this, but it's over. Okay?"

"Why?"

"Because it wouldn't work. I tried not to be harsh about it. But I can't put it any clearer than that."

"Can we be friends?"

He closed his eyes before answering. "I don't think that's a good idea either. Let's just remain on the level of co-workers."

"You asshole! I'm tired of your shit! I've given myself to you and this is the thanks I get. You're self-centered and mean!"

"You can accommodate yourself by never speaking to me again." He was not surprised she would come off that way.

She slammed the phone down in his ear.

Jonathan rested his elbows on the dinning room table, putting his hands over his face after hanging up. The nerve of her trying to accuse Summer of stealing money from the company. It was bad enough she was pointing the finger at Nadia but it sent him over the edge when she brought Summer's name in the conversation. He didn't know why she had it in for Summer, but he would soon get to the bottom of why there was so much tension between the two women. He'd learned from Nadia that Jackie had disliked Summer ever since she started working there in January.

* * *

Monday morning, he called Nadia into his office. He knew once he cleared it up, everything would be fine and he would then be able to eliminate her from the equation of being a thief.

"Nadia, did you lose your pass card?" he asked.

She reached into her purse and pulled out the card. She held it up. "Nope, here it is right here."

"Could anyone have gotten a hold of it?"

"I don't think so, Jonathan. I usually keep it in my purse."

Whomever lifted her card must have returned it before she discovered it missing. he thought.

"Nadia, the person who stole all that cash from the seventh floor last week seems to have used your pass card to enter and leave the building." he said, leaning his bottom against the windowsill. "Everyone we talked to that was here after seven within the time period the money was stolen checked out clean. The only missing link is the purpose of your card being used. You stated you left work at five every evening and didn't return until eight the next morning."

"Yes, that's right." She stared quizzically at him.

He folded his arms across his chest, looking directly into her dark brown eyes. She seemed sincere. She made no manifestations of being guilty.

"Typically, we would terminate a person with so much incriminating evidence against them but since I don't believe you'd steal from me, you'll keep your job."

"Thank you, Jonathan."

"But now I'm going to ask a favor of you,"

"Sure."

"That you be so kind and let me know if or when you find out who it was that used your card and almost left you to take the fall."

She closed her eyes and opened them again. "I will, Jonathan."

When she left his office, via Kim's workstation, she stood in the corridor, planning on how she would whip Renee's ass for setting her up. She knew who the culprit was. Renee had taken the last few days off and now Nadia knew why. She had told her not to rob the company after Renee hinted that's what she planned. She didn't listen. As soon as she caught up with her, she would be one sorry sistah.

Jerome returned to Maryland at six that evening. Darryl and Brenda met him in the seventh floor conference room and they discussed the revised charts of the stock list. After going over the charts, Jerome stood to leave, buttoning his Brooks Brothers jacket.

"You didn't have to drive all the way back down here from New York. We could have discussed this over the phone." Darryl told his boss.

Jerome smiled, displaying the Wesley dimples. "I need to catch up with my brother and gather some documents from my office. I forgot them last week." he said.

"Any time to spare afterwards?" she asked.

"I'm sure that can be arranged since my brother doesn't monopolize all of my free time. I won't be leaving until Friday morning."

"Call me when you finish up with Jonathan." she said as they walked down the hall, side by side.

He winked at her. "It would certainly be my pleasure."

She stopped at the elevator and he made his way down the hall to his corner office. He opened the door with his key, snapped on the light and began searching through unorganized documents on the corner of his desk. Though the place was in shambles, Jerome still knew where to find everything.

Nonplussed, he scratched his head, knowing the draft of Benson Germaine's interview for stock recommendations should have been in that pile. He looked around but still did not find it anywhere on the desk.

"Ah ha! What are you doing down there." he said, kneeling down to pick up a stack of papers from the floor. Once he lifted them, he spotted something gold on the floor. He picked it up right away, realizing it was an expensive earring. His father had bought enough gold jewelry for Jerome to know this was a very high quality piece from the mines of South Africa.

He knew it didn't belong to his mother. What was it doing in his office? It had been nearly a year since the time he laid Brenda on his desk, a memory he found pleasure is conjuring. He stuck the earring in his pocket and left.

Once he arrived at the guesthouse, he told Jonathan about the earring.

"You said you found this in your office?" Jonathan asked, examining the earring. "Sure it doesn't belong to one of your women?"

"Yes and I don't know what it was doing in my office."

"Maybe Brenda dropped it." Jonathan suggested, knowing the deal with his brother and Brenda, although Jerome tried to hide it.

"This is a rare design. Besides, Brenda's ears aren't pierced."

Jonathan flashed his brother an impish grin. "And how did you know that?"

Jerome admitted, "I've kissed those ears enough, that's how I know. Review that tape again. See if you guys can zero in enough to spy that unknown woman's ears. Something tells me that there is a link between that money missing and this mysterious earring appearing in my office."

"How do you figure that?"

"Well, when I went into my office, things just seemed out of place. I work on the seventh floor. As if someone had been in there. The person was looking for something and apparently didn't find it in my office."

"As junky as your office is, I can't see how you'd discover that."

"My office may be junky but I know where I leave everything."

"I'll review the tape again. In the meantime, I've replaced the money while I investigate this. Dad doesn't need to get involved. I have things under control as it stands. If he finds out, a lot of people will go down, people that may be innocent."

"I agree. He's not gonna care who he gives the axe."

* * *

The planned getaway finally arrived for Summer and Jonathan after a long, stressing week. By Friday evening, both were spent from the busy week. Marketing had been promoting all five of their publications and tens of thousands of new subscribers were calling and mailing in requests for subscriptions. *Latino Outlook*, one of the newest publications had the most reply from new subscribers.

Summer had been handling the deposit for not only *West Africans in America* but *Ethiopian Journal* because the deposit clerk had taken sick leave three days that week. During the summer is when most people called in sick or planned vacations. She worked two hours overtime each of those days because the figures for *Ethiopian Journal* were so huge. The journal brought in over ninety thousand each day.

After completing the deposit recap worksheet for the journal, she made her way to the fifth floor and distributed copies to their accounting department. Most of the employees had already gone home for the weekend and she had to slide the copies under their office doors.

Once she returned to the fourth floor, she gathered her personal belongings and prepared to leave, thankful Jackie and everyone else in the department left at five. It was so peaceful around there when everyone was gone. During normal hours, there was so much noise and activities that it would sometimes give her a headache.

She checked her watch, noting that it was time to get home to her father.

"Long day?"

She spun around and there was Jonathan, leaning against the doorframe of the deposit room. Her eyes started at his Nike-clad feet, traveled up to his blue denim jeans, white Polo shirt and stopped at his freshly tapered hair. He was stunning even in casual wear.

"Very long day indeed. I'll see you tomorrow afternoon, Jonathan." she said. She couldn't wait until Saturday. She wondered if this would be it. Would Jonathan make her a woman? At that moment, an old cut performed by Betty Wright echoed in her mind entitled: *Tonight is the Night*. She was not born when that song was created but her father played it so much, she learned the words of it.

She attempted to pass but he stopped her, grabbing her upper arm. His strength was incredible and just then, a surge of passion shot through her. She wanted him to take her right there on her desk. She hoped he would. His grip was strong, making her hot. He was one hundred and fifty percent male!

"Not so fast," he said, his lazy glare resting on her face. He let out the sexiest chuckle she had ever heard erupt from a man.

Jonathan's Summer

Before she could react, his lips had captured hers in a warm, wet, arousing and passionate demand. She offered her tongue willingly, the fire in her body making her weak with desire. She could feel the tingles starting from her breasts and spreading until they reached her toes.

She had to break this because she wanted to rip her own clothes off at that moment. She broke their embrace, pulling slightly away. "I have to check on my father." she whispered, passion in her voice. She could feel his hard member pressing against her but this time she did not try to stop it.

"Besides, you don't want us to be seen."

Just suppose Jackie came back looking for him? Their relationship was supposed to be a clandestine one but it seemed others in the company were catching vapors as to what was going down between them. Nadia even told her that a woman in her department who'd had a long-standing crush on Jonathan inquired about them because she saw them talking outside one day.

He laughed. "No one is here except us, baby. This is Friday and it's a beautiful evening. Nobody wants to hang around on a night like this on Friday."

Summer felt a little uneasy being in that enormous office alone with this dangerously sexy man. Jonathan had such an affect on her that there were times when her first impulse was to run in the other direction when she saw him headed her way. Her desires had reached the level where she could no longer control them.

"But I still have to get home to my father." she repeated.

He laughed carelessly. "Boy, do I envy that guy. I long for the day when you'll be telling someone that you have to get home to me."

"Jonathan, you're one of a kind."

"So are you, Princess. Anyway," He glanced at his Rolex. "I have to rack up and get out of here too. I'll see you at your house in a couple of hours."

"My house? Why?"

"Didn't I tell you." He grinned impishly. "I spoke with your father this afternoon. He told me to stop by the Chinese restaurant and pick up something on my way."

Summer narrowed her eyes. Seems Jonathan and her father were constantly scheming behind her back. Only two nights ago she had caught her father talking secretly to someone on the phone. When she investigated, checking the caller ID to see who called, she spied Maurice Wesley's name on the display, which meant Jonathan was the person that called.

"What do you mean? Spill it, Jonathan!"

"He invited me over for the evening. I guess he wants to have that man-to-man with me before I go trekking up to Frederick with his princess."

Summer couldn't control the laughter that suddenly bubbled out of her. She knew Jonathan must have spoken to her father if Chinese food was on the menu.

"You win, Jonathan. I'll see you then."

CHAPTER FOURTEEN:

Summer couldn't get home quick enough to tell Nadia everything. She greeted her father with a quick kiss and darted upstairs, not stopping until she reached the phone on her nightstand.

"Oh my goodness!" Nadia screamed. "He's on you, girl. If Jackie ever found out, she'd lose her damn mind." It would be Nadia's pleasure for Jackie to find out that Jonathan was on another woman, especially Summer, the one she hated most.

"I took your advice about watching my back. I've been checking behind myself, making sure that I don't make one mistake. It's getting to the point where Jackie doesn't scare me anymore."

Jonathan had built up her confidence so much, she was realizing that Jackie didn't have as much power as she once believed she had.

"Yeah, sistah. And don't let her think she intimidates you either. But Jose just walked in from work. I gotta go. You get ready for Jonathan's grand entrance."

Once Summer hung up, she changed from her red slacks into a black satin short-sleeved dress. She pulled her hair into a French roll, allowing strands of curls to hang carelessly down her back and around her shoulders. She sported a pair of gold hoop earrings and put on a smear of mahogany lipstick.

"You're beautiful." She looked through the mirror at face of the voice that spoke behind her. Her father stood at the entrance of her bedroom, smiling, hands shoved in his pockets.

"Princess, that's how I'd love to see you look every day, not like some kid who lost her parents."

Allen Douglas had seen the change in his daughter's appearance and disposition since meeting Jonathan. He was a little concerned because she was new to this dating thing but happy someone had helped boost her confidence. Jonathan was slowly pulling Summer out of that shell. Even if she and Jonathan never married, at least she would have experienced love. He still secretly hoped for grandchildren one day.

The doorbell rang and Allen put up his palm and told her, "You stay here and get pretty for Mr. Wonderful." He laughed and headed down the stairs to open the front door.

"She's upstairs, Jonathan." Allen told the younger man. "She'll be down soon enough."

Jonathan shook hands with Allen once he placed the food on the dining room table. "How's the big guy." Jonathan joked, giving Allen a light pat on the back.

"*Old* guy," Allen corrected. "Couldn't be better. That daughter of mine takes excellent care of me. She calls numerous times a day from work and can you believe this," Allen leaned closer to Jonathan's ear and whispered, "she doesn't want me to have a girlfriend. She's so protective."

"Can't beat having a daughter that doesn't want some woman bringing drama in your life." Jonathan said, breaking into a laugh.

Summer strutted into the dining room.

"Okay, what's going on now?" She placed her hands on her hips as if she was on her way to disciplining them both. "You guys scheming again?"

They both turned around, each with a guilt-ridden look on his face.

"Who, us?" Jonathan said playfully.

"Yes you."

Both men glanced at each other and at her.

"Nothing's going on." Jonathan was the first to speak up.

"Yeah, we were just talking about the playoffs last week." Allen added.

"I'll bet you were. Where's the food? I'm hungry."

Summer's appearance didn't escape Jonathan's notice. Gradually, she had changed from over a month ago. He was satisfied with what he saw – was satisfied then, only now she was even sexier. He tried not to let Allen catch him staring at her legs but every time he realized what was going on, his eyes were already trained on her legs. *She's fine! She's fine! I'm so glad she's mine!*

Summer could feel Jonathan's eyes on her. She loved the attention she got from him. No man had ever paid that much attention to her. Ever! No wonder Jackie was so crazy over him. Well, she lost a good man and he didn't belong to anyone. Correction: he did belong to someone, *her!*

They sat around the table, Allen and Jonathan dominating the conversation, discussing basketball, fishing and other sports that Summer had no interest in although she couldn't help feeling good inside seeing the two most important men in her life getting along so well.

"You seem like a three-pointer type of guy," Allen told Jonathan once he said he was never good at scoring field goals during the time when he played basketball in high school.

"Naah." Jonathan waved his hand. "I love basketball but I was never perfect at it. Never made most valuable player."

"But you coach right?" Allen said, slicing into his egg fu yung. "You have to be good at it."

"I'm better at the rules of the sport than I am at playing it."

"Is that why you're such a good boss?" Summer had to interject – say something to stroke her man's ego.

Jonathan rewarded her with an infectious grin and mused silently. *I'm also a good lover and would make an excellent provider for my wife and ten kids.* He laughed at where his imagination had taken him before taking a sip from his wine glass. Summer really knew how to lay on the compliments. He had always been a confident man but she had a respectful way about her that could drive a man to jumping through hoops for her. She was the type of woman that would make a man want to run home to her.

By midnight, the three called it a night. Summer and Allen were too tired to watch the movies Jonathan had brought from his parents' enormous DVD collection but promised to take a rain check.

"It sure was nice having you over," Allen shook hands with him.

"It was nice being able to have dinner with you." Jonathan said, his eyes trained on his girlfriend's face the entire time.

Allen noticed the eye contact and chuckled. "Well, let me get up to bed. You kids have a good night."

And he was gone. Finally!

Summer and Jonathan stood on the porch. For moments, no words were spoken between them. He had no reservations about telling her what he'd wanted to tell her since the day he met her. He looked into her regal face. She stared up at him, longing for him to kiss her. She still had not mustered up the courage to initiate a kiss.

"Summer?"

"Yes?"

"I know this may seem a little premature, being that we haven't known each other long. But there is never a time limit on when a person is supposed to feel something for another person."

"Okay." she said with that smile that melted him every time.

"But I love you."

She gleamed. He said he loved her! Jonathan Wesley in love with Summer Douglas. She was the luckiest woman in the world.

"I love you too, Jonathan."

He closed his eyes, those words spoken from her like soothing music. His ears begged to hear those words again – heart longed for them.

His head came down, lips met hers. Her arms went around his waist. Each time they kissed, he captured a piece of her heart. She knew this was love and she could not deny it.

* * *

That same evening, Nadia paced around her living room, debating whether or not she should strangle Renee or turn her in to the boss. Since Jose had gone out on his Friday night outing with his boys to play pool, Nadia used this opportunity to call Renee over and inquire about what she had done. Several raps on the door shook Nadia's daydream.

She made determined strides to the door, knowing it was her so-called friend. Renee was incorrigible and Nadia chided herself for not using her better judgment when it came to befriending her. She knew something was up with that chick when she first started working for the company. Renee just had a way about her that told Nadia that she could not be trusted.

"Yeah, whaddup?" she said, snapping a wad of bubble gum, stepping into Nadia's three bedroom apartment.

"Don't 'whaddup' me like you don't already know why I called your scandalous ass over here, Renee." Nadia folded her arms across her ample bosom and eyed her. "Why in the hell would you use my card to rip off the safe and leave me to take the heat?"

"Prove I did it!" the other woman shot back.

"Maybe I can't prove it but I know you lifted my card the day we went to McDonald's and ordered food. When I told you to reach in my purse and get the twenty I had in there so I could pay for the food."

"That don't mean I did that shit!"

"You know what, I ought to tell Jonathan what the real deal is."

That threat shook Renee scared. She didn't want to lose her job and more than that, she didn't want the powerful, influential Wesleys on her ass. Knowing Maurice, he would take her to court and demand every penny she stole.

"I'm sorry." Renee hung her head, feigning humility.

"Sorry isn't good enough, especially since I could have lost my job. And you would do this to me after I gave you money! My own hard-earned money! Good thing Jonathan didn't believe I could be that dishonest. Otherwise, I would have been fired. I've been on that job over six years and I'll be damned if you'll ruin it for me."

Renee took a seat on the sofa without being invited to sit down. She regarded Nadia with apologetic eyes.

"I didn't know what else to do, Nadia." She choked back fake tears. "I told you I owed Stix a lot of money."

"Apparently, you owed him more than you told me, to clean out that safe in the accounting department." Nadia stood akimbo, staring down at her. "And I told you not to rob the company. I ought to just turn you over to Jonathan."

"If you do!" Renee shouted, suddenly jumping out of her seat. "I'll get you for it."

Nadia pranced to the door, opened it. "This so-called friendship is over. I want nothing more to do with your sneaky ass."

"That's what the fuck you think!" Renee shouted back, passing her on the way out.

Nadia slammed the door behind her. The argument moments ago kept ringing in her head hours later. She wondered why losers always found their way to her doorstep. She used poor judgment when it came to choosing friends sometimes. Summer was the only friend she had chosen who proved her true friendship in return. They had been close friends since tenth grade.

When she thought of Summer, she calmed down. She would not tell her about Renee's stealthy deeds. Not yet. But she needed someone to talk to so she picked up the phone and dialed her number. Allen answered the phone.

"Is Summer there, Allen?"

"Yeah, darling but she's outside talking to Jonathan." he said. "Want me to tell her you called?"

Nadia thought about it. "No, just tell her I'll see her tomorrow."

"Are you okay?" he said as if he could feel her pain through the phone.

"Yes, I'm okay. I was just calling to check on Summer."

He decided to let it drop. But he knew something was disquieting her. She was like a daughter to him – he had known her a long time. He had only brought one child into the world biologically but in an emotional sense, he had two children, Nadia being the other daughter.

"Okay, darling. You have a good night."

"Sure."

The next day, Nadia and Summer hung out. She had put her plans for Jose on hold so that she could "help a sistah out". She had known about Summer's little getaway with Jonathan since the time he made plans to take his woman up to Frederick.

Nadia felt like a kid in a candy store once she and Summer reached Victoria's Secret on the second level of Wheaton Plaza.

"Nadia, I can't let people see me going in here." she protested.

Nadia grabbed her by the wrist, yanking her into the sexy apparel store. "You better start behaving like the sexy woman you are. You know you got a little freak in ya. Besides, every woman deserves to treat herself to at least one of Vicki's naughty wears."

"So does that mean that men have a little dog in them?"

"Nothing but the dog!" Nadia laughed.

"Exactly."

Nadia ignored her and went to a rack, pulling a red negligee from the assortment. There was no way Summer would get cold feet now. She was going to get sexy for Jonathan tonight! It was time she got her groove on.

"You and I are about the same complexion. I look good in red and I'm more than convinced that Jonathan will find red on you to be not only sexy, but it will make his dick so hard, he'll have no choice but to lay it on you good, girl."

"Red is for hookers!" Summer protested.

"And you're gonna be his hooker tonight. Make that nigga fall crazy in love with you! Girl, men love this shit!"

"May I help you?" asked the store clerk and Summer felt embarrassment take over. Nadia was a trip when it came to drawing attention. The white store clerk seemed to regard them as a couple of ghetto sistahs who were probably from Southeast, DC and didn't know how to conduct themselves in public. All thanks to Nadia Cruz. It was bad enough the clerk had been watching them since they entered the place.

"Yes, as a matter of fact." Nadia spoke up, ignoring the woman's apparent disdain. "My friend here needs something suggestive, sultry and sexy to turn on a handsome thirty-eight year old CEO of one of the largest black organizations in the nation."

"Oh, the three Ss?" the clerk raised her brow and smiled, knowing that they were definitely there to spend some cash. For her friend to be dating some CEO of a company meant money and that was all she paid attention to. "Come right this way. I have just the thing for you."

"All that bitch can see is the commission she's gonna get from all this." Nadia whispered to Summer and she laughed.

Embarrassed, Summer punched Nadia's arm. "Ouch!" Nadia shouted.

"Why are you trying to put me on the spot?" Summer whispered as they followed the clerk.

"Because if I don't, you'll wish I had once you're up there with Jonathan tonight. I am trying to help you out. You're talking about driving miles to a secluded ranch and spending time with one of the sexiest black men on the planet. What if you end up spending the night?

"Are you going to wear those flannel pajamas that button all the way up to your neck?" she cracked, referring to some of the most hideous nightwear she had seen her friend wear. Summer needed to come off that juvenile kick she had been on all of her adult life. She was a woman now – and that meant she needed to start acting and dressing like one, especially dealing with Jonathan, the real man he was.

"I'm not going to wear any of this stuff for him!" she protested.

"Just take it with you. It's always nice to be prepared in case you decide to give him a little entertainment once you're up there."

The clerk reached her destination, turned around after pulling a red laced garter set from the rack. "He'll love you in this," the woman said, noticing Nadia's wink of approval without Summer seeing it.

The clerk winked back at Nadia. Summer's eyes grew large. Who even said she was going to go play with Jonathan? Nadia had been desperately trying to get this to happen ever since May. All she wanted was to hear all the juicy details once intimacy did transpire between them.

"How much?" Nadia asked.

"Fifty-two."

"Perfect. Give me that in a size six." Nadia ordered with a teasing look on her face.

The woman got a six from the rack and asked if that would be all.

"Yes!" Summer spoke up, knowing that racy garment would ignite enough fire.

"Actually, no!" Nadia piped in. "How about some nice fragrances? What would you suggest?"

"*Heavenly* or *Divine* are still pretty popular. They're soft and sensual." the clerk said, leading them to the fragrances.

"I think *Divine* will do." Nadia said, spraying the test bottle on her wrist. "Why don't we go for it with the lotion and the perfume."

Summer rolled her eyes heavenward. But she knew Nadia was enjoying seeing her best friend off on her first episode with a man.

"Do you have any sexy high heels?" Nadia asked once they went to check out.

"And why would you ask me that?" Summer returned with a giggle.

"Because you need some sexy pumps to go along with that set. I know just the shoes. We'll head over to Hecht's once we're done here."

What could she say? Nadia was not giving up and fighting with her would only exhaust her. Not only that, she harbored a secret desire to turn Jonathan on. She somehow knew that he would enjoy seeing her in that outfit. How could a man that emanated such a sexual aura about him not appreciate seeing the woman he loved in that daring apparel Nadia had picked out?

Nadia picked out these hooker-style leather backless pumps from Hecht's. She had Summer try them on.

"You got some little feet, girl," Nadia commented as Summer easily slipped on the six and a half shoes she had picked out. "And a man loves a woman with small feet."

"Gosh, Nadia. Do you ever quit!"

"Shit, I'm no quitter!" she tossed back. "Now let's get these and you'll be set. Sexy outfit, shoes, perfume! Bam! You're set, girl."

Summer pulled up in front of Nadia's place. She turned to her and said, "Now use that ammunition and use it correctly! This is your big chance and after this day, you'll have Jonathan's heart, his soul and his dick will have your name tattooed all over it."

Summer burst into laughter. How could she claim a powerful man like Jonathan for life?

She had only an hour left to bathe and change. She put the sexy apparel in her bag. She put on a gray and blue Howard University tee shirt and a pair of jeans shorts with dark blue Keds on her feet.

The doorbell chimed. Summer's heart stopped. She headed downstairs and could see the top of his head through the window of the door. She flung open the door. He wore a pair of dark blue Dockers shorts and a gray Ralph Lauren shirt.

The moment the door opened, he grabbed her, kissed her possessively. Good thing her father had gone fishing with a friend of his. No telling how Allen would have reacted to such a play on Jonathan's part.

"Let's go!" he announced, taking the small overnight bag she held. "Time is slipping us by."

Yeah, this man has plans!

He led her to a burgundy Lexus truck that she had never seen him drive before and they headed to Frederick, stopping once to pick up some fast food. The drive to Frederick took an hour and some change. Finally, they reached a long, winding road and were suddenly surrounded by rural area. They passed two houses during the ten mile drive up the road before reaching the Wesleys'.

"This is a vacation paradise." Summer commented as he escorted her from the truck. "But it looks as if rain might decide to pay us a visit." She looked into the clouds.

"If it does, it'll only cool the passion that's been existing between us since you got in that truck."

She punched his arm playfully. "Jonathan, don't be a dog."

"Nature, baby." He grinned wickedly. "Only part of a man's nature, especially when he has a woman like you around."

He removed the keys from his pocket and opened the front door. The place was small, cozy. They stood in the living room. The only furniture in the living room was a sofa, chair, oak coffee table and a twenty inch colored television that sat on a stand near the stair case. The kitchen was right through an archway decked with colorful beads. They sat down at the small table for four after heating up their lunch in the microwave.

Jonathan's mother had left a list of work for him to handle. Summer eyed the long list that had been placed on the kitchen table.

Jonathan headed to the barn. He got the mower, hopped into the seat and began riding the fifty acres of land surrounding the house. Summer collected wooden baskets from the barn and began picking tomatoes, onions, collards and green beans from his mother's enormous garden.

Once Jonathan was done, he went to the other side of the garden and picked beets, okra and cabbage. Summer noticed an apple tree nearby and decided she would pick the apples.

Jonathan's Summer

After they were done in the garden, they went inside, dusted the furniture and vacuumed the floors.

"Why doesn't your father hire someone to do these chores?" she asked, returning the broom to the pantry.

"Because my mother doesn't like anyone here. My sister Theresa and I are the only ones she will allow in the house without her being here. She calls this her little home away from home. When she's in town, she comes up here and tends to this place by herself. My sister offered to come but because I was bringing you, I didn't want her to accompany me."

"So you wanted to have me all to yourself."

"Now you got the idea." He put his arms around her, giving her a light peck on the lips.

His kisses turned passionate after the first peck, his tongue riding over her lips and into her mouth, down her neck. Kissing her made all of his nine inches of shaft respond. He could no longer wait. He had to have her.

He could smell the fragrance of *Divine* on her neck. Summer tilted her head back, feeling him light her furnace. He made her so hot! She would allow him to take her. But she had to take a shower first. She wanted to be nice and fresh when this happened although it seemed nothing mattered to him except making love to her.

"Can I go up and shower now?" she asked.

"Sure. While you're doing that, I'm going out to the garage and see if I can get that old Toyota started. My dad says he's been having problems with it starting."

"You guys have about ten cars. Why is your father so obsessed with that old thing?" She had seen the old Toyota in the garage when he opened it to remove some tools.

"Because he loves that old Cressida." He laughed. "Try explaining anything to my father. He's not trying to hear it."

She darted upstairs to shower. She took the master bathroom. The upstairs held three bedrooms and two bathrooms. A small family would fit comfortably in the house.

Once she stepped from the shower, she heard an engine rev. She looked out the bathroom window and saw Jonathan sitting in the car with the driver's door open and the hood up. He got out, headed back to the hood and closed it. He drove the car down the road. She could see the metallic silver vehicle disappear down the road and hoped he didn't go too far and get stranded and have to walk all the way back.

She noticed he left his cell phone on the bureau in the master bedroom and knew that if he got stranded, he would not be able to call her.

She put on the sexy garment Nadia insisted that she own and threw a matching satin robe over it. Since Jonathan was down the road, taking a chance on that old car, she decided she would turn on the television in the master bedroom. She took a seat in the lazy boy and watched old an movie, waiting on him to return.

CHAPTER FIFTEEN:

The promising thunderstorm began and Jonathan still had not returned. One minute, the sun was shining, the next, she heard a clap of thunder. She looked out the window and the clouds were so dark, it frightened her. She began wondering if she should go out and look for him, he'd been gone almost thirty minutes.

Just as she was about to put on her clothes, she heard the sound of a car coming up the road. She peered out the window and spotted headlights headed in the direction of the house. She watched him drive the car into the garage and exit. Rain was now coming down in sheets and he ran towards the house, trying not to get too wet. Suddenly, there was no sound on the television. Summer turned around only to realize there was a power outage. She heard the door downstairs slam and footsteps heading up. The house was dark although it was only seven p.m.

She looked around. He was heading upstairs. She could hear him stirring around in the other room. Then she could see the glare of a flashlight heading towards the master bedroom.

"Summer, is everything okay?" he called out.

"Yes." she said.

He came into the master bedroom. "I know you're probably frightened but I'll get some candles and we'll be fine."

He opened the closet and grabbed four candles while she held the flashlight. He lit the candles and took one downstairs and another to the bathroom, leaving one in the master bedroom on the dresser and another in another bedroom.

Once he returned, he pulled his shirt over his head, preparing to take a shower.

"Maybe we should go home." she suggested.

"Maybe we shouldn't. When storms hit in these parts, driving can get pretty hazardous. The roads are too muddy. Just sit back and relax. I'm going to get out of these wet clothes and shower up."

He removed his shorts. My goodness! she thought, eyeing him once he pulled off his boxers. He was hung! Seems his concentration was on taking a bath at the moment.

Once he stepped into the shower, he smiled. Her look of approval had not escaped his notice. She liked what she saw. But she would like it even more once he was done showering. He would show her.

So he wanted to ignore her! She would show him that she was not to be ignored. He had come into the room, lit the candles and stepped into the shower without noticing that she wore a satin robe – he hadn't paid any attention to the fact that she had changed her clothes. She hadn't dealt with Nadia's craziness all morning for nothing.

She heard the showerhead cut off. It was time to make her move. She opened the door, slipped into the steamy bathroom without him hearing and closed the seat of the commode. She sat on the seat and crossed her legs. Jonathan was still in the shower stall. He slid open the door and stepped out.

He stopped cold. There she was, all beautiful, sitting there with those big legs crossed. A smile played at the corner of his mouth. *She wants to play this game! She'll soon find out that she's not dealing with some boy here!* He finished drying off. Admiring the red garter set she wore.

"Hey!" she said.

He toweled his face, facing the mirror. He turned around and said, "Yes?" A look of passion was in his eyes. His gaze swept over her in a way that told her he was ready.

"Like my outfit?"

He threw down the towel and before she realized it, he lifted her effortlessly, tossed her over his shoulder and headed into the bedroom. He playfully dropped her onto the bed. She giggled. "Jonathan!"

"Jonathan, what? Hunh?"

"I didn't know I was arousing you." she said innocently, noticing his hardened shaft.

"Yes, you did." He smiled.

He began kissing her toes and she didn't know that a man could toy with that part of her and make her hot. "Ooooh!" she said, closing her eyes. His exploring tongue moved from her feet, traveling up her legs and to her thighs, stopping inside, tasting the wetness between them. She moaned again, louder this time. He pleasured her and she didn't know how much time had slipped by as her head spun, causing waves of passion to overwhelm her. She felt his tongue on her breasts. She held his head, caressing his short waves. Her tongue went into his ear and this time a moan escaped him. She was learning what he liked.

His hands found the bud of her pleasure and began toying with it. She cried out, calling his name. That's what he wanted to hear. He guided her hand to his huge shaft and she felt the throbbing of it in her palm.

His hand found her womanhood again as he placed his finger inside her tight sheath and it seemed she had never had a visitor there. His shaft grew even stronger. Both knew it was time – there was no leaving the house until they made love.

Rain relentlessly pounded the windows and they could hear thunder rolling as the soft light of the candles displayed their shadowy figures on the walls.

He eased atop her and slowly placed himself into her hot, wet sheath, closing his eyes as he could feel her tightly enveloping him. He felt he would come to a climax right then and forced himself not to. Her body was warm, soft and tight.

Summer could feel his member dividing her in two. She had never felt this much pain before. She tensed.

He slowed down. "Are you a virgin?" he asked. She nodded and what he believed was now confirmed in her response. He toyed with the bud between her thighs, making her wetter. He wanted this to be a pleasant experience for her. He couldn't plunge into her and go buck wild like he could with other women. In fact, he had never been with a virgin before. Since he started having sex, he had always worn protection. With Summer, he didn't.

She cried out, sinking her fingernails into his back. This time, pleasure was prevailing and the initial pain was dissipating because Jonathan made her so wet.

He began stroking, his member touching her bud, causing her roller coaster to rise and her passion heighten. She could feel strong tingles because of what this master was doing to her. He was obviously very experienced in pleasing a woman, she thought. Because he had mastered her body, knowing what she needed. He had made love to her mind long ago, catered to her emotional needs and now he was physically satisfying the hell out of her. Those tantalizing tingles suddenly turned to strong spasms and she never realized climaxing felt so gratifying.

Hearing her loud moans, he could no longer hold it. His shaft erupted, spilling his seed deeply within her. His body immediately weakened, all of his energy draining for the moment. His breathing was labored. No woman ever wore him out this much. Summer's fruit was satisfying and delicious. His groan resounded throughout the small, quiet house as he climaxed.

"My goodness, baby!" he shouted, slowly removing himself and lying next to her. He glanced over, still feeling her body quake next to him. "Are you all right?"

"I feel wonderful." she said, sleep beginning to claim her. Jonathan did wonders for her body, quenching the sexual thirst that had been ignored too long.

Jackie allowed the telephone to ring seven times before the answering machine picked up. She hung up without leaving a message. It was bad enough he had been ignoring her for weeks, now he totally pulls a disappearing act! She knew his strategy because she had dated him last summer. Knew he had to be out with another woman. During the time they were seeing each other, Jonathan had the tendency to take her on weekend excursions or somewhere secluded, such as his father's cabin down in Halifax, Virginia. She wondered whom he was taking down there now. Wondered if maybe he had treated some bitch to a night out on the family's boat. Imagining him on the deck with another woman wrapped in his arms angered her.

When he was not out with her, she always knew where to find him. He would be home kicking back with a glass of wine or at the office having a meeting with some of the big-timers; or home sleeping. It was after eleven, where the hell could he be?

She called his cell phone and an automated message stated: "Message 2296, the party you are calling is either unavailable or out of the calling area."

She slammed down the phone, bit her bottom lip so hard, she drew blood. Another thought came to mind as she picked up the phone and dialed Abu's number.

"Hello?" Abu's voice cracked from slumber.

"Abu, this is Jackie." she said desperately.

"What's up?"

"Do me a favor and call Summer's house and see if she's there."

A long pause ensued as it seemed he pondered over whether or not he should do that. "Why can't you do it?"

He already knew the answer to that. Because she hated that bitch! "I'll explain later. Now call that tramp's house and find out if she's there. Call me back once you're done."

Abu said he would.

On the fourth ring, Allen's jovial voice answered.

"Good evening, Mr. Douglas. Sorry to bother you this late but my name is Abu, one of Summer's managers. I need to speak with her. Is she there?"

"No, Mr. Abu, she's been out since earlier today. I don't think she'll be back until tomorrow. Want to leave a message?"

"No, thanks. I'll try tomorrow."

After hanging up, Allen looked over at his female company. She asked, "Who was that this late at night? I know it wasn't Jonathan."

"One of Summer's bosses." he said as he sat down next to her.

He leaned over and began kissing her. He knew his daughter was in good hands. Jonathan was a good man, the type Allen always wished his daughter would end up with when the time came for her to choose a man. His attention was on this fifty-two year old gorgeous Latino diva named Maria Jiminez. She had been spinning his head for the past month now.

Abu called Jackie back as promised.

"So what's the deal?" she rushed.

"She's not home. Her father says that she's been out all afternoon and probably won't be back until tomorrow."

"Thanks." she said before hanging up.

This was no coincidence. Both of them could not be reached in the same night? She looked at the clock, it had struck midnight. If Summer was out, who else would she be out with? They had to be somewhere holed up together. She picked up the phone again, determined to talk to someone. She ditched the idea of even calling Gwen because she didn't want to hear the sarcasm. She called Lisa, her best friend who didn't work for their company.

"How do you know he's out with that other woman?" Lisa wanted to know once Jackie explained her reason for calling.

"Lisa, I told you that he's been ignoring me since the company picnic. This asshole's been acting like I don't even exist. And you got this homely looking girl who works in my department all of a sudden coming to work all diva'd up. She's trying to get him, I'm telling you."

"Jackie, you might as well forget about him. If he's turned to another woman, you don't have a chance anymore. You act like he's the only man on the face of the earth. It's like storing all your eggs in one basket."

"Lisa," Jackie began tearfully. "you just don't know what he did for me. I can't just allow him to slip through my fingers like that. You know all the stuff I told you last year about him. He knows I love him and he doesn't care. I can't take this."

"Jackie. Jackie, don't cry, girl. You'll get over this. Trust me. But you have to try to put him out of your mind and flush him out of your system. Otherwise, you're gonna keep tormenting yourself."

"But what is wrong with me? Why would he choose somebody like her over me? You should see her. She comes to work sometimes looking like she's homeless."

I'll tell you what's wrong with you! Lisa thought. *You're a selfish bi'atch. That's what's wrong with you. It has nothing to do with looks. It has to do with your fucked up attitude.*

Instead she voiced, "Maybe you can try having a heart-to-heart with him?"

"I tried that already. He's not tryna hear nothing I have to say."

"Then I don't know what to tell you, Jackie. Other than let it go."

But Jackie would not let it go. She was going to reclaim her man if it took all of the energy she had left. And if Summer was the reason behind him turning away from her, she would see to it that the other woman got hers.

CHAPTER SIXTEEN:

Sunday morning, Renee was determined to vindicate herself. Though Nadia said she wouldn't rat her out, she didn't see it that way. When it came down to it, she didn't trust anyone, not even Nadia because she was way too close to Jonathan. When the doorbell chimed, Renee ran to it, knowing who it was. She yanked open the door and allowed her in.

"Come in, Nadia."

At first, Nadia regarded her with suspicion. She came in, took a seat on the sofa. "What's this about? Why did you invite me here?"

Renee wrung her hands nervously. "I know you don't forgive me for that stunt I pulled but let me make it up to you."

"And what's your idea of doing that?"

She walked to the upright piano and grabbed the small velvet box that sat atop of it. Proffering it to Nadia, she said, "Take this."

"What is it?"

"A very priceless gift."

Nadia's defenses waned when she took the box and opened it. The necklace inside took her breath away. It was the necklace Roderick had bought over in Africa that matched the earrings Renee wore the day she robbed the company. But Nadia was not aware that she was missing one of the earrings.

"Renee, I couldn't possibly take this. Roderick would strangle you."

"So that should tell you how much I treasure our friendship." she shot back with a warm smile. "You like it?"

"I love it. But…"

"I'm sorry, Nadia." she cut in. "I acted desperately. I guess I didn't think of anyone but myself. I don't want to lose you as a friend."

Nadia stared into her tearful eyes, sympathy taking over. To her, here was a young woman like herself who had struggled all of her life and was only trying to make it, though she didn't go about it the right way. Both Renee's parents were drug abusers and she had been raised by her over-bearing grandmother until she was fifteen, the year her grandmother died and she found herself on the streets.

"Just promise me one thing," Nadia said, clutching the box to her chest.

"What ever I can do to continue having you as a friend, I will."

"You won't be helping me, you'll be helping yourself. Anyway, don't get yourself in debt again. Leave those niggas uptown alone, they're no good. Do yourself that justice."

"I've learned, Nadia. Trust me on that."

After Nadia left the apartment, Renee stared out the window as the car pulled out of the lot.

Once Nadia stopped at a light, she put on the gold chain with the unusual charm attached. She thought Renee desperately wanted her forgiveness if she was willing to part with something worth $5,000 in U.S. currency. She wondered why she had not used the piece of jewelry to buy herself out of debt with Stix and his uptown crew.

* * *

Summer awoke to shards of sunlight peering through the sheer panels of the bedroom window. The bed was so cozy, she didn't want to get up. Her eyes opened slowly and stared into the firm chest of the man who lay next to her. She brought her eyes up and met the face of him. She glanced around the room, noticed the digital clock was blinking. The power must have been restored overnight. They had made love in the middle of the night again and it was still dark, although the rain had stopped.

She looked at Jonathan again. He was sound asleep. She began moving but realized she was sore, the throbbing pain claiming her momentarily.

"Jonathan?"

He stirred, opening his eyes. One look at her brought a satisfying grin on his face. "Yes?" he asked, running his fingers through her disheveled hair.

"What time is it?"

He reached over and grabbed his Rolex from the nightstand. "Eight. How about breakfast?"

She smiled. "Why not?"

"I'm not talking about food you chew up and swallow." he said devilishly.

They stepped into the warm spray of the shower. Seconds later, he lifted her, pinning her to the blue tile, kissing her. The water soaked them. She could see that he would never get enough of her.

"This is what I call breakfast, baby." he said, wrapping her legs around his flanks. After tasting her sweet fruit, there was no way he could ever keep from having it again.

She moaned as he held her in one arm with little effort, making love to her against the tile. She locked her arms around his neck although he didn't need any assistance holding her.

"Jonathan!" she screamed. He loved hearing her cry out his name. To him that meant that her body belonged to him.

The more she moaned, the more it excited him, causing his throbbing member to fill up, feeling the tightness of her body wrapping around him. After bringing her to a climax, he gave in to fulfilling his own passion.

After showering, Summer prepared brown sugar pancakes, a recipe her father often used. She cooked bacon and eggs. They sat at the kitchen table, paying little attention to the food and more to each other.

He picked up his orange juice and smiled. "Every storm seems to be followed by sunshine." He was referring to his life.

"I agree." she said. "But I have to call my father. I hope he isn't worried."

"I don't think so. You gave him the number to my cell phone."

Besides her father knowing she was okay, Jonathan knew what Allen was up to. He made him promise not to tell Summer about it yet. The old guy was at home getting his groove on too. Jonathan couldn't blame him.

At eleven, they packed the truck and left, heading back for the metro area. "Did you enjoy yourself?" he asked, driving with his left hand handling the wheel and his right holding her hand. "I hope to take you to Canada with me before winter comes."

"I enjoyed myself very much. I didn't know I would have this much fun."

"I did." he admitted. "Being in love is a gift, especially when you find that someone who is truly worth your time."

"I'm sure you've been in love before." Summer said, rolling her eyes.

The memory of Andrea Rose invaded his mind. He was engaged to marry her four years ago. She had been the first one he fell so deep in love with. But the love of the woman next to him exceeded Andrea's by far. Maybe it wasn't meant to be with Andrea because Summer was somewhere out there and the Almighty knew what he needed.

They talked until they were within the bounds of Prince Georges County, where Summer lived. Jonathan pulled the big Lexus SUV into her driveway and parked.

"I should say a few words to Allen before I head home."

He unloaded some of the vegetables he had picked from his mother's garden and took them inside the house.

"Where would you like me to put this basket?" he asked.

"Over there!" she pointed towards the dining room. She headed towards the stairs when she did not meet her father in the living room. "Dad?" she called out.

Her father ambled his way downstairs. He was still in his robe and slippers. She wondered why he wasn't dressed and it was one in the afternoon. Normally, he's up and dressed at seven, even on Sunday.

He rubbed his eyes, searched around for his eyeglasses. "What time is it, Princess?"

"You tell me!" she said.

She looked at him like a kindergarten teacher would a naughty student.

"Daddy, did you have a party here last night or something?" She spied two wine glasses sitting on the coffee table and oldies CDs scattered about the living room.

Jonathan understood what Allen was telling him when he said his daughter was protective. He grinned, knowing the old guy had been entertaining all night.

Summer picked up the wine glass with the lipstick around the brim and gave her father a look that said he had some explaining to do. "Who was here?" she asked.

Evading her question, Allen began looking under the sofa and chair cushions. "Jonathan, help me find my eyeglasses, son."

He came to Allen's assistance and began looking around. He found them on the floor near the sofa.

"Here they are. Good thing you didn't step on them." He handed them to Allen with a matter-of-fact expression on his face.

When they realized Summer had disappeared upstairs, Jonathan moved closer to Allen and whispered. "Was Maria here last night? I won't tell Summer."

Allen grinned like the cat who ate the canary. "Yeah, man." he whispered.

Jonathan gave him a locker-room slap on the back, laughing. "She's fine, isn't she?"

"Son, she gives a whole new meaning to the word!" he boasted. "Did you and Summer have a nice time?"

Jonathan avoided the older man's eyes when he said, "Yes, we did."

"Don't hurt her if you love her." Allen said with fatherly concern. "If you don't think this is right, don't lead her on. I don't know how much longer I have on this earth. I'll admit before I leave here, I would love to see my first grandchild."

"I will take very good care of her. I promise until the day I leave this earth."

Allen looked at Jonathan, nodded curtly. Summer returned downstairs.

"I have to get home, baby girl. I'll call you a little later." He kissed her and left.

She could not stop thinking about the night she had spent with him. She had to call Nadia.

"Now aren't you glad I talked you into owning that sexy garter set." Nadia said. "What was he like? Did he slam dunk it, Summer?"

"You are so nasty, Nadia! All you think about is sex, sex, and mo' sex."

"Sex must be wonderful because it brings about babies."

"Yeah, whatever."

"Speaking of which, I know you're not on the pill. You guys did use condoms, didn't you?"

Summer didn't say a word. Nadia said hello three times before Summer snapped out of her trance.

"Answer me, Summer. You guys wore protection didn't you?"

"Uhhh. Not really."

"Not really! Dammit, Summer, I thought you knew better."

"The moment just sort of presented itself."

"Girl, you better not let him knock you up, not yet. I mean, I know Jonathan would be responsible but you better be careful. You know he's not the type that will get lost if you have his kid, even if you decided you didn't want him around anymore."

Summer had to change the subject. "Speaking of relationships, I think my father had a woman here last night."

This time, Nadia paused. Summer said hello twice before Nadia said anything.

"I'm here. Dang. For real? You sure?"

"Yeah. She was here last night. I spotted a wine glass with lipstick around the brim. I know somebody was here."

"Wonder who she is?"

"I don't know, but I'm about to find out. You know I'm not just gonna let any old broad come in here and claim rights to my father. He's a good looking man and a good catch to some of these women out here looking for a man. Before a woman comes into my father's life, she's gotta pass the Summer Douglas inspection first."

"Girl, you need to get off that trip. Your mother is never coming back. She filed for divorce three years ago. It's time your father found a companion."

"Don't even mention my mother!" Summer bit off. "And I'm not saying I don't want my father to find somebody. I'm saying that he shouldn't be with just any old woman desperate to have a man."

"Yeah, that I understand. Hopefully, this woman isn't some dangerous broad that will hurt him."

"If she does, I'll kill her. Mark my words on that!"

Summer said that with so much conviction, Nadia had no choice but to believe her meek-as-a-lamb friend would go ballistic if some woman hurt her father like her mother had.

After leaving Summer's house, Jonathan returned to the guesthouse and all he desired was sleep. He knew it was not possible to get any rest now. His answering machine blinked swiftly, that meant numerous calls had come in. Two calls were from his father, two from one of his sisters, several from six different editors at the company. There were three calls in a row that someone refused to leave a message. The more interesting one was from the hip-hop artist whom he had been trying for months to land an interview with. This would be an exclusive, for the artist had so far not allowed anyone to interview her. He called and set up a time to interview her in her fancy mansion in Long Island. She agreed to also give him a tour of her home and talk about her love life. This was going to be the bomb of all bombs! Every single journalist was dying to land an interview with the attractive young woman.

He booked a flight to New York for Tuesday morning. That meant too many hours away from Summer. But she would understand that he still had a career, unlike other women he had dealt with who just couldn't seem to understand that there were times when he had to make a trip out of town. Nevertheless, he could not wait to return to Maryland and have her back in his arms.

As soon as he hung up from making airline reservations, the phone rang. He rolled his eyes, hearing the familiar voice. "Jonny, I called last night but you were out. Or you just refused to answer the phone, knowing I was calling."

"What is it now, Jacqueline? I'm pretty tied up at the moment." He thought about changing the phone number of the guesthouse.

"Why are you treating me like this? I just can't believe how relentless you've become in not forgiving me. Don't you think I've suffered enough?"

He always forgave her. She knew someone else had to have captured his love for him to turn totally away from her.

"Why do you keep calling me? Do you enjoy punishment? You know what I'm going to say and you just keep contacting me."

"You've been in Maryland almost two months and I still don't know what's going on."

"You know what's going on. I've told you over and over. Listen, do not call me anymore."

"It must be someone else!"

"That would be none of your concern. And if you'll please excuse me, I have to be going." He hung up.

She stared at the phone moments before replacing the receiver. She knew it had to be another woman even if it wasn't Summer. Whoever she was, would not get off that easily without a fight.

CHAPTER SEVENTEEN:

Monday morning, Summer was preparing to go to work when she heard a loud thump in the other bathroom. She hurried out of her room and down the hall to the bathroom. Allen had slipped and fell on the floor.

"Daddy, are you okay! Omygod!" she screamed, trying to help him off the floor.

"Don't move my arm. It hurts." He winched from the pain. "I don't know what happened. I got out of the shower and didn't know the floor was wet."

"I need to get you to the hospital."

She headed to her room to get her keys. She helped him get dressed and escorted him to her car.

Once she was inside the car, she punched in her work number. Jackie's voice mail picked up. She left a message stating that she would not be in because her father had fallen and needed to be taken to the hospital.

She broke the speed limit all the way to Prince George's County hospital. Once inside, she told the clerk that she think her father may have broken his arm and needed to be seen immediately. Luckily, the emergency room was not crowded.

Allen was taken in right away and down for x-rays.

She paced the length of the waiting room, biting her nails, hoping everything would be okay. Her father was not a young man and it would likely take time for him to heal. First the heart attack, now he's fallen and probably broken a bone.

The nurse wheeled him into the waiting area hours later. He was wearing a cask on his left arm. Summer ran towards him.

"Daddy!"

He laughed. "Wanna sign my cask?" he joked.

"Don't ever scare me like that again." She laughed with him.

"Princess, stop worrying. I'm not dead."

"Well, it's time to take you home." She helped him to the car and they headed home.

Once they were in the house, the phone was ringing. Summer ran to the phone. It was Jackie.

"How come you didn't show up for work today?" Jackie snapped the moment she heard Summer's voice. This was her chance to fire her and there was no way she would not take it this time.

"I did call. I left a message on your voice mail informing you that my father had to be taken to the hospital."

"Well, I didn't get the message. You were supposed to speak with me personally."

"Jackie, others have left messages and it was accepted that they'd called in although they didn't talk directly to you. What's changed now?"

"I put out a hard copy memo last week about this. And I made sure everyone got a copy of that memo. Even you."

"I don't remember you putting out such a memo, Jackie."

"Come in tomorrow and I need to see you in my office first thing." After that, she hung up on Summer.

Summer had to wonder if there was such a memo. What if she got it and hadn't paid any attention to it? If that were the case, she had just given Jackie Shannon that stick to whip her with. She didn't want to lose her job now, especially since there seemed to be a promising career lying ahead.

"Princess, can you run down to the drug store and fill this prescription?" Allen asked once she entered the den where Allen had made himself comfortable.

She took the prescription and headed out of the house. Allen began falling asleep in the chair from the medication he had been given before leaving the hospital.

Jonathan had been in and out of meetings all morning. He never got the chance to see Summer. By the time he left work, it was almost seven. Since he had to be on a plane bound for New York Tuesday morning, he went home and packed before calling her.

The phone rang ten times. He thought he might have dialed the wrong number because her answering machine didn't even pick up. Maybe she and Allen went out for the evening, he figured.

Since he had an interview with Fatima, the hip-hop artist, he turned in earlier than he usually did. At seven the next morning, Jonathan boarded a plane at BWI Airport. He wished he could have been able to talk to Summer before leaving town but he was still unsuccessful in reaching her.

He departed at La Guardia and took a cab into Long Island. Once he was there, Fatima's domestic employee answered the door.

"Won't you step in, Mr. Wesley?" said the Jamaican woman.

"Thanks."

"Miss Fatima is currently engaged in a conversation over the telephone. Make yourself comfortable. Will you be needing anything to drink?"

"Sure, I'll take some water."

The older woman made her way to the kitchen. She came back with a cold refreshing glass of water. She sat it before him on the table.

Fatima came out wearing one of her trademark outfits: a pair of multicolored jeans and an equally multicolored shirt that was seven sizes too large. Her long hair was braided in five thick braids and she wore purple lipstick.

"It's a pleasure being given this opportunity to have this interview, Fatima." he said, standing to shake hands with her.

"Yeah, I don't usually do this but I thought, what the heck. Right."

He felt very comfortable with her as she began going through her history without him even asking. She had four brothers, two sisters, raised by a single mother and a grandmother who was a big part of their lives. One of her brothers had been shot by NYPD and killed and another one had been locked up for drug possession. They had grown up in Flat Bush in Brooklyn and now she had taken her mother out of the old 'hood and bought her a home in New Jersey.

She told him that she never knew her father, who had abandoned them when she was just a baby, the youngest of the whole clan. After hearing all of this, Jonathan began doing more probing than he had to do before.

"Now, let's get into your love life. Do you have a man?"

Fatima smiled like a young girl. Hell, she was a young girl, barely nineteen years old. "Yes." she said as if her father had asked her that question.

"Lucky guy. Who is he?"

"Since I got his permission to tell you, he's Sir Smoke."

Jonathan was surprised but not that surprised. Sir Smoke had featured on one of the tracks of her debut album. He didn't know they had become a couple.

"How serious are you and Sir Smoke?"

"Serious enough to get married." she shot back, a little sassiness in her tone.

Jonathan raised his eyebrows. "Oh? So, have you guys set a date?"

"Yeah, next year." she said then laughed. "Next summer." She then showed him a huge three carat diamond ring on her finger.

"Boy, how could I miss that?"

"I'm really happy about it. I guess when the man you love proposes marriage to you, nothing else in the world matters." she said, then looked at him as if he understood.

Yes, he understood all right! Understood that Summer would be glowing with the same joy as Fatima if he proposed marriage to her. He had made love to her, told her he loved her. What was next? Marriage! After this interview, he planned to get back to Maryland as fast as he could. He would make one stop on the way to Summer's house and that would be to a jeweler.

"How does your mother feel about you getting married so young?"

"Well, she never got married and she says it's my decision. I really love this guy, Samuel, you know."

"Samuel?" he asked.

"Yes, Samuel Bryant, a.k.a Sir Smoke."

Jonathan laughed.

"Everyone else calls him Sir Smoke. But he's my Sammy."

He laughed harder. Love was really something else. He related, because Summer was "Baby" to him.

She gave him a tour of her mansion, which he took photos himself since his photographer could not make it at the last minute. He just hoped they turned out to be as professional as if his photographer had taken them. He got shots of the pool, her entertainment hall, the outside of the mansion and her huge kitchen where she loved to cook. He took shots of her making a delicious Jamaican meal.

"I really am grateful for this interview, Fatima. And hope you continue to be successful."

"I'm really glad you could come over. If it were not for me already having Sammy in my life, I would ask if we could go to dinner."

Jonathan just smiled, shaking her hand again.

By the time he left her mansion, the last flight back to BWI had already taken off. The next flight would not be out until two in the morning.

The next morning, Summer headed to work. She didn't know how this would turn out. When she arrived, she noticed Gwen sitting in Jackie's office. Yeah, something's up. She didn't know where Abu was.

Gwen got up and gave her a snide look as she passed her on the way out of the office.

"Have a seat!" Jackie ordered callously. After Summer was seated, Jackie got right down to the heart of the matter. "You've had at least eight warnings about your tardiness and your time. You've been on probation and now you've violated it with a no-show. I'm going to have to terminate your employment. I've already contacted Human Resources."

"I had to take my father to the hospital!" Summer stressed, pain overwhelming her heart. Tears streamed down her cheeks. "What was I supposed to do? And I called you before I took him to the hospital."

"Well, you know what department policy is. Like I said, I put out a memo regarding this."

"What memo? I never got one! You're setting me up, I know it!"

"You were supposed to call and speak with me personally. In fact, I can prove that I put out that memo." She opened the door and called Gwen and Arlene into her office, her most loyal employees.

Both came in, looks on their faces that told Summer they were in on this game Jackie was playing.

"Did I ever put out a memo regarding you all having to speak with me personally whenever you called in?"

"Yes, that was over a week ago, wasn't it?" Arlene was the first to speak.

"That's right," Gwen piped in. "Matter fact, I'll go and get the memo right now." She left Jackie's office and returned with a hard copy memo dated two weeks ago. She showed it to Summer.

Summer snatched the memo out of Gwen's hand and tossed it down. The piece of paper floated until it landed on the floor.

"Who you think you bucking at!" Gwen shouted at Summer. "Don't be tryna break fly."

"Gwen, don't feed into it," Jackie said, stepping in the middle. "Summer's already in hot water. Don't get yourself in trouble, just go back to your desk."

"Yeah, 'cause I'm about to put her in check." Gwen said before she and Arlene headed back into the main department.

Summer turned back to Jackie. "I can't believe your heartlessness!" she shouted, standing up in her face. "You've treated me like garbage ever since I started working here. And I'll say this before I go." She wiped her tears and added, "You kiss my high-yellow ass!" Afterwards, she stormed out of the office.

Everyone in the department heard the commotion, even Abu, who was just coming in to work late. Jackie was relieved to see Summer turn her back and leave. For a moment, she thought she would attack her.

"What happened?" Abu asked, unaware that Summer had left Jackie a voice mail message the day before. He was also unaware that Jackie devised that bogus memo as a last ditch effort to incriminate Summer.

"Remember Summer didn't call yesterday. I had to let her go, Abu."

"What was the reason she gave for not coming in?"

"That she had to take her father to the hospital."

Abu sighed, looking the other way. None of it seemed fair. And it wasn't like Summer not to call. "And you said she didn't leave you a voice message either?"

"No, she didn't. She thinks she got it like that because she's in good with Jonathan now. But this is my department."

"I still don't think we should just terminate her, Jackie. If she had to take her father to the hospital, maybe she got so wrapped up in making sure he was okay that she forgot to call. Did you find out why he had to be taken to the hospital?"

"No, and why should I care?"

Abu regarded her with a different set of eyes. She was a very uncaring woman. He couldn't deal with a female like her. A woman with no nurturing instincts could not possibly raise a man's children right. He didn't say anything as he headed over to his desk.

Summer hopped into her Chevrolet and drove around town before going home. She was so angry, she didn't know how to tell her father. She didn't want him to worry. She figured she'd wait a few days. She arrived home five hours later, as if she had been working. She hurried upstairs when she heard the phone ring. It was Nadia.

"I didn't see you at lunchtime today. What happened? Did you and Jonathan go off somewhere to get yourselves a quickie?"

"No." Summer said. She explained to her the day's events.

"I cannot believe that hoochie-mamma bitch!" Nadia shouted, her Puerto Rican accent more dramatic than most times. Summer listened to Nadia cite every four letter word in Spanish before she finally calmed down and asked, "Did you tell Jonathan?"

"Not yet."

"You gotta tell him, Summer. He will find out."

"Don't let me guess how he'll find out."

"I'll tell him!" Nadia shot back.

"What can he do? Maurice is the only person that can reverse this situation. And I doubt if he'd make Jackie give me my job back."

"That's where you're wrong." Nadia protested. "Jonathan has more power than Maurice now. He'll be taking over the company when Maurice retires in October."

The conversation she had with Jonathan over the telephone weeks ago replayed in her mind. He had asked what she thought of working for him on a permanent basis. It was all clear now. He *will* be taking over the company, and soon! Three months was not a lot of time.

"See what I mean? Maurice is in a lame duck stage now." Nadia added.

"Yeah, I see what you mean. But I hear my dad calling me. I'll call you later."

After seeing what her father wanted, she took a hot bubble bath. Once she was done, her father knocked on her door. She opened it.

"Jonathan called while you were in the tub, Princess."

"Where is he? Home?"

"He's at a hotel in New York. He left a number and said he'll be arriving back around ten tomorrow morning. He wants you to pick him up from the airport."

Jonathan had informed her Sunday night that he would be leaving for New York. She remembered. The incident with her father yesterday had caused her to forget. She called him. She didn't mention what happened at the job, didn't know how to tell him.

"Is your father okay now?" he asked.

"Yes, he's fine. I guess a broken bone won't kill him."

Jonathan could sense something else was wrong other than her father so he probed. "Are you okay?"

"Yes. Just tired. But I'm okay."

"Sure about that? I sense a little sadness in your voice."

"Yes, I promise, I'm okay."

"I cannot wait to see you again, baby. You've put a spell on me that I can't fight even if I wanted to. And it feels so damned good." She listened to his baritone melodic voice. Hearing it was flammable to her womanhood. The sweet words he spoke coupled with the fuel he was tossing into her fire.

"Well, I'll see you tomorrow. Let your managers know you'll have to take off a couple of hours for an appointment. And I love you."

"I love you too, Jonathan."

She still couldn't muster up the courage to tell him that she had been fired.

Wednesday morning arrived after seeming like decades to her. Her spirits lifted once she saw Jonathan exiting the gate. He was so tall and handsome. He must have just shaved before leaving the hotel that morning. She noticed how smooth his skin looked. His five o'clock shadow was gone. He had trimmed a little of his mustache too.

Once he spotted her standing there waiting for him, he dropped his bag and threw his arms around her. Onlookers watched, amused as the young couple embraced as if it was the end of the world.

"Darling, you're not going to believe what I have for you." he said.

They walked to her car and got in. He removed a gift-wrapped box from his bag and handed it to her. Summer ripped open the box. A 14 carat gold chain attached to a gold charm in the shape of the African continent stared at her. She gleamed with excitement and gave him a long, breath-taking kiss. Jonathan took the chain and put it around her neck, locking it.

"It's beautiful!" She fingered the charm. "Thanks, Mr. Wesley."

"I thought you'd love it since you seemed to have adored the huge gold plaque of Africa in my parents' parlor."

She started the ignition and set off for Rockville, where he lived. "How were things at *EIC* while I was gone?"

Summer thought about being terminated. She thought about lying. Then she thought about Nadia Cruz not being able to keep her trap shut to Jonathan. It was her love for him that propelled her to tell the truth.

"I got fired yesterday." she said.

"Fired? Come again."

She told him everything that happened. He listened, her explanation angering him. He couldn't believe how relentless and vindictive Jacqueline Shannon was. After hearing Summer's story from the very beginning, before he'd met her until the time Jackie terminated her, he sighed. He had sensed that Jackie didn't like her long ago. Nadia even told him so.

"Well, I'm hiring you back."

"I didn't think you could override it until your father returned."

"Summer, I *am* the CEO. Besides, Jackie had no grounds to fire you. But in the meantime, I'll have to get you into another department. I should have done that long ago. You could opt for marketing courses. We have our own educational facility on the first floor of the building."

"You'll do all that for me?"

"Yes, baby." He leaned over and kissed her cheek. "I'll do anything for you."

"So where do I go from here? Do I start class immediately?"

"The next class begins July thirty-first. In the meantime, you could handle some other duties in the company or stay home and take care of the man I'm praying that will one day become my father-in-law."

Summer frowned, giving him a quizzical look. "Father-in-law? What are you saying?"

"That I want you to marry me."

Tears of joy poured down her face. "I would love to."

"Then don't just think about it! Do it!"

He thought of Fatima and how happy she was that she was engaged to Sir Smoke. He saw that same joy in Summer. Women were something sweet to the eyes when they were loved. Like Fatima, Summer glowed with a joy that was indescribable.

"Now? Marry you now?"

"Whenever you feel the time is right. We could have an engagement and use the time we're betrothed to work on having a nice wedding or we can head over to the justice of the peace in the morning and do it. The former is what you deserve, baby. You deserve the four thousand attendees at our wedding and your father walking you down the aisle, the big reception and the whole nine."

Once they arrived at his house, he got into his car and followed her to her house. When they were both about to pull into the driveway, another car was just leaving. Summer tried to see who that was driving the familiar looking green Chevy Cavalier that just left her father's property. The driver looked like a female but she couldn't tell the age, or race of the woman. She couldn't place where she had seen that car before but she knew she'd seen it.

"How's everything?" Jonathan asked, standing at Allen's side in the den.

He looked up at Jonathan and said, "As long as my daughter is around, I guess I'll be fine. I just wish she would give her old dad some grandchildren."

To Summer, it seemed more and more each day that these two men were plotting.

"Daddy!"

"Summer, our genes are too precious to waste." he boasted playfully with a touch of pride. She noticed he glanced at Jonathan again. They were making too much eye contact for her not to know something was up. She left it alone for now. But she would find out soon enough what was going on.

Jackie was fuming when she realized her scheme might have backfired. Jonathan called her at home on Thursday morning and told her to meet him in his office first thing. Judging by his tone of voice, it wasn't going to be a pleasant meeting. She was ready to go toe-to-toe with him now. If he was calling her in there to tell her that she was wrong for firing Summer, she was ready to defend herself against him and his new tramp.

Jonathan had to remind himself to wait until his father returned before giving her the boot. He paced around his office until he heard sharp raps on the door.

"Come in!" he called. When the door opened, Jackie and Kim were in the midst of an argument.

"He told me to come down here and have this meeting with him!" Jackie shouted on Kim. "You just mind your business."

Kim then looked at him and said, "I'm sorry, sir. I thought you were on the phone and she just barged in here. I didn't know you had called a meeting with her."

"That's okay, Kim. I should have informed you."

Kim relented.

"Now go back to your desk and do your job. Instead of wondering who is coming to see Jonathan."

"Jacqueline!" Jonathan's voice warned.

She turned to look at him then at the petit Asian woman who still stood at the door.

"Will that be all, Jonathan?" Kim asked.

"Yes, Kim and thanks."

She closed the door, leaving the two of them in his private office.

For a minute, Jackie thought it could be Kim that was seeing Jonathan, the way she had been protecting him all that time. This was not the first time Kim had pulled that. Two weeks ago Jackie had come down to his office and the woman told her that he was on an important phone call and couldn't be bothered. She knew it was bull – Kim just didn't want her down there and refused to allow her to go into his office.

Kim sat back at her desk, wanting to slap Jackie for her rudeness. She just didn't know that she came so close to getting a beat-down. Jackie could bully that young girl in her department and all those folks down there in that customer service department but she didn't scare her. Blacks weren't the only ones who could hold their own. Kim had grown up in Viet Nam and she was no stranger to a good down-home fight either.

"What happened?" Jonathan asked.

She tossed him the folder she'd been clutching. Yes, she came prepared for this fight. "Review that!" she snapped.

He sat down at his desk and opened the folder, reading all the warnings Jackie and Abu had been giving Summer. He shrugged, closed the folder and looked at her. "So?" he said.

"So she's been warned. She didn't call Monday until later that day and she knew what would happen if she did that."

"She did call!" he objected.

"She did not!" she tossed back.

"I listened to a tape that records voice mails. I had that system installed a month ago. I did it because it protects employees. So, she did call. So you have no right to fire her. Especially while Maurice is on vacation. The only time you would have had grounds would be for something gross, such as stealing from the company or a fist fight. A threat to do bodily harm would constitute grounds."

"I don't believe you listened to a tape that recorded some voice mail." she challenged. She knew she had been caught cold busted by him but would fight tooth and nail on this one.

"Oh, I heard the tape, Jackie. That same day, my father called you and told you to give him a call."

Her face showed the embarrassment she felt. She knew he must have been right then.

"Did you ever call Maurice back?" he asked.

"Yes, I did."

"Should I go on? Naming all the folks that called you over the past few weeks?"

"That would not be necessary."

"Now, Summer is still an employee in this company."

"Hold up!" she said, a palm raised in the air. "This is my department, Jonathan. I handle it the way I please. You see she's been warned." She was determined to use something against Summer, to win.

"Oh, is that what you think? The woman's father was in the hospital." he stressed. "I hadn't realized how callous you were until this shit happened. I guess I underestimated your ruthlessness."

"Ruthlessness!" she tossed back. "I have given Summer Douglas lots of warnings and plenty of chances to straighten up her act."

"In what way?" he asked, reclining in his chair, hands folded behind his head. This conversation was not annoying him, it was amusing him. He wondered how far she would go to win this now.

"Do you know how many times this girl has been late?"

Jonathan grabbed the folder and looked at the dates she'd been late. He knew why she had been late all of those times because she had told him all about how her father had been sick.

"It looks to me that each time she was late or absent was during the time her father was recovering from a heart attack. Seems you would be more sympathetic, being that you've proposed to the company a publication about good health for black people."

She narrowed her eyes. "Don't patronize me. And I won't continue treating her as if she has special privileges. That wouldn't be fair to others in the department."

"You know, I doubt seriously if you'd treat Summer with preferential treatment."

CHAPTER EIGHTEEN:

"And what's that's supposed to mean?" She threw her hands on her hips.

He looked directly into her eyes, leaned over the desk toward her and said, "I think you know what it means, Jackie. You're not an idiot. You're too conniving to be stupid. And I'm aware of the dislike you have for that young woman. In the meantime, if Summer wants to continue her employment at *Ethnic Information Corporation*, she'll be placed in another department."

"I knew it!" Jackie spoke as if it was all confirmed now. "You're fucking her, aren't you?"

"What I do in my personal life is none of your business, Jacqueline Shannon. And contrary to what you believe, you'll have to deal with the decisions I make in this company. My decision about Summer is final. No one will be able to reverse that."

She let out a loud laugh. "I don't believe this! You chose that virgin over a real woman like me. How did it feel, Jonathan?" she said, leaning over with her face inches from his.

He backed away and cut her off, "That's enough!" he shouted. Silence fell over the room. He was tired of her antics. She stared at him, her eyes filled with hatred. "I've had it with you. You're a psychopath!"

"I wasn't that psychopathic when you were fucking me." she shot back. "I guess that says a lot about you if that's the case."

"I suggest you get back to your department before I change my mind about keeping you employed with this company." he said. He had to end this and as long as he would allow her to continue this fight, she would.

"Fine!" she said, grabbing Summer's file.

"And leave that file with me!" he demanded.

Without speaking, she tossed the folder on the desk and stormed out of the office. He was so furious when she left, he hadn't realized how curt he was with Kim when she came into the office and told him that Ricky Channing was waiting for him. He had forgotten all about meeting with Ricky that day. The men were supposed to be heading up to Pennsylvania to check out some property so that they could build an annex to their corporation. The company was constantly growing and could no longer accommodate the growing number of employees. Office space was becoming limited although there were seven floors.

"I'm sorry, Jonathan." Kim said.

"I'm sorry for being rude, Kim. Tell Rick I'll be right out. I just had an ordeal with Jackie."

"That's okay." She smiled. "She accelerates a lot of people's blood pressure around here. Your father can't stand her."

Jonathan raised a brow at Kim's comment. Other than the scene at his house, Maurice had never gotten that angry with Jackie. Even then, his father had told him to give her another chance and that he was getting too old to be bed-hopping between relationships.

"He says she's a bully. And your father thinks that the only bully around here should be him." she laughed, recalling how Maurice made that comment.

He laughed with her. "Well, that sounds like Maurice Wesley all right."

Jonathan put on his Armani jacket, grabbed his briefcase. He met the senior vice president sitting on the leather love seat in Kim's workstation waiting patiently.

"Boy, it looks like you've been through some shit!" Ricky said the moment he saw Jonathan.

They heard Kim laughing behind them as they exited the office.

"Jackie just won't give up, man." he told him as they headed toward the elevator. He spoke close to the older man's ear so that no one could hear what they were discussing.

"She wants some more of that golden rod you laid on her last year. You know what the deal is with that." he responded with a chuckle.

Ricky was sixty-two years old but Jonathan could swear sometimes that he was much younger. He had that carefree way about him that most men his age no longer possessed and there were times when he could talk to him about more subjects than his own father. Maurice was all about business and how to make more money. Ricky was all of that but he had an affable way about him. Jonathan could talk to him about women all day long.

"Well, she's not getting it anymore." he said resolutely.

"Try telling her that!" Ricky said, gyrating his hips as they stepped onto the elevator.

"Man, you're never gonna grow up." Jonathan said as they rode down the elevator.

"So what's been going on with that cute one that just started working here back in the winter?"

"Rick, I'm not surprised that you would remember when Summer started working here."

"I've been paying attention!" he shot back, as if Jonathan didn't already know that.

They headed to Ricky's Mercedes parked in the executives' parking lot. He released the locks, using the remote.

Once Jonathan was inside the car, he had a confession to make. "I'm in love with Summer."

"Come again!"

"I said, I'm in love with Summer. I asked her to marry me the other day."

Ricky chuckled as if Jonathan had lost his mind. "Sure you wanna do that?"

"I'm positive."

"Then go for it. Hey, love only comes around once. And with the shortage of good women nowadays, I say you're making the right decision."

"Do you think Summer's good for me?"

Ricky pulled out of the parking lot, headed down the street and hit I-95 north before answering. "Honestly, I think she's a good woman. Hell, if I was thirty years younger, I'd take her myself. But it would behoove you to get Jackie as far away from you as you can. Tried to warn you about that girl last year but you had your head so far up in her coochie, you weren't trying to hear what I had to say."

"I don't even want to think about it, man. Take the exit for I-83." he said as the Benz purred up I-695.

Jackie was still fuming when she returned to her department. How could he treat her this way on behalf of some slut. She had given her heart and soul over to that man. No woman had what it took to complete his life. Although Summer was no longer in their department and she didn't win this fight, she would win the other one. This time, she had backup. She could count on Abu for assistance.

Over the next three weeks, Jonathan had been in and out of meetings and interviewing celebrities. He had done all that and managed to keep the company running smoothly with the help of higher-up employees, the presidents of the departments. He'd had several conversations over the telephone with his father and briefed him on everything, including Jackie's latest stunt.

His father listened then reminded him not to take any action until he returned. Jonathan wondered why Maurice kept insisting on handling this.

Summer decided she would take the marketing courses offered in the company's educational facility. Jonathan paid her a higher salary than she had made in her former position.

"How's class, kid?" he asked as they drove.

"Exciting. I hadn't realized how many ways you could market a publication. You know what? I think it would be good to promote the less circulated publications in the well-known ones." she said as they parked in front of the guesthouse. "Maybe the one I proposed can be marketed in *Nubian Entertainment* or *West Africans in America*."

"That's what we plan to do." he said as he opened the door. "See, we're on the same plane, Summer."

Once they were in, she glanced around the small, comfortable flat. It was a nice place for a married couple with no children. It had two master bedrooms with en suite bathrooms. There was a living room, small den and kitchen. The larger bedroom had a deck. That was the room Jonathan used.

"This is so neat." she said, taking a seat on the sofa in the living room.

Jonathan took a seat next to her. This time, she leaned over and began kissing him. That took him by surprise. She was not as shy as she used to be. She straddled his lap. His shaft responded to her soft buttocks resting on his thighs.

"You're itching for some, aren't you, Summer?" he spoke into her ear before lightly kissing her neck, moving down to her breasts.

"I want it." she spoke into his ear, unfastening his slacks and handling his huge shaft. He tilted his head back, resting it on the back of the sofa, savoring in the pleasure she was rendering. He could feel her soft lips all over him.

He could no longer stand it. He wrapped her in his arms and began kissing her all over, removing each piece of clothing as he explored each part of her. Soon, she was completely nude as he stared down at her lying on the carpeted floor.

"Come." she said.

He smiled, lifted her from the floor, carried her to his bedroom, gently placing her on the bed. He began removing his clothes. This time, she forced him on his back, straddled him. She eased atop him and began slowly riding up and down on him. He closed his eyes, groaning loudly. She was spinning his head.

"My goodness, girl!" he shouted when she started making him climax. He tried not to but her sweetness was too much to handle. She moaned as her pleasure overcame her. Her body quaked from the spasms. She rested herself on him as their breathing returned to normal.

"Jonathan, I love you." she spoke softly. Night was falling and she could see her own shadow in the darkness.

"I love you too." he said before kissing her all over again. He couldn't stay away from her. This was too damned good to be true.

They went at it again, reaching the height of passion, both sweating as they changed positions, him behind her, slamming her from the rear. "Oh!" she cried out. "Oh, Jonathan! Stop!"

Her plea made him stroke harder, faster. This was the phase where sex was becoming more raw and uninhibited. It added more spice when they changed their style of making love.

"Are you really going to marry me?" he asked, slowing down his pace.

"I've never been asked that before."

"Is that a yes or a no?" he asked, picking up his pace.

"What do you think?" she retorted playfully.

He picked up his pace more, began stroking her harder. She could feel him harden and fill up again. "Teasing me?" he asked, stroking her without stopping.

"No!" she cried out as her body lurched forward from the force. "What are the consequences if I was?"

Oh, she wanted to challenge him, he thought, his strokes going even faster. He pulled himself away, flipped her over and got on top of her. He draped her legs over his shoulders and began stroking again.

Their passion slammed down without warning. Both shouted out. He could feel himself draining again.

He lied beside her. "You're one delicious dish. You're an entrée that a man won't ever be able to stay away from. And if you tell me you're not going to marry me, my heart will tear into pieces."

Summer kept laughing. He was so playful sometimes.

"Where's the ring?" she finally asked. "I want a big rock that will blind anyone who dares to glance at it."

His grin widened. He turned toward her, resting on his side. "You asked for it." he said.

They lied there in the darkness, each in their own thoughts.

Finally, Jonathan broke the silence and said, "Before I forget, the idea you gave me in the car about promoting the *Ethiopian Journal* as a feature inside the *West Africans in America* was a great idea. I love your ambition. You'll not only be my wife, you'll be my partner for life. And I hope you never stop being my girlfriend. I'll try your suggestion in October's issue."

"I thought wife carried more weight than girlfriend?"

"It does. But something is more naughty about the word girlfriend. Girlfriends do things wives stop doing after getting married."

"Like what?" she asked.

Like the way you pleasured me in the living room a couple of hours ago! he thought. He voiced, "Girlfriends are uninhibited and naughty, like I said."

"And you think I'm naughty?"

"Yes."

"Jonathan?"

"Humn?"

"Why are you testing all the ideas I've been giving you?"

"You're more a part of this company than you realize. My father wants to talk to you when he returns in two weeks."

"The untouchable Mr. Maurice Wesley wants to talk to me?" she joked.

"Don't underestimate yourself, baby. I think my father is quite impressed with the idea you proposed to me back in early May."

Summer was overjoyed to hear that bit of news. She was still not aware of what was going down behind her back though and Jonathan couldn't tell her. This nagged him, that he could not kick Jackie out of the company.

Maurice had finally returned home, spent from his flight. He'd had a wonderful vacation with Donya but there was nothing like his own comfortable bed at home. Those beds in the staterooms were nice and the hotels were fabulous but there was just something about his own bed that reminded him of a comfortable pair of old shoes.

Once the older couple returned home, they retired to bed shortly after. He didn't awake until seven o'clock the next morning by his ringing phone. At first, he thought it was the alarm and he reached over and slammed it but it did not quit. It took him a minute to realize that it was the phone ringing.

"Will you be in today, Dad?" Jonathan asked.

"Of course, I will. Thanks for waking me. This old worn out body of mine just doesn't respond as well as it did when I was your age."

His son laughed. "Well, everyone's expecting you in today. Editors and writers are anticipating your return."

Maurice hopped out of bed, showered, dressed and kissed his wife goodbye. He could only grab a cup of coffee and toast from Nelda's kitchen before leaving the house.

When he reached the office, he was greeted by eager employees, asking questions about his trip and welcoming him back. Although his time as CEO will soon end, people were still kissing up. He met his sons, Jonathan and Jerome, who was home again to work on a future article. He closed the office door for privacy and the three men sat down at the round table to talk.

The phone rang. Maurice picked it up. "Yeah, I'm aware of that. I understand." he spoke. He listened again before he seemed to cut the person off. "I will see to it."

Jonathan furrowed his brows in confusion, listening to his father's conversation. He wondered whom he was talking to. Jerome seemed to pay no attention as he was engaged in his own short conversation on his cell phone.

Once Maurice hung up, he turned to Jonathan. "Who's on the schedule today?"

"The editor-in-chief of *West Africans in America* and a writer for *Ethiopian Journal*." Jonathan said. "Other than that, Ricky Channing." He laid down the schedule Kim constructed after reading off the list.

Maurice waved dismissively. "I'll deal with RC later." Once Jerome clicked off his cell phone, Maurice asked, "How's the market?"

"Bullish!" his youngest child boasted. "I'll give you some advice once you finish your meetings today. But in the meantime," He glanced at his Rolex. "I have to get cracking. I have a lot to do before returning to New York." He left the office and headed to his corner office on the seventh floor.

Once he reached his office, his telephone was ringing. He sat his briefcase and laptop near the door and headed to the phone.

"If you're wondering who ripped off your accounting department, you may try talking to someone who works in the *Latino Outlook* department." an unfamiliar female voice stated without greeting him.

Jerome remembered the stolen cash from the safe on his floor. He knew it had to be an inside job and this was probably a lead to finding the thief. "Who is this?"

"Never mind who this is." the voice curtly answered. "The question you should be asking is who I'm referring to that works in that particular department."

"Does that statement infer that you'd tell me if I asked?"

"Maybe."

"Maybe? Listen, miss, I don't know who the hell you are but I don't have time for kiddie games. Goodbye."

"Wait!" the woman pleaded, startling him, causing him to take a seat at his desk. "If I told you, I might be looked upon as a rat."

Now he was certain the person on the other end worked for the company. Trying to coax her, he said, "No, ma'am, I wouldn't view you that way at all."

"But the person who ripped you off will. You see, I'd like to remain anonymous unless."

"Unless what?"

"Unless we get together."

Now Jerome was certainly interested in that proposition. This female with that sultry voice had his full attention. And she was offering to get with him. If only her appearance matched her voice, he could have more than one thing going: finding out who ripped them off and getting himself a new piece. Variety was always his spice of life.

"Get together and do what?"

"I've liked you for a long time, Mr. Wesley. And now that I have something you want, maybe you'll give me what I want."

"Now that we've established what I want from you, why don't you tell me what you want?"

"Are you a virgin or are you just plain dumb? You shouldn't have to guess what I want."

Jerome chuckled wickedly. His curiosity didn't relent. He asked, "So when are you and I getting together?"

"Tomorrow night at eight." she said. "Meet me at the Red Grays restaurant and I'll give you what you want – only if you promise me I'll get what I want."

"You win, baby."

"I'll be wearing a pair of blue jeans and a red top. You won't miss me."

Jerome hung up, still chuckling. He looked at his calendar and thought Wall Street could go another day without him.

This mysterious woman had him going now. He thought it would be worth it to take another day off. One thing he hadn't realized while he was speaking with the woman while his door was halfway open was that Brenda stood behind the wall and she had heard everything he said. She ran to the bathroom, hurt and angry that he was still a playboy. All the Wesley men were that way and Jackie could attest to that fact.

CHAPTER NINETEEN:

By ten, Maurice and Jonathan were sitting in on their first meeting. It wasn't until three o'clock that afternoon when the father and son sat down to have lunch.

"Now that we can take that long-awaited break, what's going on with Jacqueline?" Maurice wanted to know.

Jonathan explained everything that occurred since his arrival. He explained what Summer had told him since she started working for the company. Maurice shook his head, disappointed. He couldn't believe how she had turned out. When she first started with the company, her attitude was humble. But she had turned out to be the ultimate witch.

Maurice should have known however. His family was unaware that he'd had a one night stand with her, two months after her employment started with the company. That following summer, a year ago, she fell in love with Jonathan. If Maurice fired her, she could retaliate by calling Donya Wesley and telling her about the affair, knowing she had nothing to lose. Maurice would have more problems on his hands if Donya took him to court and took half of everything he owned because of his adulterous deed.

Maurice grimaced at the guilt, his memory recapturing the affair. He long ago realized Jackie would take a lateral position in order to make a vertical move – he and his son were examples of her agenda.

"Son, I believe in giving our young people a chance. I saw something in Jacqueline and at that time, it wasn't trickery. I thought she could have been a great asset to *EIC* because of her background and education. Maybe I misjudged."

"Don't shoulder the blame on this one, Dad. She had a lot of us fooled."

"Now what about Summer? Think she's trustworthy?"

Jonathan smiled. He and his father never had that many conversations about women and it was refreshing to have this one, especially about Summer.

"I do think Summer's trustworthy."

"And is she worthy of my son's love and affection?"

"Now where did that come from?" Jonathan regarded his father with an impish grin.

"I'm your father. I see that look in your eyes. The same look I had when I met nineteen year old Donya Lovette. Just the mention of her name makes me go crazy."

"Don't forget." Jackie reminded Abu.

Abu nodded. "I won't. I just wish you stop reminding me of something you've told me a million times already." She could hear the impatience in his tone.

"Because this could mean a promotion for both of us, Abu." she said appealing to his greed. "You stick with me and I'll stick with you."

"How do you know Summer hasn't already informed Jonathan about her idea?" he asked. He knew she had to by now. He didn't tell Jackie but he had seen them at Montgomery Mall two nights ago. They were headed into a movie theatre. Seems they had become a couple and most times, couples informed each other. Being that Jonathan was the new CEO, why wouldn't his own girlfriend tell him about a proposal she wanted to pitch to the company?

"Our idea!" she corrected him, smiling slyly. "Because she's not that smart." Jackie raised her wine glass to her lips. "Even if she did, I have backup, she doesn't. You will tell Maurice that the idea was ours. And she'll look like a thief. Besides, how can she prove it isn't ours?"

"Jackie, Maurice is a smart guy." he shook his head, negative. "It's really tough to pull the wool over his eyes. And what if Jonathan does believe Summer and backs her up? You know he'll take his son's word over ours."

Jackie smiled and leaned back in her chair, staring across the table at him. "That's when you'll declare that Jonathan would say anything to back up his little piece over there. And Maurice stands plenty to lose if he goes along with his son."

"Like what?" he wanted to know.

"Never mind about that. Just play your part and we can't lose."

Maybe, Abu mused silently, she wasn't as bad as she seemed and he stood a chance with her after all. He had begun giving up hope but she was rapidly restoring the hope that had waned. He yielded with a slow, determined nod. His aim was to get that promotion and eventually get Jackie. Hell, she wasn't perfect but she was still a damned good catch. Now that Jonathan had his sights set on Summer, he found it easier to agree with Jackie. Maybe she would see the light and realize who was the better man between the two.

The next day, Jerome threw on a pair of black Dockers and a white pullover. He didn't want to wear a suit, was tired of the inhibited feeling he got from wearing a suit and tie all the time. Besides, this was not a formal occasion and the restaurant was a greasy spoon type of establishment where he would look totally out of place if he stepped in there all G'd up.

"Where's the playa headed off to tonight?" Jerome turned around at his brother's voice, staring directly into his amused eyes.

"Thought you were resting. And that's a question needless to ask." Jerome retorted.

"Well," Jonathan came all the way into the living room and took a seat in the arm chair. "since I know Brenda's pissed with you for what ever reason, I can't help asking who you're going out with this time."

It always amused him how his brother could change women more than some changed their underwear.

"Concentrate on turning that jail bait you screwed around with into a woman, Mike." Jerome shot back, slipping on his loafers.

"She's more woman than you think. And all two hundred of the hoochies you've slept with don't add up to one single Summer Douglas."

"This is more of a business activity." Jerome changed the subject. It was none of his business where he was going.

"So why not tell me?"

"I'll let you know later. But it's almost quarter to eight and my appointment is at eight." After answering, Jerome grabbed the keys to his second car, a two year old Lexus coupe and headed out.

He parked in front of Red Gray's restaurant, thankful there was a place to park. He found the woman of interest sitting in a booth by the window and joined her. He stared at her without blinking. She was a gorgeous one. Her skin reminding him of brown sugar, light-brown beautiful piercing eyes – as if she searched his soul. Her shoulder-length cold black hair swept around her bare shoulders. She was donned in a pair of jeans and a red blouse with thin shoulder straps. He shuddered, his rod rising. He tried ignoring his natural instincts at the moment.

He slid into the booth, facing her. "It's your idea so let's get the business portion of it taken care of and work on the pleasure. I don't have a lifetime here."

All he wanted to do was hit this and be gone!

"What do you want to know?" she asked.

"Let's start with your name," he said, resting his arms on the table, folding his hands.

"Renee Lyles."

"Really? I thought you might look like a Maria or something. You look Hispanic."

"My mother was Hispanic and my father is black American."

He nodded and his gaze swept over her a moment. "I've never heard of you before and can't recall ever seeing you. But you stated you work for the company."

"You've probably never seen me because you're busy dealing with the big timers in the company. And I do work for the company. I've been there almost a year."

"Which department?"

"*Latino Outlook.*"

"Oh, by the way, you mentioned something about one of your fellow co-workers breaking into the petty cash safe."

"Right." her eyes lowered to the table when she added, "Nadia Cruz,"

That name set goose bumps all over his flesh. He and Jonathan had discussed Nadia's pass card being used to enter the building. He thought it looked suspicious but Jonathan was so naïve for thinking otherwise.

He asked, "What's led you to believe that?"

"It's simply a belief. Since that time, she's been pampering herself with expensive stuff. Now Nadia comes from a poor family in Puerto Rico, the same neighborhood my mother came from and I'm sure she wouldn't otherwise be able to afford things like that."

He glanced down at her hands, spying the seven gold rings adorning her fingers. "Is your Daddy rich?" he asked.

She released an infectious laugh and answered, "Not at all."

"So how do you afford all that gold on your hands? You got a wealthy man at home?"

"Do you have a gold-digging woman at home?" she shot back.

He had to admit, he had set himself up for that one. He didn't answer, just stared into those hazel eyes.

"But I don't have a man." she lied.

"Really?" He regarded her with a stern look. He didn't believe she didn't have a man. Who was she trying to bullshit? "So what's this Nadia Cruz all of a sudden buying herself that's raised your eyebrows?"

"Clothes, jewelry…you name it. She's got this expensive gold chain with this unusual-type charm attached to it. It looks like something your father would give that special woman in his life, it's so tight."

"How do you know?"

"Pu-leeze!" She rolled her eyes. "Everyone in that company knows how much gold your father brings from Africa."

"I'll keep my eyes open." he said then thought about getting to his brother with this news concerning Nadia.

"Promise you won't tell anyone what I told you."

"But you do realize we have to get to the bottom of this."

"Just don't tell anyone I was the person you got the information from. I really like Nadia a lot but she shouldn't get away with this."

"Once this is all investigated, we'll have to bring all witnesses and those accused to the table. I don't know if I can promise that. Not only that, I can't understand why you'll rat on her if you like her so much. Was this a ploy to get me to go out with you?"

"What makes you think it's all about that?" she asked, offended that he seemed to treat her like a whore. His comment was so condescending, she wanted to slap the taste out of his mouth.

"That was part of our phone conversation. Don't you remember?"

An old cut entitled: *I Second That Emotion*, by Smokey Robinson and the Miracles suddenly flowed through the speakers.

"I love that song. My grandmother used to play it to death." she said, rocking to the rhythm. "Will you dance with me?"

He stared into her flawless face and thought, *what the hell!* He took her hand, led her to the dance floor, joining other couples who were hand dancing to oldies part of the evening. The couple danced closely as Renee deliberately brushed her bra-less bosom against his hard chest several times during the song. He knew she was doing it on purpose. She was one of those chicken heads that was just out to get what she could from a man but he would show her that he didn't succumb to gold diggers.

When his resistance finally dwindled down to the point where it no longer existed, he had her in a motel room several hours later, blending with her.

Afterwards, he had to admit, she surpassed most of the bed partners he'd been with. If it were not for Trojan making condoms, he would have a slew of babies by now. And he always brought his own. No telling what conniving woman would punch a hole in a condom and try to pin some kid on him.

When he had his first woman, he was twenty and the woman was thirty-eight. He thought back, fourteen years ago, resting his head on the headboard of the bed, his hands folded behind his head. His mother was hurt and angry when she found out her baby had fallen in love with a woman who was only ten years younger than herself.

Jerome arrived at the office at eleven the next morning and informed Jonathan what Renee told him – omitting the important detail of who the informant was.

"That still doesn't explain Nadia did it." Jonathan argued, not being able to imagine her stealing a penny from anyone.

"I'm just suggesting that we should call her in here and question her."

"I've already done that. And she told me she didn't do it." he insisted.

"Call her again!" Jerome ordered. "By the simple fact that her pass card was used that night should speak for itself."

Jonathan relented, picking up the phone. He called her extension. After hanging up, he looked at his brother with disdain.

"What?" Jerome said.

"She's innocent, that's what."

Jerome rested his palms on the desk, standing over Jonathan sitting behind the desk. "What if she's guilty? What are you going to do? Terminate her or make her pack back the money?"

"Let's work on proving it first."

They heard a knock, their conversation was interrupted. Jerome sauntered to the door and opened it. Nadia came in, took a seat in the chair facing the boss. Immediately, the brothers recognized the charm around her neck that matched the earring Jerome found in his office. Jerome looked at Jonathan matter-of-factly. Jonathan felt a surge of pain overwhelming his heart as he spied the piece of jewelry. It couldn't be, he thought.

He was so stifled for words, Jerome had to speak up. "Nadia, you are aware of the time the money turned up missing from the safe."

She nodded affirmatively and he continued. "In a situation where so much evidence we have against a person proves they could be at fault, we have no other choice but to take action. And in your case, your pass card was used and you couldn't provide us with a plausible explanation as to why. We have no recourse but to handle this."

"What are you saying?" she softly interrupted, fidgeting with the gold charm. Both men noticed her nervous gesture at the charm and shot glances at one another.

"That you're suspended without pay until you can tell us what really happened." Jonathan interrupted, finally finding his voice.

Nadia leaped from the chair and burst into tears. "Please, Jonathan! Don't do this to me. I swear to you, I didn't steal that money. I swear!"

"And you can't tell us who used your pass card that night?" Jerome cut in.

Nadia thought about Renee. She couldn't rat on her. Renee seemed so remorseful and she shouldn't tell on her. "No." she said. "I just know I didn't."

"Will you be able to pay back the money?" Jerome asked. "You're being held responsible because your card was used."

"Where would I get that kind of money from?" She had given Renee most of the money she saved up. Jonathan proffered her a box of tissues and she snatched one out of the box and wiped her tears.

"Nadia," Jonathan spoke up, tired of his brother's callous treatment. "Leave your card with me. Go home and I'll call you later."

Nadia looked at Jonathan, her eyes tearful and frightened. He felt her pain. She was not the person who did this. Maybe she knew who did it and maybe she didn't. Her face had turned red from crying and her breathing accelerated to a continuous hiccup. Finally she said after strained silence, "Okay." she reached into her purse and handed the card to him.

"Maurice doesn't have to know about this." Jonathan consoled. "And I'll tell your department manager that I gave you leave for family emergency. We'll straighten this out."

"Okay."

"Damn!" Jonathan exploded once she was gone. "Jerome, I hate treating her like that."

"You did what you had to," his brother said with a smirk of victory. He never liked Nadia. She was one of the only chicks in the company that didn't ogle all over him like most of them hoes did. "And you need to get over that soft spot you have in your heart for women. *All women!* That's the reason you can't seem to get rid of Jackie. They know you'll give in and feel sorry for them. Jackie knows one day you'll forgive her."

"That shit ain't fair!" Jonathan tossed across the room at him.

"Yeah, it is."

"I still don't believe Nadia did it."

"If she didn't do it, she knows who did. They used her card. She's covering for whomever the thief is."

"I still can't…" Jonathan sunk his face in his palms, resting his elbows on the desk.

"You know anyone close enough to her that could pull a trick like that? Taking her card out of her purse possibly?" Jerome asked.

"What is that supposed to mean?"

"Summer, maybe? Little Miss Innocent. They *are* close friends."

"You're beginning to sound like that damned Jacqueline. And it's scaring me."

Jerome was in a sense hating on his brother for landing such a decent woman and he always ended up with the no-good ones. All except Brenda, whom he still hadn't figured out why she was angry with him.

The door swung open. Maurice stepped in. He sat his briefcase near the door and sauntered to the coffee maker. Both sons became quiet. Neither of them wanted him to suspect anything. That would mean Jonathan was not handling the affairs of the company to his father's satisfaction. He didn't suspect anything and the three men sat at the round table, looking over several designs that were going to be featured in *Ethiopian Journal* the coming month.

A week after Maurice's return is when Jackie and Abu were called in for their idea. The editors had been monopolizing so much of his time that he couldn't get around to everyone that first week. October could not come fast enough for him. He was ready to hand the company over to his son.

She and Abu walked down the winding corridor, heading to the fourth floor conference room. Neither of them talked, both absorbed in their thoughts.

When they entered, Maurice was sitting at the table while his son sat across from him. Maurice stood, shaking hands with the pair.

Jackie took a seat at the table and opened her briefcase. She had done some research of her own, therefore her presentation for a publication on behalf of African American seniors had been polished. That idea still did not belong to her! After beginning her speech, her nervousness abated. Soon, she was speaking with so much conviction that if Jonathan hadn't known better, he would have thought it was her idea. The Wesley men listened in silence.

Once she completed the presentation, Maurice followed with three short claps. "I like it. I really like it." he said, glancing at his son.

Jonathan furrowed his thick brows, glancing at his father. What disturbed him was that his father seemed to buy this bullshit.

"Where on earth did you come up with something so fascinating?" Maurice asked.

Jonathan rolled his eyes heavenward. He imagined what she'd say before she voiced it. "Both Abu and I put our heads together." She smiled.

"Yes, sir." Abu interjected. "We both have parents in their sixties." he said, appealing to the older man's interests. "In Africa, we're taught the importance of caring for our ailing and aging parents. What better way to boost your subscriber database than publish something exclusively for older blacks? How many publications out there are exclusively for older blacks?"

"I agree," Maurice said.

Jonathan couldn't believe the slick shit he was hearing. Maybe Abu's custom taught their young to care for the older ones. But Jackie hardly liked her own mother, let alone loved her.

Once they left the room, Maurice shut the door, turning to his eldest child. "What is really going on here?" he asked.

"What are you saying, Dad?"

"Are you certain Summer Douglas came up with this?"

Jonathan raised his voice in frustration. "Dad, I faxed you that idea long before Jackie came to me! I believe in her. I know it was hers. Somehow, Jackie found out and bit her."

Maurice waved a hand, dismissing his son's comment. "I've been trying to figure out for some time how Summer ended up knowing about coming to us with ideas."

"That I can't explain. But what I do know is that Summer came to me with that idea first."

"Did she tell you while you were on top of her, Jonathan?"

"Dad!"

Maurice interrupted him, raising his hand. "I just don't want my son using his manhood instead of his sound judgment. That's not how I became CEO and founder of a large publishing company. Instead of behaving like some horny teenager, you needed to be concentrating on business. And not inviting some young, fresh thing into your bed after hours. Especially someone who works here."

Jonathan didn't realize his father was speaking from personal experience when he referred to those types of affairs within the company. If he had used his better judgment, they would not be standing there right now debating back and forth about whose idea it was.

"It was long before I made love to Summer that she came to me with this. And how dare you come off like that to me. I love that woman! I thought you liked her. You said she was a 'nice kid', don't you remember?"

"I like her. But I don't like trickery. I thought about it while I was in the Caribbean and thought it could have been Jackie's idea from the get-go."

"Dad, can't you see what's going on? Jackie is conniving."

As if he didn't know that!

"I understand your relationship with her didn't work out. But that's no way to get back at her."

This was all too confusing to Jonathan for him to try and figure out. He stood there, staring down at his father, who stood two inches shorter. He couldn't believe his powerful, intelligent father could be so easily persuaded by a Jezebel like Jacqueline Shannon. *If only Abu hadn't agreed that it was their idea.* But how could he prove it wasn't theirs in the first place?

Finally, his father spoke up, shaking his thoughts. "So how did Summer find out about proposing ideas? This was not common knowledge in the beginning. She was one of the first ones to pitch a proposal."

"I don't know, Dad." Jonathan had never thought of asking her that. It didn't matter to him. It was a good idea, one of the best he'd heard and why should that make a difference now. The idea could afford them even more business.

"But you know that the suggestion wasn't granted her. It was an appeal made to department heads, editorial, writers and marketing. If I find out she's eavesdropping on meetings and discussions she's not invited in the way she may have been doing with Jackie and Abu, I'll handle her myself.

"Don't think I haven't noticed how she slips around here, pretending to be passing out documents to others in other departments and pretends she's not listening to their discussions. I always knew there was a reason she was so alarmingly quiet."

Jonathan sighed heavily, staring angrily at his father. He just didn't understand. Summer was not the conniving one of the two. Without a word, he marched out of the conference room, leaving his father behind.

He headed over to Summer's place later that evening.

CHAPTER TWENTY:

Jonathan pulled up in front of Summer's house. She galloped excitedly down the porch steps and to his car. She hopped in. One look at his expression and she knew something was not right. He'd been driving in silence for two miles before she inquired.

"What's going on?" she broke the annoying silence. Most of the time, they had everything in the world to discuss.

"When you brought that idea to me back in May, it never occurred to me to ask you something."

"Well, you can ask me now." Her innocent tone of voice was tearing a hole in his heart. He couldn't stand disappointing her but he had to or his father would, more heartlessly.

"How did you find out about proposing an idea for a new publication?"

"I overheard it."

"From where?"

"I was distributing copies of the deposit recap sheet one day and overheard Mr. Wesley and Larry Gaines discussing it. I didn't mean to but I just got so excited. Are you angry with me?"

"No." he said.

But he knew Maurice was furious. He couldn't understand how his father could have been so easily tricked by Jackie. Something seemed out of the ordinary. His father was a smart man. He had never been that easily swayed.

"Jonathan, what's wrong?"

He couldn't lie to her. He loved her so much and he had to break the news to her. Even if it didn't work out, he would have been given a chance to have found a good woman.

"My father is really disturbed about it. He thinks you may have been eavesdropping."

"So my idea goes out the window because of what he thinks?"

"Not so fast, baby. We will work this out."

"Jonathan, don't tap dance around my question! I need to know. This means the world to me."

"Will you let me handle it from this point, Summer?" he snapped, annoyed. "It's out of your hands now. I will see to it that before he leaves, he sees you as an asset to *EIC*."

Tears streamed down her soft cheeks. He didn't believe in her. She knew she was wrong to eavesdrop but this wasn't fair. When he noticed her tears, he pulled over and parked. He wiped her tears with his thumb.

"Just take me home."

Jonathan grew disquieted, but controlled it. He couldn't show how annoyed he was, for she didn't deserve two blows in one night. But she had to trust him. He had done all he could to prove to her that he loved her. How could she behave like she didn't believe in him now? He turned over the ignition.

"Fine, if that's what you want." he said.

During the ride to her house, neither of them spoke. When he pulled over, she stepped out without saying goodnight. He watched until she was safely inside the house. He sat in the car another ten minutes before pulling off.

He cursed while driving down her street. But he would handle this situation with Jackie before he returned to Greenville to put his house up for sale. He would not allow that witch to get away with this.

When Summer walked into her living room, she found her father with Nadia's mother. The woman sat on the sofa like she lived there, handing Allen his pain pills, a glass of water in her other hand. Summer slammed the door, startling the older couple.

"Ms. Jiminez!" she shouted. "I didn't…" She looked at her father with an accusing stare. "Daddy?" She could see Maria Jiminez was quite comfortable in their house.

He was caught! Cold busted! He had thought she would be spending the night with Jonathan so as soon as he came by to pick her up, Allen watched out the window until the black Jaguar disappeared down the street before rushing to the phone and calling his woman over. He felt like some teenager sneaking around behind his parents' back. He understood his daughter loved him but it was time for her to quit treating him this way. He would put an end to it now.

"I met Maria at the picnic, Summer." he said.

"How are you, Summer?" Maria asked.

Summer looked from her father to Nadia's mother. She knew they had met at the picnic. But she missed the part when they decided to hook up and become a couple. Why had she been excluded from this info? She'd bet Nadia knew all about it, had probably encouraged it too. She would also bet that her friend set them two up.

Nadia's father had died of lung cancer one year after Summer's mother marched out on them. Nadia was like a daughter to Allen. Even when she married Jose, she wanted him to walk her down the aisle but Allen insisted that her older brother should be given the honors.

"I'm fine, Miss Maria. And you?"

"I'm with your handsome daddy." She patted Summer's cheek and she couldn't help but laugh at Maria's apparent boldness. "Life couldn't be better."

She had guts! She openly admitted to this man's overly protective daughter that she was his woman and no one could change that. She could only reckon with a woman like Maria. But she was a loving woman, like her daughter. If Summer had to choose a step-mother, she would choose someone like Maria.

After speaking with them, she headed upstairs and called Nadia, who had some serious explaining to do. She first told her about the conversation she'd had with Jonathan an hour ago.

"Summer, if you don't believe in Jonathan, you're a fool." Nadia said, knowing he was fulfilling his promise of coming through for her and keeping her employed. She winced at the thought of almost being fired.

"He's gotten what he wanted from me, my virginity. Now he's letting me down easily to make it appear what it isn't."

"You enjoyed it as much as he did." Nadia cracked. "Besides, if he wanted to dump you, what makes you think he wouldn't be cocky enough to drop your ass cold? He's handsome, rich and could have any woman he wants. He doesn't have to be nice. He could act as arrogantly as his brother. Added to that, you see he dropped Jackie without looking back."

"I don't know." Summer rested her head in her hands. "I just believe that he and Jackie were in on this together. He took my virginity and my idea and set her up to fire me. They've known each other longer than I have known either of them. I've been used."

"But he hired you back. And he sent you to class. He won't do that unless he thinks it's worth it. Can't you see that this man loves you?"

"I don't want to talk about him and that scheming whore anymore. They got what they wanted. I'll continue attending class because it is my future. Maybe I can run my own publishing company one day."

"That's the spirit, girl!" Nadia cheered, a hint of sarcasm in her tone. "Be optimistic and business-minded. But be optimistic about love too."

"Speaking of love," she changed the subject. "I think my father has been seeing someone." She wanted to see if her sneaky friend would admit that she matched Maria up with Allen.

"Really?" Nadia giggled.

"Yeah. The woman is very beautiful. I met her just an hour ago. She was here."

"What's her name?" Nadia asked.

She was really laying on the innocent act thick! Summer thought.

"Oh, come on, Nadia. I know you better than you know yourself."

"I confess. When you went to Frederick with Jonathan, I convinced my mother to spend the day fishing with your father."

"From what I discovered when I came home, she spent the night."

"I didn't see that one coming though, Summer, I swear. But my mother and your father had been having long conversations on the phone and going out together. I could see they liked each other. My mother has changed since she started hanging out with your dad. I mean, they saw each other briefly at my wedding but had never talked."

"I take it that you're happy for them."

"Very. And you should be too. Come on, Summer, don't be so resistant. I know how protective you are over your father since your mother left. And how you chase all those old hookers away when they try to get a piece of him."

"That's not an issue. But I'll admit my father is also a changed man since he's been going out with your mother. I didn't know what was going on with him at first. I'm happy they don't have that longing look of loneliness in their eyes anymore."

"At least there's a flame going on in your house though it doesn't involve you." she attacked, knowing Summer would defend herself. She wasn't done with this conversation about Jonathan and Nadia wasn't letting her off the phone until she convinced her that he was a good man.

"Nadia! He's a Scorpio. It's his nature to sting!"

"Let me finish. Please give the man a chance. He's all about you. At least wait and find out what happens before you give up on him. I can attest to his loyalty myself. By the way, did you forget I'm a Scorpio too and I don't sting?" That comment hurt Nadia's feelings. Their zodiac was one of the most passionate, loving of all those in the chart.

"How can you attest to his loyalty?" Summer asked.

"Well, from one *Scorpio* defending another, Renee was the one who stole the cash from the accounting department on the seventh floor. The bitch stole my card from my purse and used it to enter the building.

"When security checked all the activity entering and leaving the building, they found out that my card was used after seven. This all ended up in the hands of the boss, Jonathan, that is. He could have fired me right then, and his brother insisted on it. But he didn't."

"But why won't you tell Jonathan that it's Renee? And you're always telling me to level with him. Geez, Nadia, I don't believe your ass sometimes."

"Because she will eventually gather enough rope to hang herself."

"That still doesn't make it right. You could have lost your job. Did Maurice find out?"

"No."

"I still think you ought to tell on her."

"I'll consider it. But first, I have to give back the five thousand dollar gift she gave me."

"What?"

"She gave me this matching gold chain and charm to the earrings she so adores."

"That doesn't sound right. Was that some hush-hush present? She didn't give you that from her heart."

"I think it was a hush-hush gift to keep me from telling on her."

"Yeah, you straighten that mess out." Summer yawned. "But I better get in bed."

"Okay. See you at work tomorrow. We're having lunch together right?"

"Yes."

"And at least think about what I said regarding you and Jonny-bear."

Jonathan hadn't slept for two days. He couldn't get Summer out of his system. In the past, he found it easier to go on, even with Jackie. But Summer had put something on him that he couldn't shake. After allowing the phone to ring eight times, he slammed it down, nearly breaking the receiver.

"That little virgin you took must have locked you tight to have you trippin' like that."

Jonathan turned around swiftly at his brother's sarcastic tone. He didn't know his discontentment was that obvious. Jerome stood at the entrance of the parlor. Jonathan drew in a long breath and ran his fingers down his wavy hair. He was badly in need of a hair cut. His short waves were now becoming short curls.

"What makes you say some crap like that?" he asked Jerome.

Jerome removed his reading glasses, placed his journal atop the end table near the leather sofa. He sat next to his brother, regarding him with brotherly concern. He didn't deserve the stuff this woman was putting him through.

"I believe you love her and something is wrong in your relationship, Mike. Though you refuse to tell me what it is, your behavior is shouting."

"Oh, no shit, Jerome!" Jonathan roared. "I thought you'd gone back to New York. When are you getting out of here? I'm tired of looking at you every day."

"And I thought you'd gone back to South Carolina." Jerome tossed back, amusement dancing in his eyes. "But I had to come back because something got screwed up. Again! I'll be leaving once it's resolved. I also need another dose of Renee Lyles before I drop her ass. This is a 'for the road' fuck. Know what I'm saying."

"No, I don't know what you're saying!" Jonathan said, jumping up from the sofa and heading to the bar. "You're sick." He poured a glass of wine.

"You're even sicker if you let a fine ass babe like that get away from you. What are the chances of you meeting a clean woman like that again? You placed your flag on that coochie, man. Finding a grown woman that's still a virgin is about a zero, zero, zero, zero, point one percent chance. You're lucky if you find one that's only been with less than ten men all her life."

Jonathan's Summer

Jonathan sometimes couldn't figure out if Jerome actually sat up and thought about some of the smack he talked. How could anyone sit around thinking of stuff like that to say all the time? He shouldn't be on Wall Street, he should be hosting his own stand-up comedy show.

"Jerome, she won't even answer the damned phone. I know she has caller ID. She knows I've been trying to reach her."

"Then call from another phone." he suggested. "Eventually, you'll catch up with her. But don't give up." Jerome admonished, slapping his back affectionately. He grabbed his journal and reading glasses from the table and headed back to his bedroom, shutting the door behind him.

Unlike his brother, Jonathan couldn't sleep. He tossed and turned until daybreak. Lucky for him, his father had given him a break and he didn't have to report to the office unless he wanted to. He took the break, knowing that when he returned in late September it would be a long time before he could take time off.

His desires were coming on strong, merciless. What was even worse was that a large eight by ten photo of her sat on his nightstand next to his bed. He turned away from the photo. He couldn't let it end this way. Each time he looked at the picture, those big, seductive eyes stared at him. He would miss her dearly if he lost her.

The next evening, Jerome took Renee to the movies. He would treat her to small, insignificant things but he was not stupid enough to palm her any cash, although she kept tossing hints his way about what she wanted and needed. After the movie, they checked into a cheap motel and climbed the mountain of lust again. Afterward, they sat up in bed and talked most of the night.

She began complaining about him not taking her to at least a four star hotel or even his crib and he held up his palm, silencing her complaint. He didn't want to hear it. She decided to change the subject then.

"You know, Nadia is back to work." she said. "I thought you and your brother would have fired her after what she did."

Jerome played with a few strands of her hair while answering, "My brother claims we didn't have any solid evidence against her."

"How much proof do you need?"

"Expensive clothing and jewelry aren't." Why did women always talk about things a man didn't want to hear?

"But you said her pass card was used that night and she couldn't explain why since she's supposed to have left work at four."

"She could have forgotten something and returned to the building. Maybe she got scared and decided not to tell us she'd come back."

"Scared of what?" Renee raised on the pillows, looking into his large, piercing eyes.

"Scared when she learned someone had robbed the safe. Under normal circumstances, she probably would have told us she came back."

"I still don't buy it." she protested.

Jerome couldn't understand why she was so hell-bent on getting Nadia fired. He didn't come to the motel to discuss that office. He had planned to spend the entire weekend with her but her nagging propelled him to take her home and check out of the motel Saturday morning instead of Sunday.

"Will you call me?" she asked before hopping out of his Lexus.

He could see this hoe was desperate to land a wealthy man like him. Either that or she was catching feelings.

He nodded curtly and said, "I will." He pulled off without walking her to her apartment or making sure she got in safely. He didn't have to treat her like a lady – she wasn't of the caliber that she should deserve such treatment.

When he returned home, Jonathan was sitting in the den, working on some notes. When he realized his brother was home, he took a break.

"I thought you'd be out with Renee or some other chicken head until you headed back to New York."

"I decided to cut it short." Jerome answered, tossing his keys on the coffee table and sauntering back to the front door to answer it.

On the doorstep stood Terence, the young man who did various chores for the Wesleys. "I need you and Mr. Jonathan's keys. Saturday is the day I clean all the vehicles." the young man explained.

The brothers handed Terence their keys and he left.

"As I was about to tell you, Mike, Renee is starting to crawl under my flesh and I can't stand it." He was not as patient as his brother and didn't intend to be.

"All women crawl under your skin, even the one who gave birth to you."

"You got a point there, big bro."

"I know that nagging can be a bit much." Jonathan agreed. Summer wasn't a nagger and that was one of her finest qualities. "But what is this chick doing this time that's worked your nerves?"

"That bull about Nadia. I don't know why she won't drop it."

"So you think it's bull? How did she know about Nadia being a suspect anyway?"

"She was the person that told me how Nadia seemed to have a lot of money since the safe got robbed."

"And you put two and two together?" Jonathan added with a sigh. "The money and then the matching necklace to the earring you found in your office?"

"What I can't understand is why is she so willing to sabotage Nadia."

"You know Nadia was up for a promotion before the robbery incident." Jonathan informed.

Jonathan's Summer

"I don't think Renee cares about that since she's not career-minded and doesn't seem to be striving for a higher position."

"Then she could be simply hating on Nadia because she's trying to move up."

When the doorbell rang, Jonathan got up to answer this time. Terence had finished washing the cars and vacuuming the interiors.

"Thanks, Terry." Jonathan said, writing a check.

"That's not necessary, sir." Terence said.

"I insist." Jonathan said, handing him the check. "Jerome and I don't live here. Normally, you have five cars to clean but today you had seven."

Terence grinned after receiving the check Jonathan handed him. He then handed the older brother a small paper bag.

"What's this?" Jonathan asked, peering inside the bag.

"Items I found in your cars, sir. I'm sure you wouldn't have wanted me to toss them."

After Terence left, Jonathan dumped the contents of the bag on the dining room table top. He picked out an ink pen and his video card he must have dropped in the car by mistake.

"I think the rest of these things belong to you, Rome."

Jerome left the oval-shaped bar and joined his brother at the table.

"Where did that come from?" Jerome asked, referring to an earring he was sure Jonathan had in his possession.

"That's the earring you found in your office."

"I gave it to you."

"No, you didn't."

"Yes, I did!" Jerome argued.

They looked at one another. Suddenly, the same idea came to mind as they both headed to the study at the same time. Jonathan was the first to reach the desk. He opened the drawer. Under a heap of papers was the earring Jerome had given him. Jerome stood akimbo and stared at his brother matter-of-factly.

"Maybe this could answer a lot of mind-boggling questions, Rome. Who's been in your car recently?"

Jerome sunk into the high-backed black leather chair. "Renee."

Jonathan cocked a brow and grinned, showing his pearly teeth. "And all the time, you thought Nadia was capable of such a gross act."

"What are you going to do?"

Jonathan shook his head. "Nothing."

"Nothing?"

"That's right. Because this one's on you."

"But it's your company."

"I have another situation with two employees I have to straighten out. So my hands are full."

"I'll handle it." Jerome relented.

CHAPTER TWENTY-ONE:

Abu ran to his ringing phone. Once hearing the familiar voice, he raised his eyes to the ceiling. This was the last person he wanted to hear from. He wanted out of this now. He didn't realize how deeply he had gotten involved.

"Are you there?" the voice asked.

"Yes."

"Now, I want you to do everything I told you or your ass will be on the line along with your career and everything you've worked so hard for."

"Okay."

"So just do what you're told. Is that understood, Abu Sosseh?"

"Yes, it's understood." he said before hearing a click on the other line.

That phone call shook him scared. After hanging up, he turned over his plate of dried fish and white rice. He cursed loudly. Damn that Jacqueline Shannon! How had he allowed her to drag him down with her? But he had to do what he was ordered or there would be severe consequences.

Monday morning Summer entered the building and was on her way to class when she nearly collided with Jonathan Wesley. Her eyes were fixed on his broad chest until she looked up into those sharp, piercing eyes.

"One thing about you that's changed since I've met you, Summer Douglas and that is you're able to look me in the eyes."

She took a step backward, his presence causing her to tremble a little. She had been successful in dodging him for over a week now. "I need to go to class. I thought you left."

"Would thinking that I left have anything to do with the fact that you've been avoiding me so long?" he asked and that no nonsense tone she was familiar with was back. "I just gave up calling you after five unsuccessful days of trying. But I knew you wouldn't be able to hide much longer. I'm a patient man. And I'm not going anywhere unless you come to Greenville with me."

"I can't. My father…"

"Your father will be fine!" he interrupted. "He has a life now. Something you thought about doing until you quit trusting me."

She gave him a perplexed stare.

He added, "Oh yeah, Summer," He grinned. "My reliable sources told me what a lovely time your dad's been having with," He raised his head and pretended he was trying to remember. "Maria Jiminez. Isn't that the woman's name your father is seeing?"

Summer was going to kill Nadia for telling Jonathan everything. She could imagine the conversation that transpired when Nadia told him about Allen and Maria.

"I didn't say I didn't trust you?" she defended.

"Verbally, you didn't 'say' it. But your actions shouted loud enough for me to get the message." He smiled.

"What do you want, Jonathan? I was never good enough for you."

"I want you, Summer and you are good enough for me."

She looked away, tears sitting in her eyes. She wanted him but had been feeling quite insecure lately. He was powerful, wealthy, handsome and strong. Why would he want an insignificant like herself? She was beginning to believe that she would not measure up to the Wesley standards as the wife of one of the sons.

He noticed her tears and his heart immediately went to her. "I want you to marry me and come to Greenville with me and return to Maryland once I take over the company next month. My house in South Carolina is already under contract. The new owners will be demanding that we move out in two weeks because it will be all theirs."

She didn't miss his inclusion of her when he talked about having to move out of the house in Greenville. But she didn't feel like debating – wasn't one of her better characteristics. She was even weaker this day to feel like fighting with anyone. He took his palm, placing it under her chin, guiding her eyes to his.

"I'm not taking no for an answer." he said.

Others passed them on their way to the bank of elevators on the first floor. Some stared curiously while others nudged each other, knowing looks on their faces.

"Why?"

"Because I love you. It's as simple as that. Can't you accept that? Or do you believe that I'm not capable of being in love with such a beautiful princess?"

Before she could answer, he had her in his arms. He held her as if he thought she would vanish if he let her go. Her tears came on strong, soaking his crisp white shirt. She could smell his fresh cologne and after shave. She missed that smell! During the time she was away from him, she thought her heart would quit beating and she would die. She felt the tight muscles in his chest flex as her head rested in it. A new set of passersby saw the interaction and smiled at each other. The three women were from Somalia and had just migrated to the United States and Jonathan had given them jobs as columnists for the *Ethiopian Journal*. They were convinced they were going to be working for a wonderful boss.

"Listen, I still have the material you gave me at the restaurant that night. At eleven, I want to see you in the third floor conference room." he said.

"Then what?"

"Trust me, Summer. You will find out when you get there."

She couldn't guess what he had in store for her but she agreed to meet him at the time and place he suggested. She trusted that he had something pleasant in store for her.

It was ten o'clock and Abu still had not reported for work. He had not called either. Jackie was worried. She didn't know what was taking him so long. Each time someone passed her office, her head jerked up. Where was he? She picked up the telephone, dialed his home number. This was the fifth time she called and he didn't pick up so she tried his cell. She could not reach him by that either. She hung up, staring out the window, hoping she would see his car pulling into the employee parking lot. It was filling up and she could only spot four empty spaces in the huge parking lot.

Jonathan joined is father in the conference room on the third floor. He took a seat at the table across from him. He was still angry with his father for how he had handled this situation. Since then, words spoken between father and son were few.

"Okay, Dad."

"You're relentless." Maurice said with a straight face.

"I am when it concerns something I strongly believe in. All I'm asking is that you give Summer a chance."

"That's all I'm willing to give." Maurice said aloofly.

Jonathan didn't care whether his father was interested or not, he was going to make him hear her out. Not only did it bother him that he bought Jackie's so-called idea as being original, he hadn't even given Summer the chance to present hers. That was unfair.

The old man was stubborn! Jonathan thought. He needed to retire long ago and allow the new generation to take over, that being himself. He looked through the transparent wall of the conference room and spotted Summer stepping off the elevator. She was back to her big tee shirts and she wore a pair of loose jeans. Just then, he remembered the hip-hop artist named Fatima wearing jeans that seemed too big.

Her beautiful crown of hair flowed freely down her back. She walked with a confident strut as she made her way to the conference room. Jonathan knew then that he would be a fool to give up. Something about her had changed, he couldn't place it. He felt himself respond and growing aroused watching her. He rubbed his hands together because he didn't know what else to do with them as he moved toward the door to greet her. His father noticed how much his son loved this woman. He turned away, not wanting his own emotions to start manifesting.

"Good morning, Miss Douglas." Maurice greeted tightly.

"It's nice to have you back, Mr. Wesley." she said meekly.

"Thanks. Have a seat."

The men sat across from each other while Summer took the head seat. Jonathan slid her the documents and Maurice noticed she didn't even look at them.

"Show your stuff, baby."

That term of endearment assaulted Maurice's ears. He stifled a smile. He often called Donya "baby".

Summer cleared her throat, still not reading the notes she had given Jonathan. She had misplaced her own and until this day, could not remember where she had put them.

"In March of this year, my father fell victim to a cardiac arrest. During this time, I was frightened he would not make it. But he recovered. It was after then that I realized my father needed to eat right, exercise and take care of himself."

Maurice's undivided attention was on Summer as it seemed this presentation was more of a personal thing to her than business. At first glance, she looked like a seventeen year old but the words she uttered spoke volumes of her intelligence and wisdom. Her sincerity captured his full attention. Unlike Jackie, who gave a boring encyclopedic presentation on the same subject, this woman before him was involved in what she was saying. He compared it to first-person narration. Maurice could see her heart was involved and this is why her project was a perfect one in the end.

In conclusion, she said, "My father also needs to get away, take vacations from time to time. This could even add more years to his life."

Maurice had to interrupt for a moment, there was a question he wanted her to answer. "Summer, how did you come up with the idea about creating a column for sexy black seniors?"

She grinned bashfully. Jonathan knew and he nodded his approval. It was okay to tell Maurice.

"Other than my Dad, you and your wife, whose appearance belies her age."

Flattered, Maurice could only find such truthfulness amusing. When he asked Jackie that question, she never directly answered it, yet they had the same ideas.

"Anyway, all of that came up and the possibility of creating a column for grandparents of the month. That is, in case a publication of this nature does materialize."

Once she was done, Maurice stood up and shook her hand.

"What do you think, Dad?" Jonathan asked, a serious expression on his face. If his father didn't see the light this time, he would insist that he see an ear specialist.

"I'm fascinated by it." Maurice answered. "Her presentation was great. Now I know who is telling the truth. I'll get the team started on this project a week from tomorrow." He then nodded at his son, meaning to have Kim construct a schedule to give to the team. "Jonathan."

Jonathan nodded in return.

"You will?" Summer asked, nearly leaping through the roof.

"Young lady, I know talent when I see it. I'd be a fool not to publish this. Summer, how about you join the editorial team for this magazine once it sets in motion? In the meantime, you'll be promoting other publications and maybe writing for them if you'd like. And you'll be rewarded handsomely for your responsibilities."

Summer looked at Jonathan.

"Go for it, baby. You have what it takes."

"Yes." she said, shaking Maurice's hand.

"Jonathan." Maurice nodded at his son again.

"Dad." He nodded back.

Summer watched Maurice walked down the hall. Ricky Channing had just come out of an office across the hall and the two men headed toward the elevator. Once they were gone, she turned back to Jonathan.

"What did he mean when he said he knows who is telling the truth?"

Jonathan knew he would have to explain this one day. He told her to have a seat before he started.

"Jacqueline came to Maurice with the same idea about three weeks after you did."

"She did?"

"Yes. But she stole it from you, Summer. I don't know how she did but somehow, she got to it. I don't know if she overheard you talking about it or what."

"Is that why you were asking me if I'd discussed it with anyone other than Nadia?"

"Yes, that's the reason."

It suddenly dawned on her that she had lost her copy of the presentation shortly after informing him of it.

"Oh, you know what?"

"What?"

"My copy was in my desk drawer when I worked in her department. I wonder if she took it?"

"That's a strong possibility."

"I didn't know she was that mean. I knew she didn't like me and all, but I didn't know she would go that far."

"A lot of us don't until it's too late. But don't you worry about that now."

He sat back, his gaze sweeping over her. She smiled. She had learned him and knew when he wanted something.

"Summer?"

"Yes?"

He scooted his chair closer to her, took both her hands and said, "Will you marry me?" In one fluid motion, he reached into his pocket and pulled out a ring.

"Yes!" Her eyes widened at the huge diamond staring at her from the black velvet box.

He placed the ring on her finger and took her into his arms.

The three Somali women who'd seen the display of affection in the lobby happened to pass the conference room.

"They're at it again." one told the other.

"I see." the other said as the women all giggled, on their way to meet with the editor-in-chief of their publication.

Jonathan and Summer noticed the women. They laughed. Jonathan turned back to her and said, "Hey, don't get lost. I've got another surprise for you. So when you get off today, I need you to meet me in my office."

"Okay." She grew excited, wondering what he had in store for her this time. He had already given her two surprises this morning. Her father always told her that events come in three's. She had a surprise for him too but she wanted him to give her that one last surprise before she gave him hers.

He kissed her again before she left. Once she stepped on one elevator, Abu stepped off the one right beside it. He joined Jonathan in conference room. They shook hands and kept standing. This would not take long so there was no need for either of them to sit.

"To be frank, Sosseh, I thought you were too slick and conniving to have any morals in that sorry-looking body of yours." Jonathan cracked, still disquieted by the fact that he almost lost the woman he loved because of this man scheming with Jackie.

"Well, after that phone call from you Saturday, I thought long and hard about it. I just couldn't allow this to continue to go on. I hadn't realized how much she had me wrapped around her finger. She's a dangerous trap, man."

"And it's easy to fall right into a trap like Jacqueline Shannon. I can't blame you. She's a fine piece of work." He laughed. "But wicked, nonetheless. Anyway, thanks for sharing the truth with us."

"You're welcome."

"And you'll get to keep your job. However, you understand you'll be on probation for at least six months."

Abu nodded, lucky to still have his job. It was also inevitable that his cohort would be reproved.

Jonathan's Summer

After his brief meeting with Abu, Jonathan headed to Jackie's department. When he entered the open area, everyone stopped what they were doing and stared at the clean-cut handsome man wearing the dark blue Armani suit. He was only six-two but his strong presence made him seem even taller, his height capturing the attention of most.

Though not looking directly at them, he noticed two young customer service reps wearing smiles while they stared. He paid no attention to the nine pairs of eyes pinned on him, including Gwen's, who should also be placed on probation because of her harassment of other employees. He would deal with her later. Right now, he was about to handle the ring leader, Jackie.

As soon as he was gone, everyone began talking to the person next to them.

"Some shit about to go down." Gwen leaned over and told Arlene.

"I know it was gonna get down to this." Arlene said.

"Wonder what's up?"

"I donno, girl. But you can tell he didn't come down here for a family reunion."

Gwen was bugging to find out why he had come down to their department and marched in Jackie's office. She would find out from her girl later what the deal was. The look on his face told everyone present that he was not happy.

"I knew something was gonna jump off after what happened between her and Summer." Arlene told Gwen.

"I know."

Jackie's door was halfway open when he approached. She was looking at the marketing screen on her monitor when he entered without knocking. Once she heard the door snap shut, she turned around, admiration gleaming in her deep-set eyes. He was always pleasant on the eyes, even when he wore a straight face, such as the one he was wearing this time.

"What a pleasant surprise," she said with a smile.

He took the chair facing her desk while she swirled around to fully face him. She knew he would come around one day. He locked his hands across his lap after crossing his legs in a figure four.

"What can I do for you, Jonathan?" Her question was a literal one and he knew what she meant. She may as well forget it.

"A few days ago, I spoke with Abu. And he told me an alarming story about the proposal you presented."

She feigned ignorance and said, "I'm not following you."

"I don't like games, Jacqueline. You know I'm referring to you stealing Summer's idea."

She squirmed a bit in her chair. "How could I steal something from someone I'm not around? Unlike the possibility of her stealing Nadia's pass card."

"You have no proof of that." he shot back. His irritation was rising. He had arrived at the point where he could no longer stand her.

"The same way you have no proof of me stealing." She grinned and cocked a brow.

"Should I call Abu in here?" he asked and she became silent. Still, she refused to admit that she had stolen another employee's proposal.

He could see she was not going to make this easy for him. At first, he had not wanted to be harsh, hence firing her. He thought she would show some remorse and he could demote her or place her on probation. He was even considering placing her in another department to save her pride. But she had too much arrogance and an unbearable ego.

With that in mind, he said, "There are three people who can attest that it was Miss Douglas's idea. Two of them had known she'd come up with it before I even arrived here in May."

She narrowed her eyes at him. "So? That still doesn't say much."

He took a deep breath. It was over now. "You know what? Get your personal items and have this office cleared in an hour." He stood, buttoned his suit jacket. "And I'll be so kind as to save you a trip to Human Resources and take your pass card myself." He held out his hand.

She snatched open the top drawer of her desk and grabbed the card, tossing it at him. It missed his hand, landed on the floor behind him. When he bent down to pick it up, she leaped on his back, trying to wrestle him to the floor.

"I'll kill you, you bastard!" she screamed, trying to wrestle him down. After struggling with her a couple of minutes, he was finally able to toss her from his back. She sailed across the room and hit the wall next to the window. That was too bad, he wished that heifer had hit the window and sailed out of it.

"Jackie, what is wrong with you?" he asked.

Her bosom rose and fell as her breathing accelerated from anger. "You Wesley men!" she shouted. "You've all used me, fucking me and then dumping me." She began gathering her things from the desk, tossing them into an empty box.

"No one used you, Jacqueline!" he protested.

"Yes, you all did! But I'll get you for it. Especially your scandalous father. You wait 'til his wife finds out about this."

Jonathan couldn't believe what just came out of her mouth. Was she crazy? She was upset, not crazy.

"About what?" he asked.

Jonathan's Summer

She stopped packing long enough to answer. "About the episode he and I had on top of his desk late one evening, before I even knew you."

She thought she might as well spill it now, for she had nothing to lose at this point.

This bit of information shot his anger through the roof. It felt like a thousand knives had stabbed him all over. He was most angry with his father, who ought to know better, than he was with her. He didn't know Maurice had slept with her.

"Jerome too?" Jonathan asked, sympathy slowly replacing his anger.

"No, but the jerk tried! And when he learned I was in love with you, he was smart enough to back off."

"Jackie, I'm really…"

She raised her hand, dismissing what he had to say. She closed her eyes and said, "Save it, Jonathan. At the time, I thought I was doing what I had to in order to move up. That's how I ended up in this position in such a short time working here. But I've learned a lesson. Especially about men." She grabbed her box and passed him without another word, leaving the office.

He stood staring behind her after she left. He could feel everyone in the department staring at him, wearing looks of curiosity. Now that Abu was placed in another customer service department, he had to choose a tentative manager to handle the department until a permanent decision was made to hire or promote someone.

He looked around the department until he spotted a young man named Chris who had worked his butt off for four years as a customer service representative. He should have long ago had that position but because Jackie used her femininity to appeal to the big boss at the time, Chris had been passed up for the position. Besides, Chris was not given to gossip. He needed someone who would maintain a professional example to those they supervised.

"Christian McGavin!" Jonathan's deep voice resounded throughout the department.

The young man's head jerked up. "Yes, sir?" he said, getting up, heading right over to Jonathan.

Others stared curiously, wondering what the hell Chris did to warrant the big boss coming after him now. They had already seen Jackie leaving the department with her things.

"Can you step in here a minute?"

"Yes, sir."

"Thanks." Jonathan said as he closed the door of Jackie's former office. "And I would prefer that you call me Jonathan." he said. "Sir is a title reserved for your own father."

Chris smiled nervously.

"I am going to need someone to take over this department as customer service manager. Since you have seniority and have dedicated your services to this company, I feel a promotion is in order."

"Thanks!"

"It would be up to you to take the position permanently or tentatively. Just let me know in a week what you plan to do. But this week, I will need you."

"Thanks again, Jonathan." he said, shaking his hand.

"No, thank you." Jonathan said. He then looked around the disorganized office. "And do what you want with this place, just as long as it doesn't look like this anymore."

Chris burst into laughter at Jonathan's reference to the junky office Jackie used to occupy.

Once he was done speaking with Chris, he opened the door, stepping into the department. He didn't care if he put others on the spot. Some of the nonsense in that company would stop if others realized he didn't take any mess. If they wanted to behave like children, that's exactly what he would treat them like. He scanned the department again until he spotted Gwen. She was already looking at him. He motioned for her to follow him into Summer's former office.

Once they were inside, he got right down to the heart of the matter. "I'm going to have to give you a written warning about your harassment of other employees."

"What did I do?" She played innocent.

"Gossip is considered harassment." He named four people in that department who had complained about harassment she had been guilty of, including Summer and Chris, whom she called "white boy" all the time.

She was speechless. Jackie, her shield was gone and there was no way Gwen would be stupid enough to challenge him like her friend had. She took the reprimand humbly, thankful he didn't terminate her.

Once he was done reprimanding Gwen, he marched to his father's office, not stopping until he was through Kim's workstation and right at the door of the private office. He entered and slammed the door behind him. Startled, Maurice looked above the heap of documents covering the desk and his eyes landed into the angry countenance of his eldest child.

"What in the hell." Maurice said, baffled, wondering if his son had lost his mind.

"Dad, you better think of some way to explain to my mother how Jackie landed on your desk with her panties down one night. If you don't Jackie will. And when she does, Donya Lovette Wesley will have your things packed by the time you get home."

Maurice removed his reading glasses, his guilt-ridden eyes staring at his son. He knew he had disappointed Jonathan. He chided his son for sleeping with

Summer but his son wasn't married, therefore he hadn't committed adultery. Guilt rode him because he hadn't practiced what he preached.

"You know about it?"

"You damn right, I do!" he shouted and knew Kim could hear his resounding, baritone voice. He didn't care that he cursed his father, the man had wronged his mother. "How could you do this to my mother? Having a sexual encounter with a strange woman other than your own wife?"

"Son." Maurice pleaded, getting out of his chair, walking around to face the taller, younger version of himself. "It wasn't something I anticipated."

Jonathan looked out the window while his father spoke. "Let me guess. Your pants accidentally came down and you accidentally fell on top of her? Or did she accidentally amble her way down to your office that night?"

"Don't talk to me that way."

"How am I supposed to feel after what you've done to my mother? And just think, you're always preaching to me and Rome about how to treat a woman and telling Debra and Theresa not to get involved with the wrong men. I guess you would know the wrong man when you see him." He gave his father a look of disdain.

Maurice turned toward the balcony overlooking the executives' parking lot, staring into the distance. After long, strained moments, he said, "Forgive me for not being the perfect father."

"I don't expect perfection. I expect honesty. Isn't that something you've been pushing into our heads our entire lives? Besides, honesty is not impossible. And you have not been honest with my mother."

"I told you it was a mistake!" Maurice was determined to defend.

"Now you better find Jackie before she finds Donya. Because not only have you hurt my mother, though she's not aware of it *yet*, you owe Jacqueline an apology. You can't go around using women. You're old enough to know better."

"Where's your mother now? At home?"

"She's up in Frederick at the farm house. And that should give you enough time to find Jackie. Because the story will be even more dramatic if that woman gets to my mother before you." Jonathan searched his father's eyes before adding. "And if you so happen to forget to tell my mother, I will personally make her aware of your adultery."

Maurice knew there was no way out of this. He knew how much his oldest son loved his mother. He put on his suit jacket and left the office right afterward. Jonathan stared out the window for thirty minutes after his father left. He could feel a headache attacking his temples. This had been one eventful day.

CHAPTER TWENTY-TWO:

"Girl, he gonna call me in the deposit room and tell me that people said that I was harassing them." Gwen informed Jackie over the phone during her lunch break. She stood in the parking lot on her cell phone. She was too afraid to make that call inside the building because someone could overhear and tell Jonathan.

Although she didn't feel like hearing Gwen's problems because she had her own, she still listened.

"Who said you were harassing them?"

"Well Summer is a given. That girl from Gambia complained that I was making fun of her accent. And Jenny and Chris McGavin, who said I called him 'white boy'."

It was true. Gwen did make fun of Chris because he was white. Still, Jackie listened. "Girl, I think Jonathan done lost his damned mind. He was on a rampage today."

"Don't I know it! How long did he place you on probation?"

"Six months. He had the nerve to give Chris your position. But girl, I'm getting out of that company. I got a feeling he is not going to be as laid back as Maurice about stuff."

That's because Maurice was doing his own dirt! Jackie thought. The doorbell rang. "Gwen, I gotta go. Somebody's at my door."

When she opened the door, there stood Maurice. Speaking of the person responsible for a lot of dirt!

"What did you come here for?" she snapped. He was no longer her boss, therefore, she could talk to him in any way she wanted.

People sure did change when they didn't have to kiss your ass anymore!

"May I come in and speak with you?" he asked. He wanted to help her. If she was too cocky to receive help, she was even more evil than his son said she was.

She stepped aside, allowing him in. Though he was no longer her boss, she could tell he was still trying to emanate a presence of power.

After sitting in the arm chair, he said, "I'm terribly sorry about everything including what happened today."

"What's done is done." she said with an air of aloofness.

"Jacqueline, I have a colleague who is willing to give you a job. I just spoke with him on the way over."

"Maurice, you don't have to do me any favors no more than I have to help relieve your conscience."

"I'm doing this because an injustice has been done to you. I don't enjoy seeing people hurt."

Jonathan's Summer

She knew he had a hidden agenda behind all this. He didn't want her to tell his wife about their one-nighter.

"I'll consider it." She calmed. "Let me have the number." She needed a job and too much pride wasn't going to help her. She had a mortgage to pay.

He handed her his colleague's business card and asked, "Is there anything else you'd like me to help you with?" He was willing to do anything, pay some of her bills, car note. Anything! Just as long as she kept her mouth shut. He would tell his wife in his own way.

She stared into the face that would be Jonathan's in twenty-five years. What she wanted was that powerful, wealthy son of his. But he could not help her with that.

"No." she said, almost tempted to beg him to convince Jonathan to give her another chance.

From the time she had left the office until reaching home, she had begun coming to terms with the fact that she could never have Jonathan Wesley back, especially since he had fallen in love with another woman. A strong feeling of wishing she was in Summer Douglas's shoes swept through her. That was scary because she never thought she would feel that way. She still envied Summer's position with Jonathan.

Maurice finally left, his heart a little relieved. Instead of returning to the office, he headed up to Frederick to meet his wife. It was time he told her what had transpired between him and Jacqueline Shannon.

Jerome drummed his fingers on the table while waiting for Renee. Since their first meeting was at Red Gray's restaurant, he wanted the last meeting to be there. Renee strutted into the restaurant and took a seat across from him.

He decided this would take less than ten minutes. He got right to the issue at hand.

"You're no longer employed with *Ethnic Information Corporation*. Here are the earrings that belong to you. One of them you lost in my office the day you robbed the safe and the other you lost in my car one day." He got up after his explanation, attempting to leave.

"Wait!" She grabbed his wrist, stopping him. She stood up before him and pleaded, "I can explain." The other earring was in her purse, and she realized that it must have dropped out somehow and ended up in his car. She knew she should have taken it out of her purse.

Jerome looked her over curtly, showing no emotion in his features. "I already have an explanation, Renee." He didn't give a damn about her, he didn't know why she thought he owed her something.

"No, you don't."

"Yes, I do. I've discussed this with Santos." he said, referring to her department manager. "And he knows you won't be coming back."

* * *

Summer couldn't wait to get home and call Nadia that evening since she had missed her during lunch. She was so excited about being officially engaged to Jonathan. He said he had another surprise for her. Since he had a late meeting, he told her to go home and he would call her later because he didn't want her to have to wait. He didn't know how long this last-minute meeting with Chris Moyer and Ricky Channing would take.

"I have some exciting news!" Summer shouted through the phone.

Nadia, oblivious to how exciting her friend's news was said, "But you have to hear my news first." she interrupted. "We're finally going to be sisters, Summer. Your father proposed to my mother this morning."

Summer couldn't believe what she was hearing. By the way, where had the old man been all evening? she thought. "Are you serious, Nadia?" She temporarily put her news on hold for the moment.

"And my mother said yes. Can you believe it?" Nadia screamed.

"I can. Now hear my news, chatterbox!" she said with a laugh. "Jonathan proposed to me this morning too. His father gave me a promotion and I'll be leading the new publication."

She knew she had to pour it all out in one breath before Nadia interrupted again. She had such a way of running her mouth sometimes, it annoyed Summer.

"That's great! Did he give you a ring, girl? 'Cause you should see that huge rock your daddy put on my momma's finger this morning! Owwww!" Nadia shouted so loud, Summer had to move her ear from the telephone receiver.

"And I'll be going to Greenville with Jonathan and we'll be back next month. But I really don't want to leave my father behind."

Nadia responded with a thunderous laugh. "Your father will be in good hands while you're gone. My mother will personally see to it. It's time you left the nest, and let someone else take over your dad."

"You're right. But I've lived with him all of my life." Summer began crying. She didn't know why she was feeling so emotional the past couple of weeks.

"In the meantime, we have to get prepared for two weddings coming up. I think a good idea is for you and your father to have a double wedding." she suggested. "Now that would be something great to put into one of our publications under the weddings column. Picture this: Daughter and father finds true love, dual wedding."

"Girl, you need to get yourself into the big boss's office with some of the ideas you've been concocting lately." She had to laugh at Nadia. The girl was such a character.

"I'm working on it! But I don't want some jerk to think I'm the one eavesdropping this time."

"Dear sister, the rules will change when Jonathan returns next month. This time, everyone who works there will have the opportunity to move up, and not just the privileged. Remember you were the one who told me that Jonathan was an understanding person."

"That I did say."

"And he's cleaning house left and right, Nadia. You know Jackie's gone. About eight people were let go today and a handful put on probation. Your girl, Renee got let go too."

"No shit!"

"Yep! Some girls from Somalia just started there. He's gathering fresh apples, honey. Fresh apples. Those rotten ones he's tossing out."

"I know. I heard he let one writer for *Nubian Entertainment* go because he wrote something in his column about a movie star that wasn't true. That reflects badly on the company."

"It does." And Summer was proud of her husband-to-be. She had to admit, there would be nothing more sensual than being married to a powerful man. And the term, Chief Executive Officer spelled power! That almost ranked right up there with being the president, especially when it referred to a world-renown company such as theirs.

Her call waiting beeped. She put Nadia on hold. It was Jonathan. She got back with her friend and told her that her "husband" was on the other line.

"Baby, are you ready, because I'm on my way to pick you up." he said, maneuvering his Jaguar down Kenilworth Avenue. He talked on his hands-free cell phone.

"I didn't think you'd be out of the meeting this early."

"I made sure Chris Moyer and Rick didn't keep me all night. I have a life."

Summer looked down at the clothing she wore. She thought, what the heck! He'd seen her in a pair of jeans before.

"Are we going to a fancy restaurant or something?"

"No, but it's better than a fancy restaurant."

"Can I wear jeans?" She didn't feel like changing.

"Sure. I should have stopped home to change but I couldn't wait to come and pick you up."

"Okay. I'll be ready when you get here."

He arrived fifteen minutes after the phone call. She opened the front door when she heard a car pull up. It was almost eight-thirty and she noted that her father still had not returned home.

He got out of the car, walked to the porch. Summer grabbed her purse and he escorted her to the car, opening the door for her.

They talked on the way to their destination. Summer kept wondering what her surprise was. She watched her surroundings and realized he was heading across the Wilson Bridge into Virginia. She wondered what was down here. He exited on Braddock Road and kept going until they reached Pope's Head Road. She noticed the winding street they went down until he turned into West Ridge View Drive. He pulled over suddenly, as they sat on a road that was surrounded by trees.

"Turn around." he gently ordered.

"Huh?"

"Turn towards the window." he repeated, referring to the passenger window.

When she did, she felt him cover her eyes with what she soon realized was a blind fold.

"Jonathan."

"Shhh!"

She could feel the car moving again. The road seemed a little hilly. After what seemed like a half mile, the car stopped. She heard him get out on his side. Her door opened. He took her hand.

"Just let me guide you, baby." he spoke into her ear.

He stopped. Guided by him, she stopped. He removed the blind fold and there was a huge colonial style semi-mansion staring at her.

"Uhhhhh!" The sight of it took her breath away. "What's this?"

"Our house." he said with a smile.

"You're kidding?" She threw her arms around him. He lifted her, her legs locking around his waist.

"I know this may be a little premature, but I will carry my princess over the threshold."

"Jonathan!" she screamed, at a total loss for words.

He opened the door of the airy, high ceiling house. He put her down and took her on a thorough tour of the house. To the left, there was a library. The living room was to the right.

They went through the living room, entering a small vestibule before reaching the kitchen. There was a family room that over-looked the kitchen on the left and to the right was a set of French doors that led to the sunroom.

They headed down to the basement. There were two bedrooms on the lower level with two full baths.

Jonathan's Summer

Summer was in awe. They headed upstairs and she noticed a catwalk. Upstairs were four bedrooms including the master bedroom. There was a double sink vanity in the master bath with a shower stall and a Jacuzzi. There were two more full baths upstairs, one that divided two of the bedrooms.

"You can actually go into this room, walk into the bathroom and enter the other room." she commented. She had never seen anything like that before.

The entire house fascinated her. She could not wait to move into her new house. Jonathan told her that this was her engagement gift and the deed was entitled in her name. She knew this had to be love.

Suddenly, the smell of fresh paint assaulted her nostrils, making its way down to her stomach. She rushed into one of the juvenile bathrooms. She made it to the commode just in time and began lurching.

Alarmed, he rushed in behind her. "Are you okay, baby?" He knelt down beside her, holding her while she ridded herself of the uncomfortable feeling stirring her stomach.

"You all right?" he asked again, turning on the water in the basin. He used his hanker chief as a towel, wiping her face. He looked at her with deep concern.

"The paint just sort of made me sick." she said.

"Oh, well maybe we should open some windows and let out some of the smell." He headed toward the catwalk and opened the balcony.

"That's not all." she said, standing behind him.

He turned around.

"I'm pregnant, Jonathan. I just found out last week."

A feeling he had never felt before and one he could not describe overwhelmed him. All he could feel was joy. The feeling was so strong, it reached his toes. He pulled her into his arms, holding her tightly. Tears ran down his face. Finally, he was going to become a father and the most wonderful woman in the world would bring about his first child. God was really blessing him. He looked heavenward before closing his eyes.

"Summer, I cannot tell you how overjoyed I am, baby."

She looked up at him. "You're not upset?"

"How can I be? I have wanted this for a long time."

This time, she wiped his tears. She began laughing and crying at the same time, noticing his tears. When she took the pregnancy test the week before, she had prayed it would not turn out positive, not knowing if Jonathan would want a child this early in their relationship. When it turned out positive, she cried out so loudly, her father woke up from sleep and headed down the hall to investigate. He had come into her bathroom and saw her sitting on the side of the tub holding the test. At first, he looked confused until he realized what it was. He was not disappointed but felt a little concerned because she and Jonathan were not married.

She cried and her father consoled her, telling her that she had not done anything wrong and they would love and care for that child, but she should inform the man responsible for it immediately. She held that news for over a week, debating how she should tell him. When he asked her to marry him that morning, she knew he would want a family. At least he proposed to her not out of guilt, but love. Now it was time to tell Nadia. She had kept this from her best friend because she knew she would go running off to Jonathan.

He guided her outside to the car, his arm draped around her waist as they walked side by side. Summer turned around, looking at the house once again before getting into the car. There was a two-car garage and about seven acres of land surrounding the house. She knew he would insist on doing for her what his father had done for his mother: hire employees to tend to that big yard and a couple of housekeepers. It seemed that was the way it was in the Wesley family. She didn't know anything about how to keep up a yard but she would not mind tending to the inside of her own house.

"Now we will have children to fill up that huge house." Jonathan said, starting the ignition.

She looked over at him and smiled. "How many children?" she joked.

"Four or five maybe. Summer, I am not upset that you're pregnant." He noticed how quiet she had become. "Why do you think I bought a six bedroom house in the first place?"

"Jonathan, I love you!" She threw her arms around him.

"I love you too, baby. I will always love you."

EPILOGUE:

"Happy birthday to you! Happy birthday to you! Happy birthday, dear Leandria! Happy birthday to you!" the crowd sang as little one year old Leandria clapped her hands and laughed. She was a cross between her father and mother, having Summer's golden complexion and long curly hair and Jonathan's piercing eyes and full lips.

"Blow out your candle, baby!" Jonathan said, standing on the right side of his child while Summer stood on the left. Leandria blew as hard as she could, dousing the flame on the candle. She clapped her hands again, her piercing scream nearly deafening her father. He laughed.

About a dozen children and as many adults stood around talking, enjoying the festivities of the child's first birthday party. Jonathan's sisters, Theresa and Debra had brought their children, a total of five.

Maurice and Donya took the child's hands, leading her outside to the deck. Others stood outside, eating and talking.

"I never dreamed a day like this would come." Summer said, standing at the island of the kitchen. They had moved into their new house when she was six months pregnant. Their wedding took place a month after Leandria was born.

"Me either."

"Summer, can you get me a towel!" she heard Donya call from outside. "Your baby just spilled grape juice all over her!"

Summer grabbed a clean towel from the butler's pantry and headed outside. Allen and Maria were in the sunroom, playing the piano and singing.

The doorbell rang. Since everyone else seemed to be occupied, Jonathan headed toward the front door and opened it. A woman stood on the porch. She was short, her complexion a little lighter than his and her hair was pulled into a French roll. She looked like she may have been in her mid-fifties. She looked familiar. He could not place where he had seen this woman before.

"May I help you?" he asked, noticing the gift wrapped box she held.

"I know this might be out of place. But my name is Cynthia. I'm Summer's mother."

This almost threw him off balance. He had to tell her to repeat what she just said. She repeated it and he knew his ears hadn't deceived him.

She noticed his powerful gaze and had to lower her eyes to the doorstep. She knew he was her daughter's husband, the father of her only grandchild. She wanted forgiveness. She knew she would probably never get it but it would not hurt to try.

He closed the door behind him so that others inside would not see him standing there talking to her, especially his wife. "Cynthia, why did you come here?" Realizing now that the reason she looked slightly familiar was because he'd seen pictures of her in Summer's family photo album.

"Your name's Jonathan right?" she asked.

He nodded, not surprised she would know his name.

"Because I love my daughter." Tears began filling up her eyes. "I know I did my daughter wrong but…" she choked, could not finish her statement.

He had no choice but to take her into his arms. He hated seeing a woman cry. Maybe she was not a perfect mother but that didn't mean she didn't love her child.

"I just want my only child to forgive me. I'm so sorry." Her tears were pouring out profusely now. He could feel her quaking in his arms.

"Tell you what," he said, stepping back a moment. "Me, you and your daughter will go into the library and talk." He led her into the house. Once she was in the library, he told her he would be back and closed the door, leaving her in there alone.

He searched for Summer and found her outside playing with Leandria and one of his sister's children.

"Summer." He approached her.

"Yes, darling?"

He took a deep breath. "There is someone here to see you."

"Who?" She frowned, wondering who that "someone" could be.

"I think you need to go and see for yourself."

"Why can't you just tell me?"

He didn't want to scare her. Maybe seeing her mother could cause an emotional tantrum so he said, "Your mother."

"My mother!" she shouted.

"Shhhh!"

Summer's initial surprise subsided. "Oh, my goodness. Are you serious?"

"Yes, she's here. She's in the library. Do you want to go in there and talk to her?"

Mixed feelings shot through her. On one hand, she felt an endless measure of joy. On the other, she wanted to fire a series of unanswered questions. She had to take a moment to calm herself. Jonathan stood by her side. His mother came over, noticing the disquieted look on her daughter-in-law's face.

"Is everything okay?" she asked.

"We're fine, Mother." he said.

"Okay now." Donya then broke into a smile. "I'll put Lee-Lee to bed, Summer. I think my grandbaby is getting sleepy. She's all irritable just like her daddy used to be when he was a baby."

The comment Donya made loosened the tension and Summer had to laugh. Once she gained full composure, she marched inside the house, Jonathan at her heels. Once they reached the library and she put her hand on the knob, he stopped her.

"Maybe I should wait out here in the hall." he suggested. "But if this gets emotional, you know where to find me. I'll be in the sunroom listening to your dad and step-mother who can't sing."

He had to make her laugh, which she did.

She closed her eyes a moment. "Okay."

One look at her mother's sad face shot down Summer's defenses. She looked so tired and lonely. She wondered how life had been treating her. Her mother sat on the small burgundy leather love seat, looking at her daughter. She was such a gorgeous woman! Cynthia broke into tears, knowing she'd missed out on so much.

"Summer, baby, I'm so sorry…" She wiped her tears. "I don't know what to say. I have no excuse or reason for doing what I did."

Summer began crying too. She sat next to her mother and hugged her. Her mother rested her head on her shoulder.

"Mommy, don't cry. Don't cry. Shhh!" Her consolation only made her mother more emotional.

"I know Allen wants to kill me and you want to kill me twice over."

"No, I don't. I don't. I still love you."

"Summer, you were always so forgiving and kind, just like your father. I don't deserve a daughter like you. Never did."

"Listen, Mommy." Summer said, drawing back to look into her mother's eyes. "You were not perfect. But you are still my mother, always will be. I'm a mother now."

Cynthia smiled, sniffling. "Yeah, I heard."

"And now that I'm a mother, I realize what motherhood is about. If I did something wrong, I would want Lee-Lee to forgive me." she paused. "That's your grandbaby's nickname."

"I didn't come here to beg myself back into your lives. I just wanted to see you and the baby, leave this present and go. Only if you want me around will I be."

Summer stared into her mother's eyes of sincerity. "I want you around. We want you here. Where do you live?"

"In Alexandria. I've been living there for eight years now. Before that, I was in North Carolina."

Summer hugged her again. Cynthia didn't have to answer any questions. It was all in the past now. Her life had turned out okay. She forgave her.

She took her mother by the hand, leading her to the door. "Come, let me show you your grandbaby."

Cynthia picked up the gift with the other hand and the women headed upstairs to the baby's room. In the crib was a sleeping Leandria.

"Her name is Leandria Michelle Wesley." Summer whispered.

Cynthia began crying again, watching her granddaughter sleep. "She's a beauty." Cynthia said, caressing the child's curly hair. "And she got that hair just like you. She looks so much like you when you were like that."

Summer smiled, glancing over at her mother. She noticed Jonathan standing at the entrance of the bedroom door from the corner of her eye. He'd seen them heading upstairs. He crept up moments after them. He wanted to make sure his wife was all right. She was! He smiled and left.

"How did you find out I got married and moved down here?" Summer wanted to know.

"It shouldn't surprise you how I found out."

"Anything could probably surprise me." Summer said with a wide grin. Her mother showing up out of the blue had surprised the hell out of her.

"No, this one won't!" Cynthia said, wiping another tear.

"Maybe. But how?"

"Well, I was at Landmark Mall a few weeks ago. And I ran into your old high school girlfriend named Nadia…"

That's where Summer interrupted her. "Oh, now I understand why you're saying I won't be surprised." The women fell into laughs, waking the sleeping child. Leandria began crying.

"May I?" Cynthia asked with pleading eyes.

"Sure, go ahead."

She lifted the baby from the crib, walked over to the rocking chair, patting her back to sleep. A sudden surge of memories of her rocking Summer to sleep came over her and she almost shed a new set of tears.

"Anyway," she continued, rocking the baby. "This Latino chick comes up to me and says, 'hey, you look just like this woman that I have seen pictures of. Do you know a girl named Summer Douglas?'."

Summer fell into fits of giggles.

"So I told her yeah. I'm her mother. Then she went all into telling me about how you got married, had a baby and was living in Fairfax, Virginia. But I had to beg for your address. She told me that Allen got married to her mother. That girl stood there for over an hour, updating me on what had been going down for over twelve years. I couldn't help but cry. She's a sweetie, though. She walked me over to the food court, sat me down and hugged me."

"I know you must have run into that hussy." Summer said jokingly.

"It took her another hour to calm me down."

Summer laughed again.

"Then she said, 'ooops, maybe I shouldn't have told you all that. Summer will kill me when she finds out I did.' I had to laugh then because the irony of it was that she had gone through all that just to realize after I knew everything that she had a big mouth."

Summer laughed and laughed. This time, she wouldn't get on Nadia's case. There was no way she could stop that chatterbox friend of hers from chatting. That was just Nadia Cruz and Summer would always keep her as a friend. As it turned out, she was happy she had Nadia.

Allen suddenly came into the room. When he spotted Cynthia, memories from years ago came flooding back. He had not heard from her since the time he got divorce papers in the mail over four years ago. However, he was surprised to see his first love sitting there caressing his first grandchild.

"Hello, Cindy." he said. He was not angry, he had gone on with his life and landed a wonderful woman.

"Al. How's life treating you?"

"Pretty good. It's nice to see you, Cindy."

Summer looked from her mother to her father.

"It's nice to see you too. And congratulations on getting married and becoming a grandfather."

"Congratulations to you on becoming a grandmother." he said with a smile.

She realized she had left two wonderful people behind. That was the biggest mistake of her life. But she could not turn back the hands of time, hence changing the past.

The moment was awkward, as both were at a loss for words what to say next. Cynthia broke the silence and said, "I'm sorry, Al."

"No need, Cindy. I'm happy. I'm sure you are. There's no need to conjure up the past. I'm sure you've had your share of pouring out your regrets to our daughter. By the way, you look wonderful."

"Thanks," she rewarded him with a dimpled smiled.

He turned to Summer. "Baby, we've got to be going, Maria and I." He walked over to Cynthia and kissed his grandchild on the cheek.

"Don't I get one too?" Summer said, sticking out her cheek.

"You'll never get over your jealousy, will you?" He kissed her cheek.

And he was gone.

As soon as Allen left, Janice, who is the sister of Maurice Wesley's housekeeping supervisor appeared in the room. "I'll take the baby now." She lifted the child from Cynthia's arms.

Summer and Cynthia left the room, walked downstairs hand in hand. They found Jonathan outside talking to his parents and tossing a Frisbee at the children at the same time.

He turned to Summer once she approached him. "Is everything okay?" he asked.

"We're fine."

"Thanks, Jonathan." Cynthia said.

Donya and Maurice exchanged perplexed glances. Summer then introduced her mother to her parents-in-law. They shook hands.

"Well, I think I better be going." Cynthia said.

"Mommy, leave me your address and phone number. We have a lot of catching up to do and time to spend together."

Now why didn't this surprise Jonathan? He knew Summer would forgive her mother. She didn't have it in her heart not to.

Cynthia hugged her daughter and took her leave. Shortly after, the house emptied of all the guests and their children.

Summer and Jonathan relaxed in the Jacuzzi of the master bathroom, each holding a glass of wine, several candles lit up around them, soft jazz caressing the environment.

"Do you know what these candles remind me of?" she asked.

Jonathan smiled, his lazy glare caressing her face. "What, baby?"

"The time we went up to your mother's house in Frederick. Remember we made love under candle light."

"How can I forget? Leandria is a reminder of it."

Summer knew too. That had to be when she got pregnant. When her cycle didn't come around the next week and a half, she suspected something was up. But she had no regrets and neither did he.

"That was one wonderful summer. But the most wonderful summer I've ever had was you. You're beautiful, baby. Come here."

She slid over, positioning herself in his lap. "You know I'll never be able to get my fill of you." he whispered into her ear.

"I love you, Jonathan."

"I love you too, Summer.

THE END!

COTTON IN THE SKY

Will learning his past destroy their love?

After spending nearly a decade in prison for a crime he did not commit, Malik Henderson is determined to start his life over. Finding his eleven-year-old daughter, Jillian is his first priority, although searching for her is a formidable task. Her mother has left the state of Maryland and relocated to North Carolina. Finding a job proves to be just as much of a challenge as no one is willing to give an ex-convict a chance until…

Kari Bonaparte has it all: successful fashion designing business, real estate and is worth billions. Though she has acquired the "American Dream", there is something that has not completed her life. She has long given up on finding "Mr. Right" until Malik appears in her corporation out of nowhere and tells her he is looking for employment. She knows without a doubt he has been sent from heaven, as she has fallen in love with him the moment she sees him and he begins his employment at Bonaparte Corporation.

Love invades – Malik and Kari can no longer ignore the inevitable as desires spiral out of control before either of them realize what is happening. Now Malik must come clean about his past and wrestles with the dilemma of whether or not she will still accept him once learning the truth.

ABOUT THE AUTHOR

Randa Wise currently lives in Manassas, VA with her daughter. She works for a publishing company in McLean, VA. She grew up in Pennsylvania and Washington, DC and is currently working on a second novel.